THE WINDING ROAD

RALPH G HELLMAN

Copyright © 2025 by Ralph G Hellman

Paperback: 978-1-968667-58-0
eBook: 978-1-968667-59-7
Library of Congress Control Number: 2025918411

All rights reserved. No part of this publication may be reproduced, distributed, or transmitted in any form or by any electronic or mechanical means, without the prior written permission of the publisher, except in the case of brief quotations embodied in critical reviews and certain other noncommercial uses permitted by copyright law.

This is a work of fiction.

Ordering Information:

Prime Seven Media
518 Landmann St.
Tomah City, WI 54660

Printed in the United States of America

TABLE OF CONTENTS

Chapter 1 1

Chapter 2 11

Chapter 3 14

Chapter 4 18

Chapter 5 22

Chapter 6 25

Chapter 7 28

Chapter 8 45

Chapter 9 56

Chapter 10 60

Chapter 11 69

Chapter 12 76

Chapter 13 81

Chapter 14 95

Chapter 15 103

Chapter 16 113

Chapter 17 123

Chapter 18 130

Chapter 19 145

Chapter 20 157

Chapter 21 159

Chapter 22 162

Chapter 23 168

Chapter 24 180

Chapter 25 186

Chapter 26 193

Chapter 27 199

Chapter 28 210

Chapter 29 223

Chapter 30 231

Chapter 31 245

Chapter 32 249

Chapter 33 254

Chapter 34 260

Chapter 35 269

Chapter 36 276

Chapter 37 285

Chapter 38 287

Chapter 39 292

Chapter 40 297

Chapter 41 300

Chapter 42 305

Chapter 43 310

Chapter 44 317

Chapter 45 320

Chapter 46 326

Chapter 47 329

CHAPTER 1

Treason. The word struck John's like a blow. His father, the man he revered and idolized, was suspected of treason, of betraying his country. It was Erik, a legend in Swedish Intelligence, who let it slip. Almost absently, as if the thought had formed unbidden. He was a highly regarded MI6 agent… though, there were whispers, rumors, really, that he might have worked as a double agent for the Russians. Erik quickly tried to brush it off, backtracking as if he hadn't meant to say it at all. Yet, the words lingered, leaving John with more questions than answers.

At first, learning his father had been a spy, it felt almost thrilling, like something out of a novel. The hints of treachery buried in old intelligence files, suggesting he might have been a double agent, that is, a traitor. The weight of it became unbearable, astonishingly heavy and suffocating.

John was wrestling with the implications of his father's past when the doorbell rang. It was Marianne, an old Swedish girlfriend becoming anew, who had unexpectedly reentered his life. She sailed through the door dressed from top to bottom in shades of beige. John sensed a trace of perfume he couldn't place. Her outfit suited her brown lively eyes, blond hair in a ponytail making her facial lines stand out and gave a youngish and fresh look. She had an elegant aristocratic carriage poise which was slightly unsettling.

"Hi, I bought you flowers," she said with an optimistic smile as if she had given something truly precious.

"How exciting, exactly what I needed," said John seemingly speaking to the walls.

Her eyes spoke volumes and gave him a look which suggested that all men had an utter disregard of the subtleties in life.

"Beginning to like the place?"

"It's not Versailles yet, but I'm working on it."

"We have to personify this," she said while she scanned the place and took note, not with pleasure, pointing at his tennis-rackets and golf-bag, "those occupy too much space."

John noticed the we-word and smiled to himself.

"Isn't it amazing after twenty years, here we are together again," she said.

"I think it's twenty-five."

"Why did we break up?"

"Who knows? Maybe we were just young and foolish."

"Which is to say nothing," a bitter smile flickered her face but she didn't push further.

"The soul wandered and intuition bloomed, said John theatrically."

"Still the poet's mind," she said smiling.

"Yeah, well back then, one tried to figure out stuff," he mumbled, as if dismissing the whole thing.

"But you seemed in a strange way mature,"

"What made you think that?"

"You were different."

"Was I?" he shrugged.

"You talked about values and honesty."

"What honesty?"

"Be honest and stick to your ideals."

"Did I? Can't remember that," said John trailing off as he recalled the thrilling adventures of his youth.

She turned to the kitchen to put the flowers in a vase and put them on the empty bookshelf.

"Makes the place more alive with a splash of color."

She looked at John and said, "but seriously, why did we end our thing?"

"It ran out, because I was too self-centered."

"We weren't truly honest with each other."

"You are right, I was too caught up in myself."

"But you were distracted," she said "and successful."

"You weren't bad yourself", he added.

"We took everything for granted, that everything would be permanent," she said.

"Maybe but wow it was fun."

"Vanity," she said.

"We counted scalps," he admitted then immediately regretted it.

"What?"

"We…kept scores, I guess."

"Score?"

"It was a joke," he said quickly, "just…the more the better," trying to brush away what he just had said with humor.

There was truth in this, in their crazed adolescence both had done their outmost to date as many as possible. A game they both had thrived in. Now, in retrospect, one could say their youth had been close to perfect, although capricious and irresponsible. Those times were non-stop, packed of all sorts of emotions and experiences, stimulated by an excess of hormones. They had acted as if life's purpose was a subject of ongoing exploration but never really found their way. But at that stage how would they, when the system is at full throttle and everything is so easy. In sum, they had been two swinging characters, with an inborn disposition of duplicity and now, considering uniting. Now the question was whether life's strivings along with the phenomenon of aging had mellowed them.

"But now I can't stop thinking we both missed out on something real because of it." "It's a sad thought, isn't it? But we were young", said John. It seemed there were untold matters, needed to be explained and clarified. During those years their relation lacked candidness, which had created insecurity of the intentions of one another. Their relationship had been complicated, a whirlwind of passion and conflict, broken off before his departure. At the time, there had been glimpses of shared dreams of building a life together. Now, their paths had converged once more, but the warmth in her eyes was tempered by caution. The years apart had created a chasm filled with unspoken words and unhealed wounds. It seemed she was having an internal struggle, what he believed were signs of nervousness, avoiding eye contact.

"Memories can be a heavy burden."

"And they are selective and subjective," said John, one of those cunning phrases he seemed to have in stock.

"But where did we fail?"

"We didn't fail, it just ended."

"It seemed the future hold so many possibilities," she said with a sad look.

"And now?"

"Now? It's not as it was."

"You mean the future is kind of narrow?"

"Well, a bit limited maybe."

"A bit cramped it is, but I'm thoughtfully optimistic about the future," he said with a playful grin.

In John's assessment Marianne was a fair, beautiful straightforward woman not entirely honest in her ambitions. She seemed easily persuaded and drawn to where dense money was involved. Not just attracted to financial craft, a desire to be among the notable heavyweights in society.

"I told my ex about you and me."

"And? Is he stigmatized?

"He doesn't approve."

"Of you or of me? "He never liked me anyhow, not then and probably not now."

"Actually, he thinks you have guts."

"He never knew me."

The story behind these words was because the famous Boris Winslow, Mayor of London, at an impromptu meeting at the Ritz in London had taken a liking of John's political and social views and asked if John could be his wingman at a forum where the controversy of immigration and integration was to be debated. Thus, John had been invited and participated in a forum of EU-potentates and had the audacity to claim that, if we continue with the politics and the scale of immigration from places with vastly different backgrounds and religions, as it were, without a consistent integration, it will have unforeseen consequences. As a result, his speech had reached the Swedish press who called him, at worst a rightist populist, at best, a potential figure in politics. In the aftermath of his intervention a media monster had been born with John as the principal actor.

The leftists described John as a neo-conservative, fascist, intellectual dwarf. The war on words was still in full rage after four weeks. A chain reaction had started, and the net went bonkers from both sides of the political spectrum. The haters dismissed him as an old hat of colonialism in their defense of multiculturism. The far-right activists thought, at last someone had spoken out. Experts were called in, talking with authority slamming John as unwise and wrong. In the tabloids Expressen and Aftonbladet he was criticized according to their manual of ethics with headlines of sensational and controversial content thereby selling more of their papers. And nobody knew why he had been in the EU in the first place and for whom did he speak or represent. After a while an investigating journalist found out about John's father had been a distinguished intelligence officer at the MI6 and all hell broke loose. "He thinks your speech in Brussels was great."

"That's good news, coming from a giant in Swedish business."

"He envies your guts and says what you did is a fast lane for politics."

"Me in politics? What does he know about me?"

"I've told him parts."

"Don't know if I should thank him, he actually published the essential part of my speech in Brussels, by the way, how is he?"

"Balding, managing his empire."

"It works for him?

"Money-wise? Without a doubt, but as a full-filled person, I wonder."

"And as a father?"

"The boys respect him, he furnishes the money, no limits there."

"So they respect him?" said John, "corruption is the right word for that," laughing out loudly.

She turned and looked out.

"Always music on?"

"It's company."

"You were always the one who took care of the music, why did you do that?"

"You remember that, that's amazing, I did it to conquer."

"And now, what kind of music do you use to conquer with?"

"I don't conquer anymore."

"Seems you just listen to pop-music."

"Not true, for example I like Puccini."

"Of course you do, you are a romantic."

"Maybe so, but not too much classic music, when violins scratch endlessly, it wears me out. I'm not schooled in the finer tunes."

"So, you don't like the Swan-lake."

"Oh, I do, saw it very early as a boy, and was impressed by the grace and elegance especially the dancers, hard to resist even for a boy." She met his last remark with a cold frown.

"I like Verdi and Puccini. Not Bach or Mozart, too mathematical."

"Jazz?"

"Jazz, I don't get it."

"Sometimes I prefer music without vocals," she said.

"I agree, lyrics aren't good enough or too stupid."

"Music is such a memory-trigger, certain songs can take me back to an exact place or moment."

"That's actually quite disturbing."

John's limited sensual characteristic was due to a lack of an artistic leaning. He would look at certain paintings, read a few poems but not tactile enough to appreciate what it suggested.

"Why are all songs about love", he said.

"What else is there to sing about?

"Well, it says something about our nature, and need of emotions."

Marianne appeared not to have noticed his last remark.

"Let's go out for a walk," she said and without warning gave him a sensual kiss.

"That wasn't a kiss for a walk."

"A kiss is just a kiss."

"No, that was a rich one".

"Maybe a warm-up."

"Before the real action?"

"Kind of foreplay perhaps."

"That's a tense and dense word."

"I think it's misused."

"Let's call it a scheduled improvisation?"

"You are such a snob," she said and kissed him again.

"Or tantric love, we procrastinate."

"What do you think it was, a kiss with intentions?"

"Well, you act on the way you think and then you begin to feel the way you think", he said as if his words were self-explanatory and didn't further explanations of what he meant. It seemed the air was thick with the unspoken word and there was an urge to let out their thoughts.

Suddenly, the room seemed to shrink as they stood across from each other at the small kitchen table. A flicker of doubt crossed her face and said, "Why did you seek me out after all these years, John? Why now"?

"When we met at that party, you kind of let me understand you could be interested."

Marianne's voice was soft but insistent.

"Why now?"

John ran a hand through his hair, searching for the right words.

"Well, I never really stopped thinking of you."

She looked at him with serious eyes.

He paused, then met her gaze. "When I left, I was losing my footing, scared of failing, a feeling of not being enough. And now when I came back, I thought that maybe…we have a chance a second chance."

Marianne's eyes softened, but her expression remained guarded. "You never even gave us a chance to work things out. You just disappeared."

"I thought I was doing the right thing," he said, his voice cracking. "I thought you'd be better off without me."

She looked away, her fingers tracing patterns on the table. "You should have let me decide that."

Silence enveloped them, heavy with the weight of years apart. Finally, John reached out, covering her hand with his. "I'm sorry, Marianne. For everything. For leaving, not fighting harder for us."

Her eyes met his again, and for a moment, the past seemed to dissolve, leaving them in the present. "I missed you," she whispered, her voice trembling.

"I missed you too," he replied, his thumb brushing over her knuckles. They moved towards one another, their embrace gradually becoming a kiss that was both tender and urgent, filled with unpronounced words that had never been said before. It was a kiss of forgiveness, of longing of a connection that had never truly been severed. When they finally pulled apart, Marianne rested her forehead against his. "What happens now, John?"

He smiled softly and said, "we figure it out, together."

But even as they embraced, a shadow persisted in John's mind. Their conversation had turned into fields he didn't want to delve into right now so he tried to look distracted and began to search for his keys. He needed to go out, no cuddling now as he had thoughts in other lanes. He had quirks about the "Jasmine-factor", restraining him to be hundred percent committed to Marianne. Jasmine, the stunner he had met in Hong Kong and who had taken up residence in his mind wouldn't go away, like a jolting stone in his shoe, perhaps it might get lost with a promenade.

"Yeah, let's go out for a walk."

"The longer the wait, the better result" she said, and they went out of the flat.

CHAPTER 2

Moments before the sound of the bell which had jolted John out of his reverie and Marianne had arrived John was standing on the balcony, listening to the familiar hum of his home city both comforting and disorienting. John's thoughts drifted through the web of recent entanglements. He was torn between two lovers. It sounded absurd when laid out so plainly. But it was more than that. It was choosing a life where he belonged. And yet, how could he even begin to decide when his past still held him hostage; A father who had been a spy, possibly a traitor; a daughter in New York living a life entirely separate from his own. How could he ever be the father she needed half a world away? He sighed, knowing the impossibility of stretching himself across the ocean at this moment. And now this, two women, each pulling him in different directions. He should walk away. From both. But he knew he wouldn't.

After more than twenty years in Madrid he had returned to Stockholm with a suitcase of clothes, golf clubs and tennis rackets and hopes of a new life would start here. The city hadn't changed, it remained achingly the same but now with an undercurrent of unfamiliarity that kept him on edge. He was a stranger in a place he used to call home, struggling to reconcile his past with who he was now.

When he thought about those years away, despite facing a few serious bumps, it had been a quite good run. Obviously, the divorce and its implications had clouded things, but that "incident" was now behind him and his ex-wife had drifted out of his life like the Voyager-spacecraft with no contact whatsoever except for matters concerning their daughter. He didn't miss her, only the times - the age. Slightly distracted he glanced at his golf bag upright and solitary along the empty bookshelf, akin to a lonesome friend, sensing it gave him an accusing look, like a dog urging him to go out. Being challenged by golf- clubs to hit a little white ball didn't bother him excessively. He had more crucial things to tackle.

Standing on the balcony a slight gust ruffled his hair. The quest of the heart loomed on the horizon and had converted to a buzz he couldn't control and left him adrift like a ship without a rudder in a storm. This love-turmoil required a swift resolution. Easily resolved with a bit of moral integrity and taking a stand. However, in consideration of his psyche it was doubtful he would do that now. If the decision wasn't yet ripe, there is no point forcing a decision. He needed to find his direction not being lured and trapped into an affair he wasn't convinced of. As a consequence, he hesitated, not because he was lost, he felt lost because he hesitated. Enjoying the breeze on the balcony, he couldn't help but think of life's casualties. Was it random in a lack of purpose or design, as no clear pattern seemed to exist? Another question arose in his mind; what had driven him to leave his country all those years ago? It hadn't been a strong-hold desire he had planned for. Somehow it came about loosely little by little. Whatever the case at the time of leaving, there were underlying reasons which had propelled his departure. He neither had parents, nor siblings. Therefore, only a nudge had been required to knock him off direction and launched him from Stockholm to Madrid like an asteroid when hit by a NASA rocket. Nothing held him back. Be that is it may, the odd thing was why he had stayed abroad so long? Especially as he had enjoyed a well-established base of friendships in Stockholm, nurtured through the years and yet, he had stayed away from it almost a lifetime. The simple truth is decisions hadn't been thought out properly.

Still on the balcony in his newly rented flat, sensing in his hair a slight gust, the new puzzle he had wrought upon himself was circling around like a moment of truth and a crucial decision was staring him in the face and steadiness was needed, like a tennis-match when you are down 4-5 and 30-40 on your second serve. A quandary that whispered in his ear, distracting him to find joy in the present. He needed to clear his head, too many loose lends ends pulling at him.

CHAPTER 3

It had so happened on his recent trip to Hong Kong, entering the lobby at the hotel Mandarin he had stumbled on Jasmine and got captivated at first sight. Half a minute later he bravely invited her for a drink, which she surprisingly had accepted. One thing led to another, and they became lovers. It was intriguing how love defied an explanation. Perhaps the mystery of Hong Kong and her breathtaking beauty, added to the story, creating a mystical flavor transforming it from a simply tale into something magical.

Jasmine, a stunner with straight lines, long black hair, long curved legs like a ballet-dancer. It wasn't just her beauty that made such a great impression, it was her directness, a natural rawness and unstudied ways of passion and eroticism she didn't seem to be aware of. She had a tender gaze and yet powerful, which made him feel he held a unique place in her world. All this together with her straightforwardness, had him spellbound in no time. It came about and struck with such force it surprised them both. He had tried to get her out of his system but with small success, she wasn't a woman you erased by sheer will.

And there was Marianne, whom he had met at a party on one of visits to Stockholm. An old flame, a spark from his past that had never fully extinguished. Their connection was instantly rekindled by memories of what once was, and the promise of what could be. Two years younger than John, in theory a perfect match coming from similar origins and tastes. A strong character and will, unwavering now as then. She wanted to be in charge and somehow, she got it one way or the other. Not a person you fritter. At the same time, a good sport full of enthusiasm, with a desire to live her life to the fullest. Despite outward appearances suggesting certain harshness she was a romantic.

For John it wasn't just about choosing between two women, also the tremor of living a life devoid of meaning. The constant search of identity, in a world where no clear answers exist. Torn by his indecision, he was trapped and paralyzed between competing desires and fears. As a result, he questioned his own character and wondered whether fickleness and lack of personal strength was to blame, which had hauled him into this. Or was it, as recent events seemed guided by chance, as his personal history saturated of unexpected events, where random played an astonishing big part in his life. This train of thoughts led him to go inside and check what effects a refreshing shower and a shave could have on his mind. He had observed that those mundane tasks had a positive impact on his way of thinking. Having showered and shaved he emerged refreshed and began to tackle a troublesome package to make himself another coffee, while waiting for the water to boil, he looked routinely on his iPhone, this voracious beast which never seemed satisfied, always challenging, always requiring attention. John wondered how one lived before BG that is, Before Google. That insatiable instrument, waiting impatiently in the pocket to be looked at, always ready, like a scout to serve, thanks to sophisticated apparatus and devises combined with other whatnots, it visualized the unknown and liberated the future of uncertainties by almost neutralizing it. Hard to digest, in view of all the different kinds of apps, media with the eternal "breaking news-titles", screaming news of wars, hunger, blended with results in sports, frivolous news, celebrities, deaths in the same moment.

Thanks to a learned capacity he lazily began to scroll when a story caught his attention; a man was held for questioning of money laundering in Estonia. By the descriptions in the article, it could well be John's uncle, Dennis Modig. The very same who fled Sweden after a girl got pregnant according to John's mother. In big letters he saw; "small fish *Swedish Smurfer avoids Taxes with Black Money among Big Sharks.*" The article claimed there existed overwhelming evidence of a great scam of money laundering and funds. According to the UK judge investigating the case, huge amounts of money apparently had passed through the Danske Bank branch in Tallinn. It dawned on John, the article might be the reason why his uncle, out of the blue, had called the other day and proposed a get-together the coming Wednesday. He couldn't remember when he had seen Dennis last time. How he had found John's number was another puzzling detail. Smurfing? According to Google, *"smurfing is a money-laundering technique to evade scrutiny from government agencies by breaking up a transaction involving a large amount into smaller transactions below the reporting threshold so that it will not be detected."*

He went out to the terrace again to get a feel what kind of day it was, scanning the view like a birdwatcher. The flat was situated on the fifth floor giving an aerial vision of buildings, cars moving about almost in silence thanks to the modernity of motors and slow speeds, trees in a perfectly straight parallel line separated from one another with exact distances like a column of soldiers. People coming and going. He watched the A-team, a Swedish term for a few unlucky bumps, who installed themselves on the same bench every day, sharing time and cheap beers, swearing curses to anyone who happened to pass their spot. After the roller- coaster of the past weeks, zigzagging back and forth around the world, had taken its tool and he needed a quiet moment of respite. Those had been his reflections until Marianne's arrival.

CHAPTER 4

They left the flat and walked down the street hand in hand sharing quiet conversations and stolen glances. The summer was running strong but still young, evidenced by light green leaves in the trees. Not that John went around checking the precise color of leaves in trees but in the beginning of July, it was noteworthy compared to the dark green later.

The magic of the seasons had always amazed John. The fact that every year, suddenly spring takes over, finishing off winter with an urge. And in early spring, when the asphalt on the streets begins to dry up, trees still without leaves but with a promise that something is going on, winter seems forgotten, that was ages ago.

The seasonal shift has a devotional touch in Sweden. Hence every year when the good season arrives, almost without warning, people are all over the place, walking and moving about. People with children who must have been tucked away during the colder months appear. The amazing month is May, when a decision by nature flowering plants start to respond, opening up to the warmer climate, as even people seemed to do.

And now in July, the blooming had culminated. Parts of the summer plans had already been executed. The initial summer rush had converted to a more experienced feeling and an urgency had set in and to act fast and profit from what was left of it. A rush of optimism still present, filling people's consciousness with projects, suggesting everybody being on a mission. And as Stockholm is framed by shimmering waters, the city radiates a lovely appeal, with boats of all sorts to be seen, seagulls circling like drones whining high-pitched calls to their kins.

Since his arrival John had done a lot of strolling around, observing the world around him with the keen eye of a sociologist, to get familiar with the city as a new resident. During these promenades he would stop for a coffee. Places where coffee wasn't just coffee. Now they offered unique taste and smells, with explanations of the origins of the coffee which was supposed to make you feel distinguished. He would sit down listening to nearby conversations, like a young girl says she is going to Sri Lanka to work for an NGO. A smart-looking guy, probably banker of sorts, with majestic self-assurance yodeling about today's great deal. A father with his son, who wants to go to Paris, "to try it out". A lonely guy in his forties drinking a smoothie, maybe after a session in the gym with the PT. These days, gyms have popped up on every block. Staying fit seemed more important than knowing the names of the planet-system or who was the president in Portugal.

If he took the mother of all streets, Hamngatan, people came at you as out of a factory neatly produced, not in hoards but steadily. Some in dark suits, eating an ice cream, passing with serious strides and no wish to be bothered in their path, as if things are being planned, or something of importance just happened or will happen in five minutes. Many disappear into NK, the shopping-center or coming out of this Swedish Harrod's. Someone passes with a huge bag wider and heavier than the holder, from Hermés, exquisitely printed, has bought something of weight money-wise and prestige, duly observed and perceived like a statement. The sun is shining, you wonder which route to take, your feet take you on an already created path, the very same you have done many times and you don't change the direction because of a mysterious superstition makes you subconsciously think disaster might struck.

In these walks inevitably he would pass the area of the Sergels Torg, a place where Stockholm's architects, together with politicians high on themselves in their self-splendid seating from a superior position, had engineered and installed a big grisly crater in the heart of the city. A place which should have been the most beautiful of them all. Instead, they created a big pit and when they were at it, during the crazed sixties, contracted a bewildering sculpture in glass, that looks like secondhand tower-lamp bought on a flea-market. This piece is now branded as "culture" which is to say untouchable. Like the paintings at the subway-station under Östermalmstorg. Unexplicable engravings, what could have been executed by a neanderthal or someone high on some kind of drug, made in concrete blocks with bullet-like holes, spread out at random, "decorated" the walls no one seemed to like. The Culturati assessed with jumbo-mumbo-language, it was great art.

He would pass a park close to his flat, watch people walking their dogs and wondering about dog-life and deducts it's like the military-service, you obey and do what you are told, waiting for something to happen. He watches from a distance, young kids playing football, one of the teams had just made a goal and he laughs at the player's celebration and the sheer happiness of the little crowd watching the game. He recognized himself in their joy and remembered how good it felt when he was seven in a football match against a team one year older, he had made the only goal of the match. Recalling we fought like hell and with a certain discipline but no real tactic. But how nimble we were, small bodies crashing into each other, running until your lungs would burst, fighting like animals to win the game. One day he passed his old school and heard the wonderful sound of children calling at each other, cries of excitement, a lovely chaotic jumble of childish voices so beautiful to listen to. He often made it to "Hallen". A Marketplace for high-enders, where food of all kinds was on show to tempt your appetite, sharpened by the smell of dill, goods gracefully exposed. A place where prosperous men and women buy their stuff for the evening, no strategic buying, only short-term food-intake for a pleasurable evening.

The lingering thought during these strolls; would the striking woman he had met in Hong Kong want to see him again when he returned? His thoughts swirled: why was he even contemplating a relationship with someone so distant in place and age? Any sensible person would dismiss the idea. To make matters more complicated, what about Marianne? The conflicting emotions and the stark contrast between the two women left him more confused than ever.

CHAPTER 5

After his visit to Hong Kong, John and Marianne had crossed paths at a party, sparking the beginning of their relationship. That encounter had set everything in motion. Now they were in the initial stage as a couple with a tacit understanding it might lead to a robust, definite relation. Their affair was a run-up and had started without a succinct beginning. Both were attentive to changes of mood and consciously or unconsciously seeking a firm grip on the relation. Cautious and watchful of any possible mistake at every curve of the road as they promptly began to catch the drift, maybe they could go the whole way.

And the truth was, John missed the sweet stability feeling of marriage, the obvious sharing of all the goods. Time wasn't entirely in their favor perhaps not *the* last chance but close enough. Both were almost fifty and a decision now could lead to serious consequences. There were facts to consider, like their status as parents. She was a mother of two boys, he had a daughter, all to be buckled in, in an eventual joint venture. As so many years had passed, they couldn't truly claim to know one another and their previous experience wouldn't count, lot of water had passed under the bridge since they had been together. Despite some reservations, considering her attitude and at times declared sentiments, she gave the impression she was all in. At first glance Marianne and John were the perfect match and they seemingly were functioning well as a pair. She gave space when needed, allowing him to meet his friends while she met hers, no prowling. Although, many years had passed and they didn't know how they would act in a broader social context and were positively surprised how time and years had made them comfortable in different settings. When young she had been dark-haired, now she was a perfect blond, always carefully combed as if she had just left the hairdresser a minute ago. This conversion of looks gave her a fresh air. She dressed according to the codes of well-to-do people, tastily not mixing colors, a bit classical, a bit Burberry, without the black and white squares. She was above middle height which meant going out with John, being quite tall, was a plus making her happily wearing high heels, well aware John had a thing with shoes and boots, which for her was the way to dress up. She had a face with straight lines which John bestowed with sparkling tributes, which fell into fertile soil. Marianne came from a family of four, a father who had been in the Navy and a mother who once had been a sensation in certain environments in Stockholm. He recalled her weakness for men in uniform, and had a pronounced interest John should go into the navy, no doubt thanks to her father's background. The outfit seemed more important to her, than his career choices. Nevertheless, she was a cheerful soul, appreciating a good laugh although John thought she sometimes was a bit sarcastic and acid. He wondered if this was because of her self-assurance and vanity as she was considered a beauty, installing her above the herd. Since young Marianne had been considered the best-looking of them all which had affected her ego to unlimited ambition of what to search for and how to find it. She had a talent to weaponize her beauty, which intrigued even the strongest men. And it was true, her sheer presence usually added extra shining in a gathering where her hearty laugh did the work. He had noticed she could gaze calmly, almost indifferently at you, which must come having been gratified in her amorous experiences of easy conquests. A passionate soul who liked to be in the center of things and knew how to seduce men, giving it all when it went along her preferred lines.

CHAPTER 6

One evening Marianne and John had gone to an art gallery on Strandvägen and instantly became the talk of the town. The exposition featured a stunning collection of black and white photographs capturing the essence of New York, each frame telling a story of the city's vibrant and gritty character. However, for many attendees, the art itself began to fade due to the unexpected buzz surrounding John and Marianne as a couple overshadowed the photographs, transforming the event into a more a special spectacle than appreciation of the displayed artistry. This confirmed John's skeptical view that people who went to these places wanted to be seen, have fun was more important than having a real go at the exposition. It was the first time they appeared as a couple. Greetings were exchanged and surprisingly John knew quite a few of the present. This news that John and Marianne had come apparently as an item, was more interesting than a few photos from New York.

"Visiting Stockholm?" asked a woman he couldn't remember her name.

"I've come to stay," responded John.

"But you live in Madrid?"

"I did yes."

"I was in Barcelona and went to Figueras Dali's museum, it was amazing."

She said it as if Madrid and Barcelona were the same thing.

"You liked it?" asked John lightly.

"What a man, such creativity."

"The area where he comes from produces extraordinary artists."

"What do you mean?" asked a man supposedly the woman's husband or boyfriend.

"There is this wind, Tramontana, making people go bananas."

"Are you saying Dalí was crazy?"

"Not at all, only that the Tramontana seems to affect human psyche."

"That's why some of his work is quite bizarre?"

"The wind, they say he was touched by it."

"That's an interesting thought," said another man who had been listening to their conversation. It was Gustav an old school-mate, highly intelligent and a distinctive way of speaking, marked by a sharp wit and a talent for irony.

"Hi John, you remember me?"

"Of course I do, how are you doing"

"Always ready for new adventures."

"You haven't changed," said John bursting with laughter.

"When I see you, I also see your slave, how is he?

"Haven't seen him since I left school."

John knew exactly what he was referring to, at the time John had a friend who always trailed behind him in class, almost like a shadow, following his every move as if bound by some unspoken servile obligation. "Here is my card, call me and we have lunch one day, have to go now," said Gustav.

They wandered through the gallery, chitchatting here and there with a few people exchanging remarks until they decided it was time to leave and did a French exit.

"Is that true, you had a slave?"

"Well…there was this guy who sat behind me during my last years in school."

Marianne smirked; "Was he is your errand boy, passing messages to your girlfriends?"

"No, he wasn't a valet like Jeeves. But he had to sit through my ramblings about my weekend conquests or thoughts on the next big party."

"Who is Jeeves?

"He is a figure in P G Woodhouse books."

"Poor guy".

John nodded. "Yeah… honestly, I regret it."

CHAPTER 7

John and Marianne walked through Fältöversten, a shopping mall as any, a melting-pot of a cross section of people. There was a dominance of older people, evidenced by walking with a stick and pure white hair color, taking the direction towards the pharmacy. The younger sort made their business to Systembolaget, the government-owned chain to buy alcohol. A few outlets to get something fast to eat, sushi-bar, pasta or Kebab, mostly served by foreigners. They went through and crossed Karla-plan, a beautifully crafted circled area with a mighty fountain sprouting out water surrounded by big solid trees.

They continued down Narvavägen and passed the Oscar-church, where he had done his communion, he took Marianne under her arm and said;"Let's go in for a moment".

Standing in the middle of the church he thought of all the times he had spent there. Early on, religion had a strong effect on him, yet now it had vanished. Although still intrigued about faith and the big questions, he had no illusions about the church as an institution, as it seemed independent of the initial religion. He considered it difficult to fit in all the sagas in the bible and contemporary discoveries of the universe. The tales in the scripts left him in cold. Even if it was argued they were mostly metaphors and admittingly beautifully described.

This time he looked at the church with a new perspective and was surprised how polished it was. A rectangular built votive ship, with rows of seats on both sides of a long aisle to the altar. On each side there are balconies, only filled at school graduations or at First Advent with thousand people.

"You believe in this," she asked him.

"Not a good question in the Lord's house," he said smiling.

"The original sin, you make me say stupid things."

"Well, not exactly, the original sin in Greek actually means *miss the mark.*"

"And?

"We aren't born with evil inclination."

John's stand wasn't completely indifferent to religious rituals but had no strong emotional response to it. His approach was pragmatic. The concept of paradise wasn't something he counted on. Now he looked at the contents of the church with a serious gaze for a while and made a sign to Marianne that he was done.

"Once at a dinner-party in Madrid, a guy said, 'Catholicism is the only rightful religion to which I said,

'that's quite a statement, you exclude all the others."

"Never talk about religion at parties," said Marianne.

"The guy was from the God-squad. They justify their beliefs and absolve the catholic church from any wrongdoing."

"And you?"

"Many years ago, I saw a procession at Easter, and recoiled, until now.

"But you told me once you wanted to be a priest."

"Yes, until I started to think for myself."

"How did it come about then?"

"Actually I can't explain why or when or where it came from."

"How old were you?"

"Eleven or twelve."

"And how long did it last?"

"About a year."

They walked in silence a while and John said, "in the beginning of Christianity, slaves were promised life in heaven as a reward in a miserable world. That's an easy sell with an abundance of poor people."

"You *are* a man of serious thinking."

"I believe religions are born by fear of the unknown, act as a scripted narrative. They shape our behavior enforcing conformity, it's as if we are all characters in a Netflix series with known ending."

"What do you mean Netflix, we are talking about religion."

"They cast certain characters, the miserable detective with a tragic past, a beautiful woman diagnosed with bipolar syndrome, a misunderstood villain who is just too good-looking to be truly evil and a lost son coming back after surfing the waves in Bali etc. it's all predictable."

"That's a bit of stretch, but you've got a knack for storytelling, maybe you should consider screenwriting." Marianne just looked straight forward in silence.

"Don't forget the sex-scene, Man comes home, Woman, in *his* pajama, waiting to be thrown at the kitchen-wall and have striking sex, ending when Woman, slowly, after the intercourse, slips down exhausted, Man goes to the refrigerator, showing crafted abs, searching a beer, wolfs it down directly from the can, before closing the door to the refrigerator."

"Oh, shut up" she said playfully. "You go from philosophical to basic instincts so easily."

"But seriously, Hollywood is responsible, as if we must have films with violence and sex as entertainment."

His mood brightened with this outburst of his intellectual craft.

"Don't watch them," she said.

"Good idea, I waste too much energy on useless thoughts," he said laughing, "should invent a recycling machine for rubbish thoughts."

"I prefer a tool that reads your thoughts," she said.

"That would be scary."

"I wouldn't have to ask what you think, if you love me for example?"

"No need to talk."

"You couldn't live without talking."

"Which is precisely what sets us apart from the animals."

"But they communicate, not as we do but still."

"Yeah, but there is a catch, speaking causes anxiety of the future. Animals live here and now, no clue what might happen in the future."

"Sounds sad how you put it."

John felt he had more to unpack, a need to express more.

"You know, I find the core vision of Christianity, stripped down to its essence, offers a profoundly pure perspective on life."

"I'm not sure I follow. What do you mean by "pure vision?"

"Well, things like... do you truly believe in the miracles, like Jesus walking on water or the Virgin Birth? Those foundational stories?"

"Honestly? Not really. Life feels too complex, too overwhelming. I struggle to reconcile those concepts with what I experience."

"I think you need a kind of... revelation. A moment of clarity that shifts your perspective."

"A revelation? Like what?"

"For me, it's been those moments of deep connection with nature. Sitting on a beach, the vastness of the sea, the rhythmic waves... it's like a direct line to something big."

"I envy you that. I can't say I've ever felt anything like that."

They reached the bridge, following the route along the water. A tram passed as a witness of old times. The architect of this space must have had a sublime taste in John's eyes, all neat and perfectly placed and planted. The trees had been there before the designer came along so he probably adjusted the design to the trees, not the reverse. A few scattered houses, a pompous museum, with a frame and size tourists mistakenly thought to be a castle. In addition, people coming and going making it lively.

Marianne liked enlightened discussions but only to a certain level, not too heavy hard-core never-ending explanations of philosophical matters in search of truth. She thought it never led to anything anyway. He agreed to some extent, after all, he was only an amateur thinker.

John wondered if she had many female friends. He suspected her personality and beauty, could be intimidating to connect with other women. She seemed to hold herself apart, never letting her guard down. Until now. Not only because of John's character, it was her age that influenced more than she wanted to admit, plus the debacle of her divorce had been as most separations, a long haul of problems, which had made more sensitive and painfully vulnerable. An intelligent woman, she knew it was time to charter a new route, and John could be the one to share her life with. To her, he was a self-reliant character and good-looking fellow. Money-wise she wasn't that sure where he stood. On the other hand, Marianne being a tough bird required and needed to be fully in love and love had to be reciprocated. There was a certain slackness in John's behavior and didn't like what she perceived as insecurity of the undertaking they had initiated.
"What's your take after these two weeks?" she asked him.
"So far so good, trying to get used to it."

"It's strange but I don't see you living in Madrid, the language and all that, you are so Swedish to me."

"When you know the language, it's comes naturally."

"Spanish sounds too rough in my ears."

"It's very effective, especially when you are angry."

"We've talked about it but I still don't get why you went away."

"Those years after my mothers' death I became out of place."

"I met her a few times, always smiling."

"Yes, you did."

"Did she like me?"

"I think she was worried you were too good-looking."

An old man passed them with a very pronounced hunch-way of walking, it seemed he would fall at any moment, they passed a bus-stop where a girl while waiting was texting on her mobile.

"What was he thinking about," referring to the man with the stooped back.

"Old mistakes?"

"Or his bloody children who never come and see him, or finish the book he started years ago." Marianne looked circumspect, as if she sensed John's insecurity in his psyche.

"So, what are your plans?"

"Plans?"

"You still have a flat in Madrid? Is it a just-in-case-scenario?"

"Well," he began but she interrupted him. "Have you really taken a decision? Full out?"

John answered a lame yes, which her antennas picked up on. With feminine intuition she wore the conversation pointedly to the essentials.

"Do you believe in this?"

"In what?"

"In what we are doing, us?"

He could quash the question, instead he paused and reflected.

"That's a loaded question, I've been here a little more than ten days and trying to get used to I actually live here, in Stockholm."

"You didn't answer my question. That's evasive and you know it."

She was right, it was a crooked answer. Instead, he could have said without dithering a strong yes but he wasn't capable.

"Having two flats cost money," she said pointedly.

"You think I live beyond my means?"

"Well, I'm not aware you have a job."

"Working on it, have to wrap it up in Hong Kong."

"Are you fleeing from something?"

"Honestly? I need something stable."

"You mean a place?"

"I mean find a meaning, a role."

"You are a mystery to me, sometimes very physical and others," and she stopped.

"Spiritual?

"Yes, something like that."

"It's true, I like hitting balls against a wall, like an idiot without a clear goal."

"You see, and then you go to deep stuff in a blink."

"Haven't thought about it like that."

Which was a lie, he enjoyed the combination of the not intellectual action of physical effort lifting weights, while listening to a thought-provoking podcast.

"The problem is, I feel I touch the surface but miss what's beneath."

"Maybe you look to hard, chasing something that doesn't need to be caught?"

She was right and had hit the bull's eye unaware of his quandary.

"You are sweet and all, but I need someone who's fully devoted," she said matter-of-factly.

Not being fully committed, her words touched a raw nerve. What he needed was a sense of inner belonging, not just a physical location but feel grounded rather than constantly reacting to life's unpredictability.

"Did you suffer all these years?" Marianne asked.

"I wouldn't call it suffer."

"But how did you manage so many years?"

"Well, at times it was tough money- and job-wise. I remember when a teller-machine swallowed my card cause of lack of funds. But overall, it has been good."

"And what about now are you good?

"For the moment I'm financially healthy. Although it won't last forever."

Thanks to a few good operations had led to a state of modest affluence. She was silent for a while and then repeated her question.

"Have you really taken a decision full-out? "You better hurry up," she said a bit irritated.

He thought he had taken a clear-cut decision and ought to feel lighter as the ambiguity living abroad, had fallen of his chest after moving back to Stockholm. Now, the looming thought of having to choose again, like a rat in lab between two lovers, haunted him and made him doubt the sagacity of his decision. It seemed a hair could turn the balance in him. And the strange thing was, he yearned for a home and feel grounded in all its senses.

Up till now, Marianne had been more muted, not enforcing a full-fledged explanations or answers, only an open line, looking casually at John and checking his answer or way of answering and observing if there were any quirks in his body-language, now she wanted answers. It took John by surprise, as she wasn't one who begged for love, she could decamp at any moment. An independent woman, with no shortage of personal security, not having been completely virtuous, it seemed she desired to pursue the right path without hesitations and know what to hold on to.

"Hurry up what?"

"About us."

John stopped walking and took her hand.

"Right now, a lot is happening, I need to go to London and learn about my father's past as a spy. On top of that, I'm dealing with the media frenzy, fix the new job, my daughter's need and the sudden reappearance of my uncle."

"That's a heavy load."

She didn't seem to notice the existence of an uncle.

"Have to attack one by one I suppose. I'm not a stunt-man, jumping into things."

"Not so sure about that, when you are excited you seem to be one."

John looked around, his gaze drifting aimlessly, not focusing on anything in particular.

"Why haven't you done this before, this thing about your father?"

"Because it's very recent I found out that he was a spy."

"And that's the reason?"

"He almost got the most famous of them all."

"Who?"

"Kim Philby, the man who tricked the MI6 for more than thirty years. He escaped to Russia a day or two before my father was going to catch him."

He didn't mention his worry about the possibility his father had been a double-agent, that is, a traitor. The main reason he wanted to go to London and find out.

"Okay," she said solemnly.

The fact his father had been a spy didn't seem to impress her either way. Apparently, she hadn't read the part in the papers and the rumor that surrounded his father.

"I'm also worried about the press. You can't argue with click-journalism," he said in unusual way getting irritated by the thought of it, "not easy to debunk."

"You think they hack your phone after what you said in Brussels?"

"I don't know but it makes me nervous to be the topic of the day."

"Address it head on, that's what my ex always says."

"Maybe I should," he said as though it held the answer to the question. After this brief exchange of somber conversation, their steps slowed down, as though their wish to continue walking had vanished.

"Listen Marianne, my prophecies aren't good, the future always surprises me." She didn't say anything, just gazed towards the canal. That he didn't have a family wasn't exactly true, a few days ago an uncle had reappeared and in fact, there were scattered relatives in England he could regain. In relation to his uncle, he had been famed as an adventurer and bon vivant who left Sweden due to a grim affair with a girl.

"Got a call the other day, I have an uncle here in Stockholm."

"But that's great," she said.

"I'll see him tomorrow."

"But didn't you know about him?"

"Not really, he disappeared, left Sweden, got a girl pregnant. The girl's family claimed he had abused her and took him of the hook so to say."

"Is it this guy called Modig? Heard the story."

Wow thought John Stockholm is a small city, although, this was within a circle of Stockholm, where everybody knows each other.

"It's that" and he paused, "when you don't have a real family to lean on, it's a bit frightening." It came out more seriously than he had foreseen but it was the truth. She had a worried look in her face.

"But all those years in Spain, how did you manage?"

"You make friends of different sorts by force."

"Poor John," she said and took his hand, "I couldn't do it," she said looking almost afraid, as if she was imaging herself in a situation of solicitude in a foreign country.

"It takes time, it's a constant adaption and when you think you got it, you become aware your reflexes are different, not opposed but different."

"I thought Spaniards are famous for their hospitality."

"At the beginning they did a better job to adapt me than I did."

"But you've told me your circles were mostly Swedish."

"There were years when some lived in curled foreign ghettos a little Sweden but thanks to my job and marriage, I saw a more Spanish aspect of things," and added, "even if you try, you are always a foreigner."

"Even for your wife?"

"For her, I guess I was exotic at the time."

"Was she that old summer-love you mentioned once, in a fragile moment?"

"No, it wasn't."

Marianne was referring to an old love-affair, which had cast a long shadow, evoking strong emotions, a romance during a summer at the coast in Spain. A platonic summer dream, where the cliché of love-at-first sight was applied. Intense moments of platonic love with only one tender kiss. In the aftermath subtle love letters were written during the following autumn and then stopped without explanation. Amazingly, the year after they met again and their relation did fly again, though the second time reality got hold of their minds, a divide due to the geographic distance and the cultural difference. That affair became a benchmark, a reference to which other affairs would be measured and affected forth-coming relations. Not that he was looking for *her* in a new version, or cynically comparing her to anyone who came onto his track, but henceforth he strived for a certain poignancy in love. "So, what did you do all those years a part of playing tennis?"

"You mean workwise? I hopped around the country, where my presence and wisdom were needed", not offering a full-fledged answer of what his job consisted of.

"And you liked it?"

"I miss the enthusiasm of those years and the conquering element, like new frontiers."

She didn't seem to absorb his last words.

"You took a different path than most of us."

"But now I'm back, as everybody else."

"And you have me."

"You know, when you are an immigrant, realizing you are on your own, you sit in a cafe like a "voyeur" dreaming away, not conscious what is going around you, watching with nostalgia a film that doesn't exist anymore."

"Sounds very sad."

"No no, it's the typical lyrics in a Tango."

"I couldn't do it" she said again.

"When I didn't belong, it was tough, feeling like an alien. But you get used to it and find ways, see people you wouldn't do in your home-country, different age-spans."

John remembered when it was completely unknown territory. Didn't know what ground to stand on, didn't know how to assimilate, no idea how to behave, what food to eat.

"I even looked different."

"You look fine, and you have me," she said and kissed him. "I'm all yours."

"But why are you with me if I may know?"

"Because you are so good-looking."

"I'm not."

"Yes, you become beautiful."

"No, I'm not" he insisted.

"Because you are charming and unpredictable."

"In that order? You like uncertainties?"

"I like the romantic John, which I hope never leaves you. Even if you sometimes get too philosophical and that's for a reason, maybe an absence of love."

She didn't know how right she was he thought.

"I could make you happy," she said. Her incisiveness made John feel the screws tightening and didn't know how to answer. He felt a sensation of surprise mixed with a vagrant appeal as there was a fleeting attractiveness to her. He thought she liked him, drawn by his intensity or simply from the way he looked at her with emotional excitement. When young, he said things like "you are my Garbo" or to that tune, which she absorbed like a sponge and demolished her defenses and took her by storm. As they were young, these matters held water for a while and had them trapped in a burst of ideal love. Both were influenced by romantic tales of men dressed in a militaristic way, rapturing a beautiful woman on a horse, to disappear to faraway places where the sun was shining, subsisting of love in some magical unpronounced way, living in a magnificent cottage with a garden full of flowers and apple-trees, having lunches under the old oak-tree while their four beautiful children were dancing around, in a surrounding of the English countryside as its best.

"When we were young, I thought you were stronger or more assertive than me," said Marianne.

"And now it's the opposite, you are the decisive one, I follow you."

There was accuracy in what she said, he was more secure in himself, in general and especially towards her.

"I have the feeling I'm the one who craves and I don't like that."

Get used to it he thought rudely; I'm not in, not hundred percent.

"In reality I don't know much about you", she said slightly teasingly.

"I thought I talked too much."

"Maybe, but you are nice to me."

"Nice?"

"Ok, you are wonderful." She paused for a moment and said, "are you faithful?"

"Where did that come from?"

"I don't know, are you?"

"That's also a loaded question."

"A loaded question? It's a straightforward question. If you can't answer, it says a lot."

John felt like he had been hit in the face. This was new, to speak like this and a subject they knew well, infidelity.

"I don't play around anymore," she said seriously.

"We are not playing" said John now also serious. Those words he had pronounced in another world, to a different person a few weeks ago.

"Love isn't an object you give or take."

"Absolutely not, it's to be shared."

She turned her head towards the water and like talking herself said, "I had a thing with a married guy, and it overtook everything, even my children, couldn't stop it."

"You told your husband?"

"Yes, he couldn't take it, he threw me out with our children inside."

"But until then, had your marriage been good?"

"The truth is we weren't the perfect couple. He thinks I socialize too much."

"Can be understood as flirting."

"I've changed, seen the damage it brings."

"You regret it? To have been with a married man?

"I've a sense of guilt but when passion takes over," adding, "you know the rest."

As a result, to what had been said loud and clear about fidelity, they continued walking in telling silence. They needed time to take it in and his thoughts went elsewhere. He knew this path like the back of his hand. Each bend, each rise, each perfectly spaced lamppost was a familiar friend. The flowerbeds, bursting with vibrant color. Even the trees, their leaves a healthy glossy green, seemed to nod in greeting. The air was crips and mild a welcome, change from the recent heat. A few fluffy clouds drifted lazily overhead. The steady rhythm of joggers, young and old passing by along with the occasional dogwalker and their furry companion was the soundtrack of these thoughts.

"Have I changed since I left?"

"No, you are an improved version."

"Have the sensation that the person I was back then is someone else."

"Have you reached the point where you think you understand everything that happened to you?

"That's a very good question and I have no answer, yet."

This was the very first time they had been more straightforward and earnest in their way of talking. Until now they had danced around the fire without explicit statements partly because of their lack of a clear goal.

But talking sincerely sparked him to speculate if they had a possibility of a happy ending together and if love was a transferable commodity. No question he wanted to look towards the horizon and a bright future but he wasn't sure with whom and that, that was the question.

Marianne looked in his eyes and was weeping, not a few tears, she was weeping big. Her eyes deep in his, John liked what he thought he saw, it was a mixture of hope and love. He also saw sadness.

"I love you," she said.

Her words took him by surprise. Love was a word John had no problem with he had thrown it around many times. You worked yourself up to a frenzy and *I love you* came pouring out, pronounced in a moment of impulse, an assertion of the moment. Her words hit him like a sudden perception of an insight that you can't play around you little jerk. Words are not just words they have a meaning. John got caught in the emotional process and was suddenly feeling something he hadn't felt before with her. He hadn't seen that one coming. He must reckon with this new fact she had popped out without warning.

"I don't go to Paris with everybody," she said.

In a recent weekend-trip they had been in Paris. Decided by an instant, they had spent three days there. You better be careful he reflected unanswered love leads to resentment. He took her hand, and they continued walking in silence for a while. Both aware that he hadn't answered her *I-love-you* with a *me- too*.

As far as he knew, or thought of her, Marianne was a free spirit with limits, she used to say. What it actually meant wasn't that clear, she adapted according to her needs, depending on the moment. Nevertheless, you better shape up, Marianne isn't the Penelope-type, waiting twenty years for Ulysses. A proud woman who after her divorce had forged her own career as home-designer, solicitated thanks to what everybody called her good taste, no over-bearing furniture, mixing old and new with discreet colors. She didn't do the wannabes, she only worked for the solid families of older traits.

John sensed Marianne was economically safe not bothering on the everyday hassle of money, furnished by an ex-husband who didn't care much about her way of life after having been cuckolded and due to heavy responsibilities. What she had said was a warning, not an ultimatum but enough to make it clear that the clock was running.

RALPH G HELLMAN

CHAPTER 8

They had been walking for an hour and began to return along the canal when John said,

"Can we go and visit the graveyard where my mother lies?

"Where is it?"

"It's on the other side of the road, close to the bridge."

"Of course."

They passed the road and went inside the encircling wall of Galärvarvskyrkogården, a landscaped cemetery. John walked firmly in silence, sat down on a bench, no words were said by either of them. After a while she took his hands.

"My plan is to lie here," he said with a mischievous grin.

"It's a beautiful place," she said with a hint of melancholy in her voice.

They left the place as they had entered, in respectful silence. She hadn't asked where his father lied, a question there was no answer to because when killed in the south of the Atlantic, his body was never to be found. They walked towards the bridge with the inevitable intention to stop for a drink at the Bryggan, a restaurant and drinking oasis just beside the bridge, when a guy approached them on a what appeared a high-tech bike. He was dressed as a genuine rapper, baggy T-shirt, baggy jeans, large hoodie with a confusing printed message and Nike footwear, although no gold-chains only casually wearing wristbands. "It's my son," she said in a whisper. "Hi Fredrik."

Not the typical name for a rapper thought John.

"Hi," said the boy looking surprised.

The situation became awkward due to the boy's obvious insecurity seeing his mother together, with what might be a new close friend to his mother. John sensed Marianne's not hidden timidness towards her son. "This is Fredrik, John Sherman."

"How was your day," asked John congenially.

Their handshake was a mix of curiosity from both sides. The boy seemed to wonder if this was one more of the endless lovers, never knowing which could be the lasting one.

"We were just talking of having a drink, maybe you'd like to join us," said John taking the initiative. Marianne looked with appreciation at John.

"Yeah, why don't you come and talk tennis here with John, he is a tennis-nerd. It's his life-priority."

"You play?" asked John.

"Not much" said the boy shyly, giving his smartphone a look.

"Maybe we could give it a chance?"

The boy looked at John making a fast evaluation, a man of approximately fifty, can't be hard to beat, only boring.

"Okay," he said in the short-cut way young adults sometimes speak, without furthering if it was for the drink or tennis.

They turned and went to Bryggan, a floating bar-restaurant, as it indeed was situated on the water. Perfectly set you wondered who's pockets at the Townhouse had been filled to get the permit and rights. A better placed outlet for a drink, didn't exist in Stockholm, a pure money-maker. The site offered a perfect view visualizing the center of the city. Close by there were stationed a few fishing-boats of older tract, giving atmosphere to the surroundings. It wasn't clear who the owners of these ancient boats were, as they just laid there, never left the place, just hooked there as per design.

In this outlet for drinkers and eaters you were obliged to order and pay, before you sat down. Fredrik was engaged on his mobile. John saw how fast he moved pictures or whatever there is on that devilish machine. Those wizards in Silicon Valley were so smart with easy entries, no cost or effort to watch anything. Life was a screen, where everything was acted upon. Constant notifications and the allure of online content distract from face-to-face conversations leading to isolation and superficiality. By a click, the world was yours. John had read that depression among adults rose, when iPhones sales spiked. Following this line of thought, John found a table and they sat down, close to a man in his sixties, sitting alone, who seemed to be looking with anticipation towards anything that moved. He was waiting for someone. His smiling face beamed with anticipation and yearning, hinting a joyful rendezvous ahead. He must have arrived a bit early, or the other person was arriving late. He was perfectly dressed and waiting eagerly. John had a Sherlock Holmes-instinct in him and was watching the man discreetly. John had often done this, sitting as a spectator in an airport or train-station, observing the people, trying to foretell the status of a passersby, general standing, kind of work or personality. John concluded this man was well off, not a top gun, sixtyish, married and two kids, worked as a civil servant, not the funniest guy in a gathering, a man of order.

John turned his attention back to the boy, striving to be detached. This tendency to console and listen stemmed from years of navigating life without a close family.

"What are you up to? Studying?"

"Not really, fixing my own company."

Not really, either you study or you don't John thought.

"Okay and which field is it?"

"I'm doing hoods."

"Hoodies, okay, selling on the net?"

"Yeah that's the idea."

"Where do you take them from?"

"Was in Portugal and found a supplier."

"Going main-stream or high-enders?"

This question suggested John knew about the business, which surprised mother and son.

"High-enders."

"I think that's smart. But you must give value for money."

Fredrik began to show a more deferential manner towards John and relaxed talking about his hoodies. His mother watched in silence how the conversation flowed between the two.

"Working on the website but you need good models."

"Which costs money of course."

"Yeah,

"Lots of competitors?"

"A few."

He didn't furnish how many or who they were, perhaps he thought it wasn't worth it. Even after these exchanges, the boy didn't appear to be on firm footing and John felt sorry for him, remembering when he was young how difficult it had been when the hormones were at full throttle and so many questions were raised, doubts about meanings and above all, the mating-game.

"The beginning is tough, not easy to find the right path," said John. There was an acidity in the boy's attitude, expressed with absence of self-assurance, maybe Instagram and other devices had killed it. The tools where you compare other people's exterior life with your own inner life. A recipe for disruptive thoughts. An abundance of social media where the beautiful people showed their edited pictures partying in Ibiza, being remembered by old loves announcing how fun they had without you. It was stalking without meeting the person. A virtual stupid world, where no one knew what was really going on. How could you show empathy in a world of images?

The conversation shifted and Fredrik mentioned his love of surfing in Costa Rica, getaway from where he was, which John had nothing to say about, he had done the same. A visible frustration like an open wound thought John. The boy had identity problems and existential issues, accompanied with possibly a late puberty, a growing boy in search of direction and purpose. Too protected, installed comfortably far away from life's realities.

"Have you done a bucket-list?"

"Sort of."

"Mount the Everest, or live with the Masai in Africa and stuff like that?"

"You know, see the world, travelling, have a gap-year"

John concealed his thoughts, it seemed in this age where instant gratification reigns, fueled by feelings whims of emotion made it so difficult for them, perhaps they had too high expectations.

"Instead of doing hoodies?

"Yeah."

"Two very different choices but with a positive approach, it's easier to find the way," said John as if he was talking to himself.

"You mean that crap of having the right attitude?"

"I would say it depends how you react to things."

"What do you mean?"

"You see what you want to see instead, if you try to be objective, you make it easier for yourself."

The boy looked straight at John. What John had said could well be for his own use.

"Well put" he said after a while.

"Think about it as of a tennis-match, if you react angrily when the ball comes at you, you'll might miss but if you adjust and take the ball with a degree of acceptance, then you might hit it back, in your favor."

The boy gazed toward the water in silence as in a sign of approval.

"Have you tried golf?

"Yes."

"Like it? It's character-building."

"Maybe but it's stressful," sentenced the boy.

"There is a study that shows there are more failures putting for birdie than putting for par."

"And why is that?"

"The scare of failure."

John decided to change topic to tennis.

"What do you prefer, fast courts or clay,"

He took some time before answering, digesting the question.

"Hard courts."

"I could fix an hour at those out-door courts on Djurgården.

Fredrik looked surprised. Another calculation if it would be worth it, play with a man who more than doubled him in age.

"Are you up for it?" he asked John.

"Tennis is a strange game, you never know," answered John with a big smile as if the match had already started.

"Fredrik has played a lot," said Marianne.

"Me too", said John smiling.

"Okay, we could do that," which was expressed with a slight defiance, like I'm going to beat the shit out of you.

Fredrik stood up, and said, "are you the one they talk about in the papers?"

"You saw the article?"

"Yeah, and I think you're right, the immigration-issue is a mess with lousy integration."

"Seems the ramifications of my remarks have become a media-drive." The leftists portrayed him as an offender of the multiculture system. John's views were being debated in full storm. It was stuff to argue about and good for sales of the papers. Luckily there were only a few images of him so he hadn't become a household person.

"I had no idea my words would cause such a stir."

"Before things are out of your control maybe you should counterpunch," said the boy.

"That's an option," said John looking at the boy with newfound respect, "although it doesn't attract me, enter that kind of scuffle."

Fredrik stood up, "have to go now, see you."

John raised and noticed he was slightly taller than the boy. Both did an estimation of the other's measurements as two boxers before the fight. After an instant both smiled, "see you on the court" said Fredrik, kissed his mother on the chin and departed. Marianne looked at John with curiosity.

"Did I say something wrong?"

"No not at all just saw the competitor in you."

"Well," he said deviating her comment, "it's amazing how many friends you make with a good forehand,"

"I think he liked you."

"I suppose he was trying to catch what kind of fish I am."

"I'm also trying to do that."

"Are you close?"

"There are moments I believe so but sometimes I feel a sense of loathing."

Naturally, the emotions a child experiences, after a parent's divorce, are little known, John thought.

He cast a casual glance at the man at the table close who was now accompanied by a woman, a perfect match for him concluded John while raising. The man looked suddenly at John and said abruptly, "Are you the one spreading lies about immigration?"

"Sorry buy you are mistaken," answered John and took Marianne to look for another table on the pier, enabling them to enjoy a better view and sit down in the outermost part of this watering hole.

The man got excited and almost shouted, "You are a racist, a privileged brat."

John stopped in his tracks, turned angrily to the man and said, "Say that again." John's voice had somehow turned into a booming resonance. Seemingly the man hadn't expected this reaction and became meek in seconds. People were staring with tensity at John and the man who had initiated this commotion.

"You don't mean that do you?" said John. It sounded like a father talking to a misbehaving son and now weighing what kind of punishment he would execute.

At that moment a man looking like a bulky weightlifter came forward and spoke with authority, "What's going on here?" It was said calmly making it clear, he was now in charge. John didn't say anything, the man and reason for this intermezzo, tried to say something but his companion cut him short and raised resolutely, took him by the hand and mumbled an excuse and began to leave the place.

"Excellent," said the weightlifter who had appeared from nowhere as if he had been hiding and now had popped out to fix a brawl and thrive in it.

"I'm sorry," said John.

"For what?" I read the papers, saw your picture. I agree with you as many others here", said the weightlifter.

This little interlude which could have ended up much worse thanks to the intervention worked as a stimulator for the weightlifter and put him in a good mood and said, "I'll invite you on a drink," and turned to a waitress without waiting for John's answer, "offer them what they want."

"That's very kind of you."

"At least someone speaks out and I thank you for it, have to work now," and left.

"Well done, you escaped," said Marianne.

"Just luck,"

"You have to be careful this might happen again."

The waitress came and they ordered two glasses of champagne. Marianne noticed John's pensive mood and weariness, "cheers, you did well there".

"The champagne is always better when its free," said John while sipping from his glass.

The incident seemed to have thrown John off distracted, caught in two minds. Marianne steered the conversation towards calm waters.

"Tell me about this uncle of yours, how did he find out about you?"

"He saw the article in the paper and somehow got hold of my number."

"When did you see him last time?"

"Don't remember, haven't seen him in years. After we both left Sweden, we lost contact. I'll see him tomorrow, cheers," said John and clicked her glass.

"But that's great."

"Enough about me, what about you, what have you been doing all these years?

"Are we talking about me now?"

"Why not, give me a synopsis of your life."

"Synopsis? Okay, no long tales just to the point."

"In chronological order please," he said smiling.

"I became airhostess by accident, flew around the world, married, got two boys and here I am, freshly divorced becoming an interior designer."

"Maybe you condensed it too much but it's a good summary for a CV."

"Tell in 25 seconds twenty-five years isn't very exciting."

"It sounds perfectly good and normal." She looked in a pensive mood.

"Was there a meaning all these years, did I fulfill my dreams?" she said looking towards the water, "life pushes us forward and one day you wake up and wonder what it was all about. You begin to doubt and regret, at least parts of it."

"Were you in love when you married, I mean in the real way?" quizzed John with half a smile.

"With hindsight I'm not sure."

Hindsight often provides a different perspective. And memories are treacherous old friends. It seemed she was in a similar situation to her son, no solid ground there but on the other hand, who was?

"John I'm not in the best mood today."

He took her hands as a gesture of affection. She didn't cry again but it was close.

"Regrets?"

"Honestly? Yes, you have awakened something in me."

"I'm sorry," he said lamely.

"Are you happy Jonny?"

"I like when you say Jonny."

"You didn't answer my question."

"I'm fine, not Christmas-happy maybe but it's okay."

"Okay? That's not the Jonny I like."

"Which Jonny do you like?"

"The enthusiastic one, full of energy."

John couldn't agree more, she was right, he had been slightly unenthusiastic towards her, due to the stone he had brought with him in his shoe from Hong Kong.

"There is so much going on right now," he said in an effort to not lie outright and this was true in a way, as lies from truth are better than invented ones he thought.

"Maybe it's me," she said, "don't worry it will pass" and she looked on her watch, "have to go now, my sister wants to talk."

"About us?" he said thinking he was funny.

"No, no, she thinks she needs a change in her life. Her husband is going on a trip for a year, to the South Pole of all places, a scientific mission and she isn't that unhappy about not being un-happy. Dinner at your place?"

"At seven, okay?"

She nodded and stood up, no words, eyed him seriously and left. He stared like in a void, conscious it's getting serious. He began to walk towards his new home. It was evident time was shrinking for a decision. He was walking a tight rope a little mistake and it would end. She was sincere and wanted to play it straight, obliging him to act in consonance, not like when they were young. He had a flashback from when he was twenty-one or twenty-two and they had been a couple, how different it is now compared to then. This time she didn't have the leading role, she followed him. This could be a turning point, given the direct words made earlier, loud and clear.

CHAPTER 9

Being left alone, he felt an urge to talk to someone, so he called his daughter in New York. Must be late morning in New York, she would make him focus on other matters.

"Hi.

"I'm going to Riverside to play tennis," she said.

"Great," he said and remembered when they had been there together.

"Are you coming to New York?"

"No, I wonder if you could come to Stockholm.

"When?

"Whenever you want.

"Have exams now but in two three weeks I can be there."

"Ok good, I'm going to Hong Kong again."

"Don't mess it up," she said.

John had told her about Jasmine, without details and above all, not Jasmine's age, wouldn't be appreciated.

"Are you okay?"

"You know what dad I really love you."

John stopped in his tracks. This was the second time this day he heard those same words, but this was different. Hear that from your daughter means responsibility. It made him feel close to ashamed and a sensation of guilt.

"That's nice of you to say, me too."

She was silent at the other end of the phone.

"Let's check flights," he said and then we talk."

They agreed he would check it out and they cut. John couldn't envision what goes around in the head of a girl, coming of age, living alone in New York. He remembered when two years ago they had been in London for a bit of tourism and bonding, they had played tennis in Regent's Park and she had fallen so bad, they had to go to a hospital. They did a scanning of her head in case there was any serious damage. Luckily there wasn't any real trouble. The doctor who treated her happened to be star in the medical business, obviated when he spoke, you perceived sheer and raw intelligence, added with empathy, exactly what you wish a doctor should be. John recalled how he had seen her suffering and wondered what consequences there might be in her psyche after that.

How did she get over the divorce? Many questions to confront like with whom to spend Christmas with one or the other? Divorced parents put their children in a hard choice-gamble. And what about the guilt gifts I gave her, to compensate. And now, at nineteen, an age when things can change in a whim, what were her feelings? Consequently, a creeping sense of guilt occasionally haunted him like a wet towel he couldn't get rid of like in a bizarre nightmare. However, as a divorced parent he rationalized and thought it's better as it is, instead of two people going at each other's throats in shouting matches. Plus, you think you are free again. That's easy-thinking and cheap. Well cheap that depends, economically his divorce wasn't precisely a win-win.

Anyways that was the past and right now he needed to channel his attention towards the up-coming trip to Hong Kong and the new job, strictly speaking making money and accordingly let go of the distraction of the mating-game. Thinking about money gave him a Pavlovian gag-reflex so he sent an e-mail while walking, to Francois Antheaume, a French distributor who would be a central figure of the upcoming launch of the start-up company, together with Ben Dunbar, the Tai-Pan in Hong Kong John had met over there with whom he had not only made friendship with but who would be the principal owner of this yet- to-be established company. Francois answered immediately suggesting John should come to Paris and arrange themselves before going to Hong Kong and the up-coming meeting with Ben Dunbar. I'll have to deviate that trip and take London first and then directly Hong Kong, thought John.

Walking upwards Narvavägen, he looked around and deduced Stockholm could give a sensation of being dull, traffic wasn't that intense. Cars and buses passed by practically in silence. No advertisements in all corners. The buildings, most of them built a century ago oozing respect, manifested in the price-tag, a clear tangible expression of privilege. Even if you couldn't visualize from the outside, he knew that behind those walls and windows, inside existed solid means, but also a enjoying an understanding of life's finer parts, albeit, who knows what's going on behind the façades. The area exuded a sophisticated quality, probably up-to date in the modernity, eco-bio-friendly, grinding their own expresso, efficient app usage, reducing waste while composting and recycling, according to John's assessment of these neighborhoods.

While walking his eyes darted here and there. It was here where he had been made and had become what he now was. Unexpectedly he had gradually come to realize that living in your home country didn't require any explanation of any sort, you accept what there is. In a foreign country you compare, analyzing what is in front of you at every turn, making judgments with a polarizing result. Your home country, gave a sense of belonging, embedded with a natural tribal affinity. That sensation was never fully felt during his time abroad, despite the quite good things that had happened. Still and to his defense, he had adapted well to a life as a foreigner and wasn't regretful. As a matter of fact, it might have been a blessing in disguise to have left Sweden, what outcome had there been if he had stayed? This was a new angle to consider. To prevent doubts and make his life puzzle easier to solve, he re-affirmed that things were turning out according to his decisions, he was where he should be.

CHAPTER 10

To uplift his worried state, with so much weighing on him, he needed to talk to someone and let off steam, thus he called his friend Carl. Thanks to identical childish playfulness, obviously not articulated when you are thirteen and immature, but they shared an affinity. Whether it was, jumping into the water, going down slopes or the tantalizing effect the opposite sex had on them, they were bound together. They even looked alike to a degree, with boyish features. Though there was a distinction between their hobbies, John liked everything with rackets and balls, while Carl's passion was horseback riding and sailing. Riding was a sport John had never understood the excitement of galloping a meadow feeling the moisture of the nostrils from a horse but envied the sensation of being weightless and powerful enough to stop the beast like a wizard.

The last years John had lost precise tracks of Carl's life. At some stage their lives had drifted apart, not been in full contact. The reason for this shortcoming wasn't clear. It was John's hope they could develop a good friendship hitting older age, recovering the lost years with a fraternity-like ambition, pick it up with no residual reserve. John liked and admired Carl's common sense and no nonsense, he was nobody's man but his own.

"Hi Carl."

"Just finishing some painting stuff."

"Painting with big brushes or what?"

"It's the house out here, every year needs a bit of my talent."

"What about sharing a moment together?

"Two persons and one thought. By the way, someone had seen you the other day and I thought I must call you and hear what you are doing." Carl had the detective's mind and was always probing you. At times he would skillfully interview you, coaxing you into revealing things that didn't need to be told.

"We could share a bite and catch up, there is plenty to talk about." They agreed to meet in an hour at the cafeteria of NK, the department-store. Carl arrived as he always did in a kind of rush or occupied with something that needed to be solved on the spot.

"Looking better every day."

"I'm sure trying."

"Many things have changed, save your looks."

They sat down, ordered a sandwich with a sensation of immediate connection, instinctively they liked each other. The gap years didn't seem to affect their interaction. They had started out on similar tracks, but now they were like two independent sailing-boats, tacking their vessels, choosing different winds. Nevertheless, as two grownups they felt a curious anticipation of how their friendship would unfold. Never spelled out but they deduced they were privileged and cherished with good constitutions and ingredients to make it in life. Carl didn't show fragilities, giving a sensation he had things figured out. Although John knew that it hadn't been easy for him, a broken family and money was never carefree. One didn't know how much substance there was to him but when Carl arrived at any gathering, he made things seem better than before his appearance and possessed a flair and style people liked. Always making sparkling cues about whatever theme was flying in the air, fingering with a common sense all could agree on but didn't find the words for. Strong in body and in mind. His father had been hugely successful but left a wife and family when Carl was at the tender age of seven. Carl's mother, because of an addiction to alcohol or other unknown reasons had also vanished, travelling Europe, in a spree of searching a man she wanted and never found. The effects on Carl of these things had made him resilient, where sentiments weren't brought to light or declared. Dealt with a tough hand he was no-nonsense, pragmatic, never marinated in negatives. Fairly good-looking with a face of innocence, not parochial. Above all, he was astute and a quick-witted opportunist, as a good sailor. John envied that talent to take charge of a sailing boat, it must do something for your self-esteem, he thought. He characteristically seemed to possess a talent for taking shrewd decisions and went about things in a casual smooth way. At the same time there was something mischievous in him but in a charming way. In terms of his professional working life John hadn't any precise insights what had been done or not done.

"Are you sure what you are doing, coming back?"

"There are moments of doubts yes."

"You'll need time to adjust."

John didn't want to reveal his real doubts those were not about time.

"Is it as you expected?"

"You soak it up differently when it's not just a visit of a few days."

"I see you sitting in Madrid romanticizing about Stockholm and now, suddenly you are here, in the thick of it."

"Exactly, you are right on."

"After all, it's here where you lived your formative years. That affects everything."

"Yes, what was created here last forever."

"It does, and of course nostalgia and memories play a part. You select certain details and install them in a gold-frame."

"I don't chase the good old days, they just appear, like the wind with precise recollections of the past."

"I think you forget how it truly was and shape it to fit your wishes."

"What about you? Restless when you lie on the pillow in the night?"

"Not really, I suppress fancy dreams."

Meeting an old friend, you are not sure if you really know him anymore, if the mutual interests and ground were in place and maintained. Besides, you couldn't be sure if the questions he put were a checklist in a puzzle, or genuine interest John thought.

"And do you succeed?"

"I would say yes, with variations."

"Variations?"

"I kind of accept what I've been given, so far at least."

"All the bruise and struggle are like an orchestra tuning their instruments, making annoying noises with the hope to reach improved heights," said John pompously.

"Still a poet's mind I see, sounds a bit thick though."

"It's cause of reading too much mixed with mellowing I gather. Anyhow I'm glad to hear you are good because many seem to be unhappy with what they are and have, despite of what looks like a good life."

"Yeah, there is a lack of satisfaction, all this about realizing yourself. Family isn't that tight anymore, people travel and when you come home after a weekend it seems dull. The affluent society, PT's and caviar."

As ever Carl had a knack of resuming things perfectly, thought John. They continued chatting away, sharing recent events from their lives and reflecting on all that had been accomplished and all that remained undone. John knew that to feel good, you needed to discern you were a member of the tribe where small talk and gossiping was a lubricant. For John, sitting talking to Carl was like therapy, it made him feel better and at home.

"By the way my uncle has appeared, Dennis Modig."

"I've met him, he is one of a kind."

"What does that mean?

"He lives with my wife's aunt. His reputation isn't perfect."

"Not perfect?"

"He is known to drivel about huge business plans without finishing them."

"I didn't know, haven't him seen for years."

"His fame is more boast than substance."

John took this in, remembering how many years ago, his mother mentioned that his uncle was something of an eccentric. And if Carl had this disquieting opinion, there must be some truth to it.

"I'll see him tomorrow."

"In any case, it's good to have family around," Carl said to comfort John after his sharp critique.

"Well, we both know what it means with no family around."

"Yes that's true."

They both fell silent, realizing they shared a similar situation when it came to family. John considered if he should tell Carl about his love quest? No, not now, no need as it might be thrown out of the window soon.

"And how do you deal with your newfound fame", asked Carl with his characteristic penchant for interviewing and a tendency to move forward putting his elbows on the table when he wanted to declare something. Obviously, Carl had read the articles about him in the press.

"You are swimming in dangerous waters."

"Haven't grasped it yet, I'm juggling other balls right now."

"Remember that Dutch filmmaker who was killed being outspoken about immigrants?"

"Yes of course."

"You better be careful, there are radicals and crazy oddballs all over the place and they can be activated."

"Activated, that's a way to put it."

"Let's forget that, why don't you come out to my house in the archipelago this weekend?"

Carl had shifted their conversation in his typical way, steering to more neutral grounds as he might have discrepancies about the hot potato of immigration and integration. With a mind like Carl's things were diverse and changed fast.

"That would be great."

"Can I come with a friend?"

"A friend?"

"It's Marianne."

"The same you went out with.? You don't waste your time," he said slightly startled.

"Old love doesn't rust."

"You were always a ladies-man."

"No, they just appear, same as with Orson Wells."

"You took the girls, but I was funnier than you."

"But you had your share, I remember when you came home after a holiday in France and was deeply in love."

"It came strong those days, like being in a wonderful stunning dream."

The word stunning made John reflect on what had happened to him in Hong Kong.

"Do you remember that doctor who cornered all the girls?"

"Yeah, Michael something, he bulldozed and seduced them with his crap of bullshit."

"I think he wanted to get laid and apparently he succeeded." John was absorbing this fact of a fellow man he didn't know.

"Anyhow, good luck with that or as we say at sea, go by your gut-feeling."

"Wow that's a funny turn."

"Well, I tend to focus not lose my time wobbling," said Carl laughing.

"Like me you mean, aside of that, remember when you said there were only two guys you would share a war-trench with? It was Johan and me, still thinking that?"

"Yeah, I remember that, have to say though, the thought hasn't bothered me since."

"What made you think that?"

"Not sure but you didn't seem to get scared so easily, not getting mad if things would turn rough."

"I could say the same about you. I think we tilted towards tough characters."

"I have more friends now, have to think about it but you still have a chance."

Which they both had to laugh at because what had been said was indeed a strong claim of respect and a professed recognition of affection towards one another.

They sat in silence a while reflecting on what had been said. "Carl, I think we missed a mentorfigure."

"You mean we are self-made?"

"We had each other for sure, you were there when my mother died."

"Maybe you don't know but you were always a good listener."

"I think I was too cautious and emotionally guarded after that."

"I never figured you out. "What stroke me with you, as serious and easy-going at the same time."

"Honestly? To me you seemed to have an inner strength which I envied I suppose."

"I'm a good actor," said Carl with the smile of his.

"Any mistakes you regret?"

"There are things I didn't do which is a mistake in a way." Characteristic answer from Carl which defined his person.

What had been said was new, it had never been pronounced with such sincerity and warmhearted nature before.

"Think I have to go now," said Carl. "I'll pick you up at the gas-station for boats in Saltsjöbaden, Friday afternoon about six, is that okay?

Just before leaving John asked Carl; "When I left Sweden what did you think of it?"

"Can't remember, probably I thought it was a kind of escape."

"Nothing firm to hold on, nothing stopped me. I was restless after my mother's passing."

"To me it looked like a whim-decision."

"Actually, it had been brewing quite some time, do something different." With hindsight, he realized again he lacked a truly satisfying explanation for why he had left.

"But why did you stay so long?"

"That's another question I don't have a good answer to."

With a sigh, he acknowledged that the past was often a labyrinth of unanswered questions.

"Do you think all these years living abroad have changed you as a person?"

"I hope not, the essence is still there, undeniably it has left a mark."

He hoped whatever dreams he had forged here still held sway. The youthful frenzy of those days undoubtedly had subsided but not entirely extinguished. This was evident in his enthusiasm for new ventures, a powerful energy and youthful spark still flickering in him.

"I do think it has instilled a more careful way of hasty undertakings.

"You've become more analytical?"

"Yeah, a bit yes, at least more patient thanks to the experience."

A thing hard to know if experience helped you or took away from you, could be as difficult as mapping the position of the galaxies, he concluded.

"I'm a slow sailor."

"Well, there is random at sea, you can't always predict the winds," finished Carl giving a fatherly look of affection. "John, you are good, and I like you."

Hearing this by Carl, stirred John and he needed it badly, it was like rain for dried out soil.

"See you on Friday."

CHAPTER 11

John left Carl with a good notion. Once at home he opened his laptop and wondered why there was a whirring sound inside. Once the mystery machine had calmed down a message came through which attracted his immediate attention, it was from Ben Dunbar about a meeting in Hong Kong.

Please search for flights in about a week, will confirm exact date soonest for our meeting.

The purpose of meeting up in Hong Kong was to establish the essential groundwork and infrastructure to launch a trading company specializing in packaging solutions. Set up frames, meet suppliers and do a budget. Work out a scheme, combining suppliers and collaborators, visit various factories outside HongKong and investigate about the possibility with a factory around Venice to be a supplier to be incorporated to the ones from the Far East which John had previously worked with and knew well. The perfect suit for John. There was also a new message from the think-tank that had shown an interest in him after John's intervention in Brussels. They were interested in "Gentleman-John", as he sometimes was called in the press, there might be a place for him within their team. As Marianne would come to dinner, John went out again, a minute's walk to a supermarket to buy some food.

The warm sunny afternoon put John in a good mood, and he set out to buy the stuff he had longed for living abroad, like Swedish shrimps with mayonnaise and toasts. And of course, buy wine at Systembolaget, a uniquely Swedish shop where they only sell alcohol. You could start a company, buy a house, get married and divorced at eighteen but not buy alcohol. He bought two bottles of French Rosé of what can be called mid-level pricewise. The State dictated these outlets, with a patronizing effect and a prerogative commission, publishing all prices, which meant all Swedes knew the standard of your wine- bottle-gift, or what class of wine you invited with.

He left this peculiar big-brother-business and went to the supermarket. Once inside looking at the shelfs perfectly filled with products in straight lines brought memories when he as a kid, worked during holidays in a supermarket to get extra-money. He had overseen the drinks, sodas and milk as a shelf-stacker, that is put goods on the shelves: fill them up in perfect squares on gondolas, hence he got always annoyed when someone bought a bottle breaking his perfectly made straight lines. Suddenly the phone vibrated with an unknown number while looking at the delicious seafood spread out nicely.

"Hi, it's me."

Listening to Jasmine's voice his brain made a tilt, and he felt a surge of excitement.

"Can you speak?"

"While I'm looking at shrimps?"

"What?"

"Just buying some food."

"I can't see you buy food."

"Someone has to do it."

"I miss you."

"Me too, great to hear your voice again."

What a banal thing to say. There was a short silence, enabling him to recap and think. He imagined her lovely face and black mane, which he in a bewildered moment had compared to a Mustang's, when he had seen her the first time in the lobby of the Mandarin hotel. He looked around hoping no one would hear him, as if doing something he shouldn't.

"I wanted to hear your voice."

Searching frantically for words he said, "I'm thinking of you all the time," a slight lie though not entirely.

"Where are you now?"

"In Stockholm."

"I can't picture you there."

"In a week I will be in Hong Kong."

"How come?

"Fix my new job."

"That's why you come?"

"And to see you."

She went silent

"How long will you stay?"

As he didn't know, he avoided to answer her and said instead:

"How I miss you Jasmine," by uttering these words he suddenly became aware that he really meant them.

"You didn't answer my question."

"I really don't know," he confessed, thinking he was becoming an expert not answering questions lately.

"What day do you come?"

"When I have the flight I'll let you know."

"Ok."

"I long to see you so much."

"Me too. You like it where you are?"

"Yeah, it's fine."

"More than Hong Kong?"

"It's different."

She fell silent again.

"Ok let me know when you arrive."

"How I miss you Jasmine," he sighed.

"Have a safe flight," she said pragmatically.

"I'll call you or send you a message."

They rung off. He smiled to himself wickedly. A feeling of elevation arose accompanied by a radiating energy, added with different images of Jasmine. After the short call he felt an adrenaline rush and perceived things from another perspective when eyeing the surroundings. Flustered he went to buy shrimps where an older woman talked to a young guy serving her. They discussed the pros and cons of buying food in big or small quantities. He sensed the old lady's need to be in contact with other human beings.

"My daughter is coming tonight so I'll invite her for a small dinner," she said.

"That's nice," said John who also was in need to talk with the world.

"She doesn't visit me often," looking both at the boy serving them and John.

John looked at the little woman, probably a widow with a daughter who didn't visit her sufficiently.

"You, young people will be like me one day."

"I hope I'll be like you," said John elegantly.

"You should meet my daughter, she is your age," now looking with straight eyes at John.

"Maybe we should," he answered, "the problem is, I already have a date tonight."

"I'm joking," she said blinking one eye, "I'm an old lonely lady and I'll like to talk."

"Nice to meet you and good luck" said John when she went away. He bought his shrimps, bread and mayonnaise, and went back home in a dreamy state.

God, I've tried but the feeling doesn't fade away Jasmine, I'm lost, a real fuck-up squeeze considering the upcoming dinner with Marianne. You must focus now, my boy. But how can I, when life isn't just some cognitive shit, it's emotional, he thought. Walking back to his flat he speculated about the meaning of the call, not reaching a conclusion. The only thing he knew was that he had fallen irrevocably in love. From the very first moment, it had ignited an immediate connection. An overwhelming sense of attraction and a profound feeling of being drawn together. Despite these feelings for Jasmine, in reality he knew very little about her, only that she worked in a great hotel, had a Chinese mother and English father but not much more. Not much about her aspirations, what she did during her free time, hadn't met her friends. He perceived her easy going and synergetic with the world in general and a person who didn't use strong words or extremes. Standing in the elevator with his purchase for a dinner with Marianne he began to read the description of elevator-security and didn't absorb one word of it, only the brand Thyssen, a name he never could dissociate with their aid to Germany's blitzkrieg during the second world war machine. Pushing himself out of the elevator and searching for the key to open the door he tried to focus on preparing the dinner.

But fate had decided otherwise, Marianne sent a message saying she wouldn't come for dinner. She didn't give any explanation. He took it as a relief to be alone and gather his thoughts. This meant he had to eat the shrimps alone. He prepared a few toasts and opened the mayonnaise-tube and began to eat. A solitary meal, these things were better shared.

Looking around the flat he had on occasions tried to figure out if he had been strong-armed by Marianne renting the apartment he now lived in. At first, he hadn't thought much of the consequence by such a decision. Nevertheless, it had released the stress-factor initially of where to live. A bedroom with an abstract painting in blue above a solid bed and eastwards a big window. A living room, connected to the kitchen and a balcony, with sufficient space for four chairs and a table where you could share a glass of wine on warm summer nights. The furniture was un-exciting IKEA, a TV-set with thousands of channels. A perfectly furnished bathroom and a walk-in closet, where he could choose what to wear in a luxurious way where his shirts and trousers could be seen. Although John wasn't a man who dedicated much time on what to wear but liked to visualize what options there were. His way of clothing had remained the same over the years, with a certain conservatism and hints of Ralph Lauren-style. His preferred colors were white or navyblue, no quilted colored shirts, nor brown trousers.

He sat down in the sofa and observed the bookshelf bared of books, which for him, a man of reading, is a flaw because the bookshelf says a lot about the person. Same goes for a visit to the toilet in someone's house and the medicines you might come across speaks volumes. The only touch of decoration was a vase with the flowers from the other day. To the right of the shelf, as a manifestation of his person, were his rackets and golf clubs. For a visitor who didn't know John, the impression would be misled by this spartan decoration. A visitor would catch, whoever lived there, had arrived recently, it lacked soul. Not an avid TV-viewer, he turned on CNN. He was familiar with the anchors and their overly perfected hairdos, the permanently grave looking Wolf Blitzer, a shouting funny Richard Quest. Apart of these two, he had the impression that the reporters were very good-looking at CNN, whose purpose were to attract attention and concluded it says a lot of our times. Even information was based on physicality and required good looks. An e-mail came through while he was sitting watching TV, it was Ben's secretary giving dates for their meeting in Hong Kong: I must check my visa at the Chinese Embassy he thought. Tonight, would be good for a solo walk, get his things thought out but renounced when he heard raindrops on the windows and went to bed instead. That night he slept in a feverish chimerical state. A nightmare like a trip, dreaming stark mind-boggling mirage, nothing to be ashamed of, only frenzied unspecified stuff. The things that appeared in his dreams were bizarre with no meaning or sense. In any case he wasn't a believer of the significance of dreams and didn't try to interpret its possible meanings, as if it was some lurid guiltiness in the subconscious coming out. For John dreaming was the brain's way of recharging it's batteries while chaotically processing all the impressions it had accumulated. He concluded he had slept in a too warm bed.

CHAPTER 12

When John woke up, he had breakfast consisting of only coffee and decided to do something about the quest of his late father and deeds as a spy, that is talk to Eric.

Eric Gustavsson was a legend in Swedish Intelligence and according to myth a man able to see around corners, whatever that means. Recently Eric had hired John for a few weeks stunt as a private eye. An affair involving "talented" people who through internet-gambling had become too ambitious and established a money-laundering scheme. Eric might be of help to get in contact with someone at MI6. Dialing the number, strangely Eric answered immediately.

"Hi it's John."

"I had a hunch you would call me," answered Eric with a raspy voice.

"So, it's true then, you see around corners?"

"That's horseshit." Eric was a man who spoke with brutal clarity, no filters there.

"I was thinking," John began when Eric interrupted him.

"You want to know more about your father," now more gently.

"Yeah, that's why I called you."

"I've already told you what I know and that's not much."

Both knew this wasn't true but being the man he was, Eric probably wouldn't give more details on the phone, as these machines left proofs of conversations and Eric's telephone was probably tapped in one way or the other.

"I thought you could help me with a name to call your comrades facilities over there in London," said John instead of vociferating the real name which was MI6.

"I see."

"I mean since I learned what kind of job my father had, it's only natural to know more about him."

"In this business, not much is natural."

Of course, anything but natural John thought.

"I think it's perfectly understandable I want to know more and what happened to him," John's tone had slightly sharpened.

"You are aware certain facts about how it was played out and what went wrong is not public."

"Yes, but when you told me he almost got Kim Philby, I really got curious and wonder if you could give me a name to contact?" said John forgetting about the discretion on the phone of such a delicate affair.

"We do cooperate in certain affairs as everybody knows, anyways I can try."

Sweden cooperated with the UK even if officially the high priests tried to play the "neutral card" in all its bearings. Lately it had been written a lot about Sweden's hold which de facto was like the rest of the NATO-countries and had joined American and UK-interests when needed for searching Soviet thugs and spies. It had become public how Sweden's Intelligence Security had worked secretly way back with the West in its efforts to curtail the Soviets. Sweden at heart was never pro Soviet Union and had obscure deals with the West's Intelligence, maintaining a neutral stance.

"I understand as much." There was a pause.

"Have you read the latest about Estonia?"

"Not much, I've read bits and pieces, strange things seem to be going on there."

"You should, what your friends were up to was peanuts compared to what is going on now. There is a machination from Russia through Estonia and now also via Hong Kong."

"We could meet, and you tell me."

"I'm off for a few days, I'll call you when I'm back."

One could only guess what off meant in his business.

"Are you going to find out or?"

Eric ignored his question.

"Have you by any chance talked lately with your uncle?"

How the hell does he know I have an uncle John thought.

"Actually, I have, he called me a few days ago."

"And?"

"Haven't seen him in 25 years. Why do you ask?"

"It seems he is involved in fishy businesses in Estonia."

"What business?"

"Can't tell you."

"Has it something to do with the article I read the other day?"

"You are right on that, any thoughts about it?" he asked with his inquisitive manner.

"I'll see him tomorrow, any trouble going on?"

"Hope not." Which didn't sound reassuring.

"When I know more details I'll call you. You might be my eyes and ears again," he said chuckling.

"What?"

"Just a thought."

The words hung in the air.

"About my father and the MI6, can you help me?"

Eric hesitated a few seconds and then said, "You ask for Alistair Wellington," and gave John a number.

"Let me know how it goes," and they hung up.

John eyed the number nervously, uncertain if he had the courage to make the call, after all this the MI6. He wasn't even sure of what he really wanted to learn about his father but the fact he had been a spy of rank and involved in the Kim Philby-case was extremely fascinating and the rumor of having been a double-agent. Moreover, what kind of individual immerses you in such a hard-core ballgame compared to the ordinary man. After a few moments of deliberations John made the call.

"Could I speak to Alistair Wellington?"

"Who is calling," asked a dispassionate female voice.

"My name is John Sherman, son of Jack Sherman" he began, hoping it would have the right effect.

"Please wait."

John waited and a second person asked.

"Could you please say your name again?"

"John Sherman."

"And what's your business Mr. Sherman?"

"A friend in Sweden Eric Gustavsson gave me this number."

"Please wait."

It took a few seconds, and he heard a man saying on the other end of the line;

"Alistair Wellington."

"I got your name from Eric Gustavsson," said John for emphasis making it clear he was no trickster or ruse.

"Is that so?"

"Precisely."

"Oh, great, how is he? Drinking and eating as usual?"

"I'm not into his private life," said John as he thought the comment was too pejorative.

"Of course not."

"I call you as I've been told a story about my father and the MI6."

"Is that so," he said again, what seemed an empty pronouncement giving himself time to reflect.

"Yes."

"John Sherman, Jack Sherman's son." This was pronounced as if he was Rees-Mogg with an upper-crust accent typically schooled in a public school.

"What can I do for you?"

John explained his case and curiosity about his desire to know more about his father and his doings at the MI6.

"You are interested to learn about your father I gather," repeating John's words.

"As you might know he died in the Falklands, when I was eight."

"Yes, I know about it, so sad," he added in an effort to comfort.

"By the way, are you related to the great man himself, the man who gave Napoleon a beat at Waterloo?"

"Actually I am. Would it be convenient you come to London?" Typical English-styled, wordings like, would it be possible that eventually and so forth.

"Yes of course."

"What do you say, in two days?"

"Think I could do that."

"Call me when you arrive, and we decide where to meet and have lunch together."

"That would be great."

"Nice to talk to you, look forward to meet Jack's son."

That was easy. Today it's Monday, could go Wednesday, be back Thursday, dinner in the archipelago Friday. As if I needed more excitement, he thought and booked a flight to London.

CHAPTER 13

A cloudy but warm enough Tuesday he went to the Chinese Embassy to validate his visa for his up-coming trip to Hong Kong. Once inside he reached the counter a young man with a tattoo like a triangle on his right temple took a serious inquisitive look at John's passport.

"Why you go so often to Hong Kong?"

At first John thought to answer such a pointless question was to say none of your business but instead said with a smile; "we are looking for Chinese manufacturers."

"Are you a journalist?" as if hadn't listened.

"No I'm not."

"Any association with politics?" he interrupted John.

The man was beginning to irritate John, so he tried to not let it show.

"Not really."

"Really?" "Just a joke."

"What kind of business," was said with a sadistic smile knowing fully well John would lose his nerves at any moment by now.

"Packaging."

After what seemed an un-necessary thorough look on the passport, raised and went into a room with his passport, came back, stamped it and gave John's passport a sordid look.

"Here, I have a lot of friends in Hong Kong," in the way he was saying this it, John felt it sounded like a warning, a bad omen of sorts.

Relieved John went out of the embassy thinking the Chinese, weren't worthy to have the embassy in such a nice surrounding on Djurgården and began walking to meet his uncle. It had so happened, a few days ago he got a phone call: "Hi I'm Dennis, Dennis Modig, by all accounts, your uncle, brother to your mother."

John had forgotten about him. The last time he had seen him was at his mother's funeral.

"Can you say that again?"

"I'm your uncle."

"Dennis?"

"Long time no see," he said laughing.

"How did you find me?"

"I read the papers and saw your name and with a little help of friends I got your number."

"Well that's great."

"I don't know what you think but I think it's wonderful."

"And where are you now, living where?"

"I live in a flat on Karlavägen."

That an uncle apparently living in Stockholm was unexpected and took him by complete surprise. His mother didn't have any other siblings: There were a few distant cousins where contact was lost way back. On the English side, i.e. his late father's family, the relations had vanished a part of a few sporadic contacts through the years, a thing he had decided to do something about.

He knew his uncle had left Sweden due to an un-wanted pregnancy with a momentarily girlfriend of high reputation to maintain. The girl came from a substantial family, who didn't accept him as the child's father and had called it a milder form of rape, if that exist. It was said he had debauched her. That was the explanation John had from his mother in subdued words. After the incident of pregnancy, Dennis subsequently left Sweden for Paris not to be seen in a lifetime. This meant John had not just an uncle, he had a cousin somewhere. They agreed to meet at his uncle's flat.

While walking on Karlavägen he was puzzled watching old women with crunched backs strolling alone struggling in their path. Not like in Spain, where you see an elderly fragile person in the street is usually accompanied. A theme one should investigate and make a thesis of the whys.

Arriving at the front door, after a twenty-minute walk, what looked like a stupendous building he rang the bell, waiting to be let in.

"Hi there, wow, as good looking as your father."

"You met?" was the first thing John uttered.

"Only briefly but important moments, was a witness at their wedding, before I left Sweden."

They went inside and John saw a smartly decorated entrance, followed by a big living room, an ostentatious piano, where upon there were classical silver-framed photos with pictures from weddings sending a message of class. On the walls hang paintings of modern art plus a few fox-hunting themes in golden structured frames. Maybe not the taste of the day but linked to a heritage with possible value in it, big sofas in light colors, a splendid fireplace in the middle. French windows with drapes in suitable colors, a complete setting conveying a perfect atmosphere of well-being.

"Nice place, you live alone here?"

"No, I live with a woman I met in France a year ago," said Dennis, now leaning an elbow on the mantelpiece. John recognized how his uncle carried himself with a certain dignity and refined in his movements and gestures or wished to. He had an air from another age, slightly dashing. An impressive commanding aspect, silver-haired and handsome to a point, must be over seventy. At first it seemed he dressed casually like a man up-to date, not like in other times, when fashion was dictated by a man's age; his outfit was navy-blue blazers and grey flannel trousers and a white shirt with a pertinent tie, tall with looks like the actor Richard Harris. Albeit looking with more precision, his clothes looked a bit ragged. Behind this rather glamorous façade John couldn't shake a feeling there was something un-easy with his uncle. He couldn't pinpoint the reasoning for such a thought but first impressions tend to stick. It was a scene which looked like old black-white movies from the fifties, where men in double-breasted suits chatted about trivial daily matters and a maid would appear receiving some ordering of drinks making it crystal-clear the existing class-differences. There was a pause, both men looking queerly towards one another. This sudden family-tied situation felt odd, as they were becoming aware that future Christmases might be spent together.

"How old are you, forty-eight?"

"Yes."

"So nice to see my little sister's big boy, haven't felt I had family since ages."

"I know what you mean."

"I'm really glad to see you."

"You left Sweden when?"

"I left Sweden when my girlfriend's family thought I wasn't good enough for their daughter."

"My mother told me."

"She did? It was a delicate business, my girlfriend got pregnant."

"So, there is a child?"

"Yes, there is a boy."

"A boy?" John repeated.

"Yes, don't see him much. He was kind of taken out of my life."

"How is that?"

"When he was born, they shut me off. My God how I tried to see him. Couldn't communicate with the mother."

"But there are laws, this is Sweden."

"It's a sad story, very difficult to explain."

"And now, you never meet?"

"Now and then only. It's heart-breaking when we meet, and a feeling that I'm some kind of monster to him. He seems determined to reject me."

"He must be my age almost."

"Let's not talk about me, what are you up to now? Live here alone, I mean any partner to share the lonely nights?"

John abandoned the idea of questioning further specifics about the lost son, it could come later.

"I just returned to Stockholm, after some twenty years in Madrid, have this job coming up and a friend yes."

"Find it easy to adapt? Have you noticed you soak it up in a different manner when you live here, not just visiting?"

"Not yet, only been here two weeks."

"From personal experience, it takes time."

"A friend told me exactly those words the other day."

"It requires a bit of patience and fortitude; let it sink in."

This new circumstance sitting and talking to a long-not seen family-member, due to so many unknowns, made them talk tentatively. It didn't feel secure enough to go too deep on personal matters. Dennis sat down in a sofa.

"For me," it seemed his uncle wanted to steer the conversation towards himself and began to talk about how he met this woman. "Was at a party in Paris, met this woman a mother of two and divorced. We decided to take our things further and live together. So, I moved back to Sweden."

"Swedish then?"

Dennis launched into a detailed account how he had been hooked up with this woman.

"Yes, it was a surprising beginning at a dinner-party. At first, she didn't take notice of my presence. It was a willy go round among mostly divorcées, males and women with antennas zooming in if there were any lions present, like a marketplace. We were presented, she didn't show any interest until I made a thank- you speech and got her interest, she approached me as if it was a game. After the dinner we left together, went to St. Michelle talked about old times and thanks to a bottle of champagne, one thing led to another and here we are."

John got the notion this was a man with that special character you find in a womanizer or a playboy with a tendency to magnify his deeds. John also was a bit startled why he had told this mating story with such detail and eloquence.

"And you, what about your friend, been together long time?"

"Not really it came about fast, we skipped the preliminaries."

"That's the best ones."

"Actually, I knew her since young, we were together on and off, now we are in a state of searching like."

"Confirming and checking if it would work out," he said as a question.

"So far so good."

"You don't seem to be very enthusiastic about her, has she a name?"

"Marianne."

"Not the Faithful?"

"Who?"

"Marianne Faithful, a famous muse of the Rolling Stones many years ago."

John pondered the word faithful in relation to Marianne. She could be more un-faithful than the contrary. If things got dull, she would leave the love-nest without too much commotion for another amorous hook-up. All of a sudden, John felt an urge to tell his uncle about Jasmine. "Actually I'm in a squeeze, met this woman in Hong Kong very much stuck in my mind." His uncle looked startled and said;

"That's more than a squeeze, you must decide, not playing around and pushing the boundaries. I know what I'm talking about, have done it myself and you end up badly."

"It's not the end of the envelope yet," he added more to assure himself than towards his uncle.

"That's a tough one though, whatever don't you worry too much, life takes care of those situations. A drink or is it too early?"

"No, it's fine."

Dennis prepared two glasses with stiff gin-tonics.

"I must give you a bit of family memorabilia, as I suppose you are not too familiar with, I think Jack, your father asked your mother out almost at arrival at the hotel when he came to Stockholm for a military congress. Your mother happened to work as a trainee during summer at the Grand Hotel."

In reality he knew a lot about how it happened. According to John's mother's account, they had spent a spirited weekend together. Promenades on Djurgården, stopping here and there for a drink or for lunch, actively getting enthused by the minute. Their brief encounter must have been of high intensity, because after he left Stockholm, your mother noticed she was pregnant. She was only twenty-one. He was an officer in the British Army from Sandhurst according to his mother, who probably wasn't aware he was also a spy.

"Love at first sight."

"Yes, absolutely, they got married in a whirl of happiness."

"A shotgun marriage at Skansen in November. A rapid ceremony held in Swedish. Jack hadn't a clue what was said during the ceremony, a part of the question if he would love her forever which was done in English. An intimate dinner at Djurgårdsbrunn with only me and my fiancée present." John didn't ask if the fiancée was the pregnant girl which it probably wasn't. Dennis continued.

"Jack's family wasn't so happy and left them to their own destiny. According to his family this hasty wedding was a social downer and didn't wish to have any part of it. As for our family, what was left of it, weren't attracted she would marry a foreigner she barely knew." Listening to his uncle John was getting a bit confounded and he began to cherish listening to his uncle painting with great brushes his parents love story.

John knew that when newly wedded, they decided to live in London. They moved to a townvillage called Richmond, alongside the Thames, beautiful parks and roedeer running around the place. Jack's salary wasn't fat being an officer, thus they lived in a little house which looked like coming out of a film from the second World War II, it was spartan but they were happy, according to his mother. After some time, his father's family began to get curious of the two new family members and wanted to get familiar with the woman their son had married so quickly and began to get acquainted with John, their grandchild.

His mother had mentioned there were times they were invited to London where Jack's mother lived in grand style in Mayfair. Jack's family was surprised how easy-going and down to earth this Swedish woman was, combined with Nordic beauty, blond hair and light blue eyes.

"Jack, what a guy, brought up in public-schools. He spoke with a stiff upper lip and the inevitable accent that goes along with it" said Dennis.

John lived there for about eight years, and went to the same school as his father, Westminster. Maybe not learned to row, play rugby and cricket but was initiated in those very English sports, a feature he hadn't been able to continue after he and his mother moved back to Stockholm.

"Do you remember much of those days when you, lived in Richmond?

"I do, especially the reindeers when my mother took me for walks in the park."

"Your father was always smartly dressed in uniform. Jack had the looks of a quintessential Englishman. If he had worn a moustache, he would have passed as a mixed breed of Clark Gable and David Niven" said Dennis laughing.

The rest as it happened, the fateful year 1982, when he was eight, was a sad story John knew too well. There was sable-rattling between Great Britain and Argentina. A dispute about the Falklands, which ended up in a war no one had seen coming. Lot of macho-talk by the dictators in Argentina, screaming about recovering "Las Malvinas". John's father was sent to South America on a mission to Peru for a sensible negotiation, avoid a possible sale of the missile Exocet to the Peruvians, which the English weren't fond of, as the missiles could end up in the hands of the Argentines, which they eventually did and John's father was sent there and to war.

John's mother listened every day to the BBC for news, no internet or mobiles those days, as talking or writing was out of the way. In general, the news was of optimistic content but between lines, there were worries as the whole scenery was at completely unknown shores very far away, a place most people had never heard of. And the oddness of it. A war between England and Argentina, they were not even close neighbors. A call from the Foreign Office gave her the news about her husband's death. John's father had been on the HMS Sheffield at the Falklands when hit by an Exocet missile of French construction. A solid rocket booster missile hit the ship's casing, killing twenty people. After his father's death his mother decided to go back to Stockholm. Consequently, John was brought up in a little flat in Stockholm, in a district with lots of green areas, went to school and forced to learn Swedish. The idea before the fatal change after the death of his father, had been to send John to a stern boarding-school in England, a thing his mother had feared immensely sending a boy of eight, to something equivalent to Harry Potter's school, with cold showers, rugby and other whatnots, supposedly making you a man where you learn to rely on yourself.

Being brought up without a father he tended to appreciate men of strong and tough nature, who didn't bother to put on coats when the weather was cold or jumped into the water without wobbling, men that talked with gusto as free spirits.

Be that as it may, in his childhood he did what boys do, played football, ice hockey or skied depending of which season. Early on he noticed he was good at sports, including a competitive stroke. And sport was a fertile ground for making friends, both items did come easy for him. After his father's death both families reconciled their mutual destinies, and even financial aid was coming through to his widowed mother occasionally. But then disaster struck again. When John was nineteen, he went with his mother to the French Alps, to Val D'Isére. His mother had been skiing with some of her friends and on a day with heavy snow, she was lost. Took two days to find her under the snow due to an avalanche. He took his mother's death in a way he became inhibited for some time. "Death" a word once distant and obscure after his father's passing, impossible to ignore with the loss of his mother. Despite the tragic circumstances of his mother's death, he found a way to navigate the complexities of life and he emerged from the experience a strong and compassionate individual. A well-adjusted straight-looking tall adult, with blond hair and green eyes that made him quite the catch. While he wasn't the top-student, his self-reliant nature helped him pass his exams. His demeanor earned him good friends and a vibrant social life. While finishing school he lived in a flat as a young bachelor, financed thanks his father's pension and funds from his family in England, went to University, was going to study sociology but was told it's bogus-science and instead studied history for three years. The years went by and due to chagrin and not sure what to make of his state being alone, he decided to look for other shores and appeared in Madrid after some months travelling around in Europe.

"I have something for you" said Dennis, raised and took a book that lied on the piano.

"It's Marco Aurelio's book of advice of how to lead a good life, your mother's."

He opened the book and randomly saw many underlined sentences, one in particular: *learn to be indifferent to what makes no difference.* This indicated an inner life he hadn't been aware of. Having her book in his hands he became aware how much he missed her and to what extent he had really known her. One should have shown more interest to her when she lived. Upon reading the underlined sentences he felt a shift in his mood and needed to steer the conversation elsewhere: He casually asked Dennis;

"Did you know my father was in Intelligence, not just an officer?"

"Yes, he almost got Philby I've been told. That man was double-spy for thirty years. Can you imagine living a double life so many years, that guy must have been in titters."

"You seem to know a lot about him, Philby I mean."

"Actually, I do, they say he drank like hell in his home in Moscow. Probably longing for his home-country he had so badly betrayed, while reading books about spies," said Dennis as if he was really informed.

"Live a double-life, must take a lot," said John thinking of himself and his love-life.

"Nerve-racking."

"What kind of man was my father?"

"Can't say I knew him; he seemed to be a cheerful Englishman. Confident without being pompous, liked Burt Bacharach's music I remember, aggressive tennis player, running to the net like the Americans did in those days with a Maxply Fort."

"I have one of his rackets said John, "but don't use it, I only use his old shoe-legs."

"Put the racket on a wall as a remembrance."

"And what about you? Are you retired or how do you manage hunger from the threshold," an expression John liked to use, copied from an old friend who had got super-rich.

"I'm playing on the stock-market, you know up-and- down." Those last words didn't come out with the usual self-assurance Suddenly Dennis seemed to be stressed, looking around nervously as if searching for someone under the sofa or a hidden microphone. Perhaps a bad day on the stock market, thought John.

"I'm not good doing trading, don't like to start my day checking the stock-market and how my portfolio is doing, if it goes up or down, I would be worried the whole day," said John.

"Perhaps you think it's an activity you don't deserve making easy money?"

"I don't have the feeling for it."

"You can learn it."

"I'm not a risk-taker," said John, and added, "in that sense", thinking again of his love-squeeze.

"You have to read stuff, get some experience with it, learn the trade."

"But no one knows in the end, it's wishful thinking to me."

"There are ways, like short selling for example, a subtle thing, you sell and then you buy back when it reaches a lower price and profit from the difference."

"That doesn't sound ethical."

"You bet against growth," said Dennis smiling.

"I went into the market once, advised by a very smart top-notch guy, who said; This is a very good fund. In a few months the market went down 30-40 %."

"Shit happens any time."

John rose and had a look at the silver-framed photos on the wing-piano, strategically put making it easy for an observer to watch what must be family-members in different stages and ages.

"They are not mine," said Dennis, "it's her family."

"Your generation seems to have lived the good life."

"Our generation thought we knew better, better and with higher morals than our parents. We thought the past was basically wrong, influenced by freedom of all sorts, free-sex and all that. And we lost respect towards the elderly and what they had done. At the same time a lack of a certain discipline, it became easy to pass the exams in school."

For John the sixties were known to a point. From his perspective it seemed like a crazed time and suspected all the hoopla about it was exaggerated.

"It felt new and different, a seismic shift." He paused and became thoughtful. "I remember a movie by Costa Gavras of the Greek coronels and was impressed. We did care about Vietnam. We saw Fosbury jumping high-jump. Thought we were an improved version of humanity. We began to travel, taking things for granted, completely egoistical, we did what we wanted, hadn't suffered."

"I thought you had higher morals?

"With hindsight, no, not at all."

CHAPTER 14

John wasn't sure if it was the drinks or sitting here in Stockholm chatting away with a family member, that affected him, heeding a sense of belonging. Suddenly, he felt a familiar warmth, a sensation he hadn't experienced in ages, after all, blood is thicker than water. Maybe the same went for his uncle, he had no one either, for him it must be good to sit with a nephew, bonding and talking away. Their conversation wandered about touching on various topics for a while, from the mundane to more abstract metaphysical stuff. Clearly his uncle was well read and had a wide-spread knowledge of different matters. At the same time, he noticed that his uncle tended to exaggerate, it was kind of grandiose big stuff, making you slightly uncomfortable. Dennis talked about his father, who had volunteered in the winter-war between Finland and Russia and in the effort lost a leg. "I remember once when your mother said to our father when he was chopping wood: "be careful with your legs" and he answered laughing with irony "I only have one to worry about." He bought a summer- place at Ljusterö, which I still have. Not a fancy place but a cozy cottage very genuine."

"Have been there a few times."

"There is a fabulous story from an island not too far away from my place, the famous opera-singer Jussi Björling sang from a distant island in the evenings, to warm up his lungs, people came out from shores far away without seeing the singer, must have been fantastic." John tried to imagine the scene.

"When my father talked about the war, he said it was so cold you could see the letters while speaking and everybody laughed." Dennis way of exaggerating must come from his father John thought.

"Maybe he was affected by the war"?

"Of course," and in an afterthought, "Finns are more down to earth, in Sweden we believe that war is something of the past, dozed off and let down our defense guard."

"Why and when did Sweden become so relaxed about a possible war?

"Sweden didn't participate in the World Wars and benefitted from it, although with a very ambiguous position, letting German soldiers be transported from Norway, via Sweden to defend Germany in the later stages of the war."

John had read about all this and how things had occurred. After the war, Sweden became prosperous, attempting higher ideals.

"Olof Palme did his part claiming a higher standard of civilization, criticized the USA, was interviewed by David Frost and got world famous. We thought Sweden was the best country in the world."

"But to a certain extent it was, no?"

"Well, it was a period of affluence and social welfare. The sixties were indeed a time of revolutionary fervor, followed by the seventies' stagnation, and the eighties, unchecked excess. Altogether it produced a generation of young adults who, with the newfound luxury of gap years,' traveled the globe like royalty. I recall witnessing this firsthand during the Australian Grand Slam in tennis, where their behavior, was like hooliganism than anything else."

Evasively, John answered, "I was too young to really know anything."

Dennis got a call and John raised and looked around as if giving privacy, letting Dennis talk alone. Once finished, John said:

"I'm going to London tomorrow to meet a guy at the MI6."

"And why is that?"

"To learn more about my father."

"Probably they can't say much."

"Are you sure?"

"Absolutely."

"I need to know, don't know what exactly."

"Well good luck," he said abruptly. Dennis' reaction to the news of the visit to London seemed to stir something in him.

"Be careful if it is one of those Eton-educated boys at the MI6, they manipulate your senses."

"What do you mean?"

"There is attraction to it, be a secret agent, not letting your closest friends know and that exhilarates your blood."

"I'm not interested in that."

"Don't be so sure, they might want to hire you, don't forget your father was one of the best in the business."

"How do you measure that?" said John wondering how he knew.

"Suppose you give valuable information to the one who is handling you." and added "I was once approached by the KGB."

"You didn't take the offer I assume?"

"No."

"Are you sure it was KGB?", John asked or was this one more of Dennis extravagant brouhahas.

"Can't say hundred percent but once, a beautiful woman with Russian accent approached me in a bar here in Stockholm and asked about my views in politics."

"What did you say to her?"

"That I don't held strong views on anything and she lost interest in me."

"You need to have guts to be in that business."

"Absolutely, think of it, you sit in a bar and a woman walks up to you and you think it's thanks to your good looks when she in reality is working for some kind of obscure enterprise."

Now was the moment to mention the Smurfers thought John.

"I happen to read an article the other day," he began.

"You saw it," said Dennis narrowing his eyes.

"Don't want to be impertinent but."

"You wonder if it's me? Yes, it is."

"It occurred to me."

"John, to be honest it's a bad thing. I've been fooled to be a straw owner."

"What's that?"

"Well, it's a person who has the legal appearance of owning something but on behalf of another."

"You mean to hide the identity of the real owner."

"Exactly."

"That's smells bad," John offered.

"I want out of it and don't know how."

"Just tell them then," said John innocently.

"Not easy, not easy at all, there are bad people out there," not saying who *they* were.

"And who were they?"

"A few months ago, I met a guy who had a business-proposal."

"What guy?"

"A guy who talked about investing in assets like real estate in Sweden and Estonia, buy commodities etc.

Said they wished to be legal and deposit cash in legitimate bank-accounts and if I could be an intermediary opening an account."

"A goalkeeper".

"Yes, I was stupid to say yes," pausing looking down he said, "I was desperate, I was going to lose everything."

"Why did they choose you? Did you know him beforehand?"

"Suppose I was under his radar as financially vulnerable. I was lured into it. We met at a few cocktail parties here and there and this guy approached me said if did what they wanted, I would get a percentage from each deposit. So I went to Tallinn, created a company, Modig Import & Export, went to the bank and opened an account. Went there a few times making deposits making it clear for any suspicious bank-manager that the company was there and doing things, until the fourth time, I began to understand it was bad stuff. My guy showed up with, what I assumed to be a Russian, I got scared."

John didn't know what to say and was fast becoming aware that his uncle was in real and hard trouble.

"As you said, I was hired as a mule and recruited as a useful idiot."

"What was in it for you?"

"He promised a good percentage and as I was in serious need, didn't say no."

"Are you the sole person who can wire transfers?"

"That's the problem, now they want to have a joint capacity for sending money, to invest in real estate."

"And then sell it rapidly and put the money into a legitimate account somewhere else."

"I'm hooked."

"No money has left the account until now?"

"No."

It wasn't clear who the man was who had bedazzled Dennis into this shady scheme and John decided to not ask. Classical case of money- laundering. You create a shell company in any offshore location and make the purchase of the property making it difficult to trace the origins of the funds. It's called layering, making it difficult to track the origin of the funds. The idea is to distance the money from its illegal origins by putting it through numerous transactions. It confirmed what John had read about smurfing and structuring, the practice of money laundering splitting large cash amounts into smaller chunks and depositing them into many different accounts, making detecting the illegal funds nearly impossible.

"What are you going to do?"

"I need to go to Tallinn, to close the account."

"If you close the account, they will not be glad I suppose."

Dennis looked down and didn't say anything, John felt sorry for him. He must be a fool or desperate to have fallen into such a trap. He didn't come forward as stupid, so maybe there was something else, instead he might be the instigator of such a scheme and thought he ought to talk to Eric Gustavsson and said so to Dennis; "I know a man who could be of help, he is working at Säpo."

Dennis gave John a worried look.

"Who?

"His name is Eric Gustavsson."

"I know him, we have met."

"Wow now everybody knows each other, soon Santa Claus works undercover in some obscure scheme" said John laughing.

"How do you know Eric?"

John told the story about gambling on the internet in tennis and how through various coincidences he got to know Eric. This didn't seem to comfort for Dennis.

"Anyways I have to sort this out on my own, sorry John but I must go now and pick up my girlfriend, she is at her mother's residence."

"No problem, I also have to go," which wasn't true.

Instead of asking all the why's about his reasoning to get himself involved in such an incredible scheme, John said, "there must be a solution."

"Yeah sure, let's be in touch, he said evasively. "Oh, I forgot, I have some letters for you. Don't know how they came into my hands, there was a box of letters in my old flat."

"Have you read them?"

"Didn't dare to but I can see on the dates of the stamps it must in their beginnings."

"And?"

"Think they are love-letters and those you don't read if not allowed."

They were standing in the hall and bade their farewells and agreed on to have a bite or something in the upcoming days.

Once outside his uncle's house on the street John saw two burly men talking in a what could be Russian. One of them came forward with a curious look.

"Do you live here?"

"No, why do you ask," John answered a bit high-pitched.

"Just asking," and then turned away.

Hurriedly John began to walk away. This smelled bad, why does someone ask a question like that in the middle of the street. His uncle was in deep trouble. Much worse than his own quagmire. Walking home he felt the pressure of the box with his mother's letters made him curious and anxious to read. Once he arrived, he put down the box and with an urge to read the letters but was indecisive, fully aware it was personal and of sensible value. After a while he took at random a letter.. It was just a few sentences, with his mother's beautiful hand writing, coming about in a harmonious flow and rhythm. John began to read.

Dear Jack,

When you left last week, I was worried about all kinds of things, that you would forget me and something might happen to you, as you didn't say where you were going.

These last days have been wonderful.

Well in case you think about me I want you to know that I love you. Yours Helen

John sat back and wondered if he should read them all or not, finally decided to do it another moment. Reflecting over what he had just read, he concluded it's always the same story, love with difficulties. At the same time, realizing how difficult it must have been for his parents. How wonderful it would be to have them to talk to. To sit back and have them around and hear their stories, their take of things. They would be old but what kind of advice would they give to him?

CHAPTER 15

John landed at Heathrow and took the train to Paddington. During the flight he was pondering over the incident on the street when leaving his uncle. He must be in hot water. No easy way out there. Putting himself in such a danger was so utterly dumb, with Russians lying in wait for you, along with the Swedish Intelligence he must have been completely desperate. He put this thought aside and focused on the upcoming meeting with the man from the MI6. The purpose of his trip to London was obscure and the outcome uncertain. It wasn't until he reached the train-station the gravity of his undertaking dawned on him. Slightly jittery, he texted Wellington, the man he had talked to on the phone.

"Good day, I'm on the train from Heathrow to Paddington, when and where shall we meet?

After ten minutes he got a short answer: "The White's, 37 St. James's Street, 14 hours."

John had never heard about the place, so he googled and found it was one of the oldest gentlemen's clubs in London, founded in 1693, considered the most exclusive private club in London. Among the members he saw Prince Charles. The clubhouse was located in the City of Westminster, close to the Ritz. From Paddington he took an

Uber, being in a state of anxiety he asked the driver if he knew of the place called White's.

"I'm black, don't know anything about whites."

Which was a logical answer and not easy to pursue further questions. The club's entrance was surprisingly unremarkable, with no hints of its renowned reputation. He saw a sign about the dress-code; smart casual, no trainers, no sportswear. Gave his name to a brittle man in want of retirement and was ushered inside. He passed a "betting book", paused briefly to scan the display of bets. One was a £3,000 bet on which raindrop would reach the bottom of a window faster. Famous or rather infamous due to the vice of hefty gambling by the men who went here. It didn't take much time to perceive this was the ultimate place for the privileged high priests of the Empire. The setting was old-fashioned though not lavishly opulent. Paintings of grave men hung on the walls of presumably affluence thanks to secure vintage money. John was standing looking around when a dashing-looking man came towards him, back-combed hair, around fifty, smartly dressed, a white shirt which John knew was for high enders by just looking on the collar, a navy-blue suit with a tie in light blue which accented his good taste and looks. He moved with a sportsman's vigor, white teeth and no belly, no fat.

"John it is?"

"How did you know?"

The man exuded charm with military dignity. He carried himself with a measured stateliness and led John to a room with mahogany walls, chimney, a painting of a woman surrounded by two angle-like children. The room was Chesterfield styled in all quarters where many cows had let their skin go to the upholstered leather sofas, not fake Chinese contemporary faked leather. They sat down and John looked again at the painting and wondered who had chosen such an item over the chimney. Maybe it had bounced from here and there and ended up here by chance. He noticed a few fellows saying hellos to members, patting their outside pocket on the blazer, as Prince Charles does where the patting becomes an act. The gesture seemed to give an assurance of some kind, not easy to understand its meaning or origin, maybe a Freudian tic or *I didn't bring my wallet.*

"We have our methods," he said smiling as if he had just won a match of some kind.

John felt the manipulative craft of the man, charismatic, soft but firm movements, he made you understand he was on a mission or in a game and if you play, you play to win.

"Drink something?" he asked when the waiter approached them.

"No thanks."

"We'll wait," said Wellington to the same man who had led John inside, looking older by the minute.

"Quite a place," said John.

"It's fascinating, White's was addicted to chance, playing cards and betting on anything, like who Lord Byron would marry."

John was surprised by the man's easy and friendly manner, as if they were old friends.

"Tough to bet on."

"There is a bizarre story about Lord Montfort, who sent for his lawyers and witnesses after having made his will, asked if it would hold good even if a man would shoot himself. He was informed that it would. When he heard this, he asked the lawyer to wait a minute, stepped into an adjoining room and shot himself."

"That's a certain rationality at least," said John amazed.

"He must have hidden some unspoken truths or debts, who knows. His ghost is said to wander here during the nights. Anyways, nice to meet you."

"Thanks for meeting me."

"I thank you, probably you don't know but your father wasn't any agent of ours, he was a damn hero. "His name is well reserved in Whitehall, almost got Philby but someone let the bastard slip away. Things can go wrong due to lack of rigor and the old-boys network of which I suppose you know what I'm talking about."

"I think I know what you aim at."

"The club-ability aspect of things and the rest."

"And we don't know who it was?"

"No, we don't," he said what John took as pure irony. If he knew he wouldn't tell John.

"You know your name triggers the alarm-bells, could wake up the bear somewhere on the steppe, by the by, I heard you met Boris Winslow and made a courageous speech in Brussels."

John was surprised how things have been circulated but after all, this man was MI6.

"Frankly, I didn't count on the media attention my speech would cause."

"Well, that's how it is these days. As I understand it, your political views are rather coincidental to ours, your views on Russia and China, Iran, the rouge countries."

"How come you say this?"

"In a random conversation I had with Boris Winslow's spin-doctor, your name was dropped by coincidence, he mentioned your account you did at the Ritz, you impressed them."

"The man with spectacles looking with suspicion at you?"

"The very same yes."

"So I'm the talk of the town," said John both amused and startled.

"Let's say it's important to work with the same sturdy material when you build a bridge."

"Nice metaphor."

"Your speech in Brussels about immigrants and the lack of adaption and our way of giving shelter but not letting them in our tribal society. The need for creating a foundation for future generations a better life and all that, wasn't it?"

"As a summary it will do."

At that point, Wellington raised a bit his voice and body as if to clarify that something of importance was to be unfolded.

"I was thinking, in some way you could work for us." John began to laugh.

"Work for MI6?"

"According to my friend Eric, you are good."

"By good you mean clean or according to your tastes?"

"Both."

"This sounds like the-tap-on-the shoulder, a pinstriped man at Lord's with an umbrella asks if you might come down and see us?" Wellington laughed at John's comment.

"Broadly speaking, we recruit through adverts nowadays, with exceptions off course."

"I see. I thought it was from Oxbridge one was vetted."

"At any rate, this is not a job-interview," said Wellington and changed venue." I'm glad to meet you, didn't know your father but heard he was the finest of them all."

"How long did he work for the MI6?"

"He began in his early twenties until Falklands."

"That's a long life of secrets."

"As far as I know he had seen it all."

"And what about you if I may ask?"

"I started at the time the Iron Curtain broke down, 1989 when the wall in Berlin was demolished."

"The official version says it was torn down by the people or was there some unspecified help?"

"They did it themselves. When the authorities announced people could trespass the border to the West their system collapsed."

Wellington looked at John as if he was trying to discern something in John, sniff out his integrity.

"Anyways, we didn't come to talk geo-politics," he said with a smile.

"At that moment a headwaiter approached them.

"What can I do for you Sir?"

"Please give us the menu and still water."

"And you sir?"

"I'll have the same," said John.

"So you are back in Sweden now, after a long stretch in Spain?"

"How do you know this?"

"Eric told me."

"Well, to answer your question yes, I stayed a while in Spain but there was this problem of not belonging."

"Didn't adapt?"

"After some time, I did yes."

"I had some business there during a few years."

What business meant in his case you could only guess.

"There were the years when ETA hit hard."

"Connected with IRA?"

"Something like that."

"What do you mean?"

"It was tough, those Basques and their independence streak" he said almost absently.

John could imagine what tough meant for an MI6-envoy, during the years ETA killed every day almost and black-mailed business-owners by means of the so-called revolutionary tax.

They rose and went to the assigned table. A glance at the stationery on the menu you got an idea of what you were up to. The waiter brought the menu and Alistair suggested:

"Let this get over with and then we talk."

John had a look at the menu so when his eyes caught a straight Tournedos it was an easy decision.

"What do you want to know about your father?"

"What kind of man he was for example."

"Can't say much about that but what I've heard, he was a good spirit. Good sportsman, especially when it came to throwing or hitting balls."

"Like tennis?"

"Tennis and table-tennis."

That's funny thought John, he saw himself a good shot at ping-pong, had competed at a fairly good level before giving it up.

"Would you tell me the whole story about Philby and how and what and so on?"

"No."

"No?"

"No, well, Philby was a traitor, fooling everybody within the MI6 and his friend Elliott. Many suffered torture and deaths because of him. Philby was recruited by Stalin's people in the thirties, worked himself high up and would become the head of counterespionage in Washington."

John sat listening, whatever might come out of this, it was exciting and observed Wellington spoke with a certain intimacy such a delicate theme.

"Your father tried to get him, but Philby was somehow informed that we were after him and escaped, that's all I can tell."

"We don't know who did that, do we?"

"No, we don't."

"And if you knew, you wouldn't tell me?

"Exactly. Although I can say the man, a certain Mr. Elliot who was sent out to Beirut to disclose,confront Philby and get a confession, was a very good friend of Philby."

"Who wasn't blunt enough," said John doing the finger-movements which indicate irony.

"I see you do know stuff, funny you mentioned blunt", said Wellington with admiring smile, "it's possible Anthony Blunt was the man who tipped Philby."

John had seen a documentary about it and wondered what else might be hidden which the BBC hadn't found out.

"I saw the documentary."

"Elliot and Philby came from identical backgrounds. In those days MI6 was a boy's network, the club- ability we call it."

"Why didn't they send an unbiased tough agent to interrogate Philby?"

"Maybe they preferred Philby in Moscow, instead of the humiliation in court."

"What does that leave friendship in the spying business?"

"Good point, Elliot ended badly after having been betrayed during thirty years by a friend."

John went silent again thinking how do these people live their lives. Wherever they go they must be aware of a treacherous option, a treacherous friend.

"The same year Philby disappeared and the Swedish coronel Wennerström got caught, the MI6 was investigating if there was a connection.

"The famous Soviet spy?"

"Your father went to Sweden some years later cause of a nervousness in the Intelligence community about possible followers. Everybody went neurotic after the Philby incident searching spies everywhere." Regardless of the circumstances his father hadn't been an amateur spy and been involved in the largest spy-hunts and conspiracies of the century.

"We all have our secrets," murmured Wellington seemingly to himself, as if being in the Intelligence business was close to normal.

"Who do you trust then? Your friend or colleagues?"

"In our trade truth and reality doesn't need to coincide and lies can convert to truths."

John's mind went wandering about and a sudden scare began to grow in his mind listening to Wellington. He had read about journalists who weren't journalists, entrepreneurs in foreign countries had a businessman's cover on their government's behalf, perhaps not a matrix-world but a mirror-like reality where everybody joined the party of hidden identities. But as John had a fluid mind recovered despite his stupefaction and said;

"The Russians must have been suspicious of the information Philby and the others from Cambridge gave away, too good to be true?"

"I see you have a mind of an intelligence officer," said Wellington with his wry smile. "Well, answering your question, you cipher as best you can and trust your instincts, not easy, as there are crooks and others who pretend to be crooks just to fool you."

"The effect of Philby and the Cambridge-Five was a psychological disaster I suppose."

"It leashed a mole-hunt, not just in British Intelligence also in the CIA and the infamous Angleton went bonkers with our incompetence. It was catastrophic and became like McCarthyism searching for moles everywhere and most importantly, trust was lost."

"How could he remain so long, what was he doing?"

"Very much a class-thing the whole rotten business."

An admittance of the immorality of it all thought John. The waiter returned, taking away their finished plates. The food hadn't been appreciated due to their conversation.

Without warning, Wellington veered into a completely different topic.

"We are investigating, a widening scandal, detected in Tallin at the Danske Bank. Huge money is laundered from state-companies in Russia becoming white."

John didn't know what to comment so he stayed silent.

"Anyways, this involves a risk to UK-security, international terrorism, weapons proliferation and cyber issues. Identifying risks at the earliest stage, preventing emerging threats."

"You cover all that?

"Yes, you see in 2014 Estonian regulators stepped into the Tallinn office of Danske Bank, it was shown that companies were moving huge amounts of money through the bank from Russia, Azerbaijan, and Ukraine, justified by nonsensical contracts. This has triggered one of the biggest money laundering scandals of all time with billions of dollars moved through the bank's Estonian branch. One company from Uzbekistan bought $2 million worth of *building materials* from the remote British Virgin Islands," he said rolling his eyes in disbelief.

"And the employees at the bank, didn't they put out a red flag?"

"Systematically they ignored hundreds of transactions."

"Why not?"

"They made big money at the branch, too sweet. It's astonishing."

"And how was it justified?"

"Not good, not good at all, the ramifications are still to be seen."

CHAPTER 16

The waiter appeared with two plates where you couldn't see what was inside the two silvered half-moons. Must be the dessert John thought.

"Now, the issue at hand is Russian money, is flowing into Hong Kong due to Western sanctions as investors look for a haven after the debacle of Estonia. I tell you this as you have the ears of one of the Taipans in Hong Kong."

This remark made John nervous, soon he'll say he knows about Jasmine and Marianne.

"Actually I'll go to Hong Kong in a few days," said John.

"For what reason?"

"We are founding a company, procuring goods from Chinese manufacturers for distribution in Europe."

"Maybe you could do things for us while you are there?

"Things?"

In an instance the man's voice had become much more kind. Wellington's intuition must have approved of John, as if they belonged to the same team. His question about working for them seemed like a normal formality as if you want sugar in your tea. Wellington didn't take note of John's last question and continued instead and said, "there is a shift in power, its' getting oriented eastwards. China stands out as the greatest long-term threat. The impact is a threat to our economic security and a threat to our national security," he affirmed.

These comments were pronounced without emotional additives, simply as facts. Wellington was steering their conversation at will like a music director in any direction that suited him or in his interest. He spoke softly and with authority, not fast but not slow. Not easy to intervene as there were no clear pauses.

"The Chinese are blending foreign investments and corporate acquisitions with cyber intrusions and espionage and corrupting insiders. Now, this is my point, we want executives to consider who they choose to do business with and who they make up their supply chains, have you done that while searching suppliers?

"In the sense you are pointing at, no," said John.

"Enter into a joint venture with a supplier might look good and making a lot of money today but perhaps not in the long-term."

Long term John mused, what exactly does that even mean in my case. Wellington seemed to be on a roll, his excitement building with every word. He needed to speak and articulate his vision.

"They weaponize the data, the stolen stuff by Wikileaks or Snowden with an army of trolls, manipulate it into algorithms to search-engines like Google and it appears as trending the information space which affects the public opinion."

Looking straight as in his own thoughts Wellington continued;

"It's a lot on our plate," not referring to the dessert Wellington had just finished as a man who seemed to consider food as gasoline, not for pleasure.

"I can see that."

"I'm also going to Hong Kong, have worries about the Triads influence in China and the business over there."

John knew the Triads were like the Mafia, a supermarket of crime, gambling, prostitutions, human smuggling, extortion, loansharking. "Imagine a supply-chain disruption by agency of the Triads, it can threat across industries. A chip shortage can bring car production to a standstill. Listen John," while leaning forward, "I just wonder if you could be what we call a pigeon stool?"

"An informant?"

"Perhaps you would like to contribute as your father did?"

"What could I offer you of interest? As an afterthought; "In what condition?"

"We do sub-contracting."

"As Snowden, the whistleblower."

"Exactly. Well, as I was saying… one can only wonder what went through that guy's mind when he fled, now sitting in Moscow asking for mercy, used as a propaganda tool for Putin."

"And the Guardian's, the newspaper didn't take care of him, what happened there?" asked John.

"Snowden must have understood when he decided to blow the whistle, he would be forced to face the music and take the rap, I mean the damage was great" and added, "John you *are* well read."

"I scan the smart phone as any when there is a moment of void."

"But in the digital age, espionage is more complicated, your footprint is all over the place, if you go to a hotel or buy something your movements are known through the credit-card."

"That's pretty disturbing."

"As I said perhaps you could feel what's going, furnish us with information as I heard, you know the Taipan Dunbar quite well."

"And what exactly should I do?"

"Detect if you sense muddy deals, clues you might consider of interest, not judging if it's good or bad and pass it on."

"What sort of information do you want?"

"You know the nose was invented for the only reason to put spectacles on said Voltaire, I'll read you something," he said looking on his mobile. It was interesting how this chief in the art of spying jumped from dead serious matters to cites or themes completely different from one another. He had an acrobatic mind steering his conduct to the goal turning with side-turns like a skier going down the slope watching for until then, unseen hinders and obstacles. John also had a bit of this, but this guy was a master.

He put on his glasses and said:

"There is this new thing, one more stretch in science, "a super-quantum computer which would change the world," Wellington read gravely; "Quantum computers will make it possible to understand complex chemical reactions that will help to design new drugs, develop new materials optimizing artificial intelligence and algorithms, cybersecurity and finance etc."

"That could affect the origins of crypto-currencies or?

"It could change everything, a new level of AI."

Ben Dunbar had touched this briefly with John when they met in Hong Kong and had been listening without fully understanding the implications of such a novelty.

"Why do you read this to me?

"It's to let you know that big wheels are churning, a delegation in Whitehall is going to Hong Kong shortly as top guns from the business community to a conference about quantum-computers."

"Okay," said John very confused by now. "I came here to learn about my father, and you talk about quantum computers."

"Well as you are going to be there, observe stuff which might in our interest. Using your instincts, according to Eric you acted well with that Gang-of Four."

John was baffled, perhaps it's the quantum activity applied on him, things weren't where or what they seemed to be and therefore by some cabalistic orders, randomly were energized.

"Is this official in some way?"

"Not really," he said with a sly grin.

"I doubt I'll be present at any meeting of this kind. And if it would happen, I would betray the man who is investing in me."

"Don't take it too seriously, let's say if you hear something which wouldn't disturb your morals and you think it might be valuable for our country you let me know, sounds better?"

"Suppose I can live with that."

"I mean, if you hear something you think is worth its salt, you let me know. No harm in that. As you might understand, when talking to Eric, we did some checks on your past and you are clean and no stains as it looks."

"What do you know about my past?"

"I would say most of it."

"Do you have a file on me?"

"Something like that yes, don't forget who your father was."

Wellington then proceeded and spelled out the essentials of John's life in perfect chronological order; schools, military service, where he had lived and where he had worked.

"Wow, how splendid. You know more about me than my best friends."

"And you are your father's son and he was damn good, that helps."

"So, there is a file on me," said John almost with awe.

"Not exactly, let's call it a rough draft."

"A draft?"

"A summarized version of your life."

"But why?"

"The moment you talked to Eric, no red lamps began to shine but we were informed, taking into account your surname, that's all."

That's all? thought John almost nauseous realizing that he did exist in the MI6 files.

And now this man was searching for intentions, where the drifts were going, a forecast or simple gossip.

"Should I let Eric know about this, he might ask me?"

"Negative, let's leave it between you and me. In our trade we can't blab to anyone, what you are doing to your loved ones, that's what makes it thrilling."

"And why should I trust you on this?"

"Good question," he said with a wide smile, "do some checks on the internet. I could even further detailed information about us if you need it."

"I tried to google you but there was nothing out of the ordinary or in the racket of spying."

"I wouldn't call it a racket really. Anyway, I'm sure you have read John Le Carré novels which are to some extent close to the truth, especially his first works but they aren't about real action. A lot of them have to do with his bitterness and lack of trust between the old Empire and the US. Wonderfully written but much is about personal relations and their problems. The reality is much worse and ugly. Tom Cruise's films are closer to the real world apart of his jumping and all that crap, in Carré's world it's a moral problem."

As an afterthought he added; "There is an ugly part out there and that sometimes leads us to the right place," he finished cryptically.

This might be beyond my own control John thought distressed. But what the hell, seize the day and by a strange force John forwarded his right hand and they shook hands in silence as a validation of a deal.

Subsequently Wellington offered suggestions of what kind of information could be interesting. He was especially interested in which companies were hot for investments, like the Volvo-deal. "Your Taipan might give you insights what's going on."

"Which he will not tell me."

"Asking a question here and there."

"Is that not a bit vague?

"Of course, but there are vibes which pour out of people's mouths, the way of saying things and when they don't say things when they are supposed to."

"What about Volvo?"

"It is owned by a Chinese company and that puts pressure on Sweden. There are also interests in SAAB and their warplanes."

"Meaning less independence for Sweden."

"Definitely, the Chinese are buying all over the world which affects governments in their decision-making, we might end up as a colony to their wishes and whims."

"What Great Britain did some generations ago."

"Yeah, but there is a difference."

"Which is?"

"We don't want to live under their authoritarian hammer, with no accountability."

"And was Great Britain at any point accountable? I mean that's relative, if you ask an Indian to name one, they see things from another perspective."

"The bottom line is," Wellington summarized, "we have to know what they are doing and that's what we are dedicated to."

Coffee was served, which gave them time to ponder the contents of what had been said.

"All this sounds a bit over the top, blurring the line between friendship and relations."

"Let's say there is word of change in ownership for example."

"As I said, don't think I'll be present at talks of that kind."

"Perhaps not but between lines there might be words and desires of strategic value. Rumors or chit-chat after a few drinks. Many years in this trade and my instincts tell me you will do good."

"We'll see about that," said John gruntingly. "I came, here to hear about my father and we talk about very different things."

"You are right but that's the thrill of it you never know what's behind the corner."

"That's true."

There is one thing I don't know if you are aware of."

"For sure there are."

"You have an uncle, I happen to know, who at the time did some work for us or more specific, for the Swedish Intelligence."

"What about him?"

"I'm afraid your uncle is in serious trouble."

"That I didn't know," John lied.

"I thought you should be aware of this, please let me know if you hear anything."

This caught John off guard and unsure how to respond.

"He is being investigated?"

"Can't tell much but I will let you know if something comes up."

"Would appreciate that."

"Are we good then?" said Wellington and raised.

"Thank you for taking your time," said John feeling he had to finish in a good mood, as he just said, you'll never know what is around the corners, well a part of Eric of course. Wellington offered a contagious smile, the charming man he was.

"Not too much fuss about our conversation, ok?"

"Okay."

"I mean we don't sing out loud to our girlfriends and all that."

John understood what Wellington meant this conversation hadn't take place, that if you are in the spying world you are on your own, no one to talk to about except your handler.

"You have my number, call me when in need."

"Need?"

"If something substantial comes up you consider might interest me. Think about it, we have an advantage, we have friends, and they don't."

"Who?"

"All the authoritarian regimes."

An ambiguous way of saying what might be obvious. Wellington waved to a waiter and fixed the bill. When they were leaving an elderly man came forward and saluted Wellington, they were presented and when the man heard it was Jack's son said.

"Your father was a patriot for sure. But sometimes, a patriot does things that doesn't look that way from the outside. We all have our debts to pay."

"Maxwell, you can't say that" said Wellington angrily.

"I just did."

"You don't have proof."

John went numb again, what were they talking about. The man looked at both John and Wellington and left them.

"What was that all about?"

"This Maxwell was your father's competitor or enemy, he claims your father was involved when Philby got lost."

"And what do you think?"

"I'm sure it's false."

"Not hundred percent?!

"There was a lot of rivalry in those days and your father seemed to have outplaced this Maxwell career-wise within MI6."

"But you can't assure me that's is false?

"The problem is these are classified issues I can't talk about."

"Sorry must go now, nice to meet you," and he was gone, the embodiment of the Spy-world, one moment a secret man and the other a normal citizen, member of the right clubs. In a flash he was back and said: "I was thinking, there is a reception of some sort this evening at the Dorchester, maybe you would like to come, Boris will be there."

"That would be fun, I mean to meet him again," John said without thinking as he was in shock after this new revelation.

CHAPTER 17

John staggered out of the club, wonderstruck, trying to grasp what had just happened, from becoming a pigeon stool, the startling fact his father might have been a double-agent, that is, a traitor. Not to forget there is a file of me in the MI6, that's almost flattering but also dangerous and he thought of Orwell's book 1984 where states surveil its citizens. Out on the street, he was struck by the mundane ordinariness of it all, people coming and going about their business. The world carried on, oblivious to the extraordinary things he was now grappling. And why should it?

His reality had shifted not the world's.

Before going to the reception at Dorchester, he had to kill a few hours. He found a nearby pub and had a lager. He finished the beer, walked a bit and was amazed at all the flowers hanging on fences in different colors, who is taking care of that he wondered, took a cab to his hotel and dozed a bit, a shower and a new cab to the Dorchester in a state of perplexity. He couldn't discern which of Wellington's revelations had shaken him more; the file about him, the murky details of his uncle's dealings, or the chilling possibility that his father had been a double-agent. The thought of it made him recoil. I need a drink he thought after battling to get out of the cab with a low seat.

Dorchester buzzed like Piccadilly Circus, a whirlwind of activity, clinking of glasses where everybody seemed to know each other. Always an inconvenience when you are dead alone. He saw a table of drinks and made his way towards what looked like a bar, it was the best thing he could do, find a drink and give an appearance of being occupied. There was a little queue in front of him. After a while he was second for a drink, a woman he knew asked for a glass of champagne. Not exactly knew but had met a moment during his last visit to London, the famous cook. During that occasion they had exchanged a few words.

"We meet again," he began appreciating how beautiful she was.

She looked up and with a sincere surprised look, yes, she did recognize him.

"Yes, we have."

"I'm not stalking you."

"I've begun to wonder."

"It's a small world."

"You think?" she said a bit testily.

"No, I don't think so, actually it's immense and the probability that I would see you again is unlikely."

"Now I remember, I liked your tie," she said, resting one hand on her hip, enhancing her attributes with eyes conveying a message as if saying look square now and check how gorgeous I am.

"Only the tie?"

"Well, there wasn't much more, was it?"

"It's in the eyes of the beholder."

"You aren't stalking me, are you?"

"Let's say I wouldn't mind but no, it's random, all the time."

"Must be tiresome", she said with a grin.

John couldn't help it but felt himself drawn to this woman.

"It's wicked, it happens so often. Perhaps there is a recipe to avoid it?"

"Haven't come across it yet," she said openly smiling.

"It's like when you don't follow the recipe making food and go by intuition."

"Generally, I go by the recipe, avoid surprises is my motto."

"Always?"

"No, sometimes I go by intuition." John liked this play of words.

"Next time we meet I invite you for dinner so you don't have to cook," suggested John.

"If we meet."

"The third time and all that."

At that moment Wellington arrived, looking satisfied, whatever a master-spy's face unveil.

"Hi John, I see you know the prettiest cook in England," he said forwarding his hand first to her and then to John.

"We happen to meet now and then," answered John.

"So, you are a friend of Alistair," said Fiona, "you work together?"

"His father worked for us," dodging the theme of Intelligence.

"Maybe he can speak for himself," she said and looked at John with curiosity.

"If we work together? No not really."

All of a sudden, the famous Boris Winslow appeared, accompanied with his spin-doctor. He wasn't mayor anymore, now he was in Government. The statistical probability of meeting Boris again or Fiona was infinitely small but here they were. Visibly, neither of the two politicians seemed immune to female charm, giving a fast look on the famous cook, especially the spin-doctor gave a dirty man's look at her.

"Nice to see again, you know each other?" said Boris, "now you know everyone, the most popular and the powerful," he said laughing at his own joke. "You did a great job there in Brussels."

"I just said my mind."

"Were there any repercussions after your little intervention?"

"The media is treating it like a wildfire, suppose I have to face it heads-on and fight it."

"No, no do as Mitterand, indifference."

"Not easy."

Boris brushed off John's comment and switched back to his previous point.

"Good, good, these two are the most influential people in this country, if you didn't know already."

It was obvious Boris knew Wellington and the famous cook.

"I happen to bump into people", said John with a cryptic half-smile.

"We have to watch you, more closely," said Boris seemingly lost in thought.

"John is here, because of his late father," said Wellington helping John.

"What happened to him?"

"He died during the Falklands war."

Fiona now looked at John with what he perceived as new interest.

"I'm sad to hear that," she said.

"Must have been a good man," said Boris. "We should meet again you might be of help."

"Yes of course," said John automatically.

"I'll leave you, must rub shoulders. Call me in case you need something," which was his way of saying good-bye and as fast as he had appeared he was gone.

"Do you mind?" said a tall man with Indian traits.

"So sorry we are obstructing you," said Wellington.

"Even writers drink."

John saw who the man was, the famous author of the Satanic verses.

"Any new book to be printed?" asked Wellington.

"Let's say I'm on the verge."

It was obvious they knew each other, this author had been safe guarded during years by English Intelligence.

"Have read a few of yours," said John gallantly.

A foolish interruption of mine John thought. His books sell in the millions.

"Is that so? How interesting, which one?"

"Can't remember the title. It was about a bizarre family in New York."

"The Golden House, was it up to your expectations?"

"I didn't know what to expect really but beautifully written"

"You talk like an editor after having refused my work," he said smiling.

The author left their little party as did Wellington, saying, "we keep in touch".

"You know Alistair?" asked John the famous cook.

"Alistair is a fellow of many things and societies."

"The establishment?"

"Definitely, he is one of the boys. And what about you, having business with him?"

"I wanted to know more about my father, that's why I'm here, got his name from a mutual friend and here I am."

She had emptied her glass, so John saw an opportunity to continue their chat.

"I'll get another glass for you."

He didn't let her answer and rapidly was back with two new glasses of champagne.

"By the way my name is Sherman," John Sherman was said imitating James Bond. "And if I may ask, how do you know Wellington, in view of his kind of business."

"He is everywhere, went to Westminster school as my father they all know each other, it's like a little golden pond, seen him since ages."

"My father also went there."

She looked at her watch, "have to go now."

"Can we meet again?"

"If there is a third time."

"And how do I contact you?"

"I'm sure you'll find me."

"But London is big."

She seemed to have a change of heart, opened her bag and produced a card, "call me when you are back in London and gave him a kiss on the chin, "let's see if there is a third time and I go with you."

When she had left, John was startled by how these things turn up in life, you meet someone where you instinctively know you like the person and vice versa. Strange this constant craving of mating, he thought. With nobody to talk to, he finished the drink and decided to call it a day to no one and searched for the exit of the hotel, walked until he passed an Italian restaurant ordered a spaghetti with tomato and went straight to the hotel, saw a bit of BBC-news, then changed to a documentary about UFO's and decided he wasn't interested in if and when or how, the aliens would behave or with which intentions. He had more prosaic matters in his head than the coming of beings from outer space. But it worked as an effective sleeping pill.

The day after he went to Paddington, bought a ticket for the train to Heathrow. Sitting looking out the window in the train without seeing the thankless suburbs, not taking it in. It had happened again he had been asked to do some kind of undercover search. It was vague as to a degree, immoral. He couldn't call it spying, that would be giving it too much stature. Another thought came to his mind, he had to check his digital footprint and be careful writing e-mails, this guy Wellington would hack him in a jiffy, probably it's already done, especially now, as I'm very much in the picture, as my uncle.

Why do I even bother about this and just say a firm no? People do these things for patriotism or money, some for both, he wasn't sure of his own, "Being a spook for what? Vanity?" It's not narcissism because whatever you achieve in the spying-business it can't be known. A stool pigeon stool, as an informer of some sort. Like the birds from the First World War, who flew over enemy territory fitted with camaras to provide information. Was he aware of what he was exposing himself to? Did he have what his father apparently had, or would he crumble and metaphorically shit in "midair" as the pigeons do? He didn't know, he had never been exposed to real peril. And what about his father, if he hadn't been the man he thought. A frightening apprehension. A silent conversation raged within and then a single decisive thought, when he arrived to the airport; Lift yourself and that chin of yours as the lobsters when preparing for a fight, be combative and regroup. No dire straits, take a straight venue and focus. Don't be too hard on yourself. After checking in with no luggage, a deceitful extra bag surfaced in his mind, his quest for his love-life. It reverberated during the two-hour flight. Was he treacherous and therefore maybe perfect for the intelligence-business and wondered if spies are born or made. But as humans rationalize their own behavior, he decided simplistically that his life was a journey of exciting sentiments. The flight back to Stockholm was without incidents, a silent airport, no spontaneous encounters, took the Arlanda-Express, a taxi and he arrived at his flat, tired of too much of everything, he dozed off listening to the sound of the traffic.

CHAPTER 18

On Friday John and Marianne took a twenty-minute train-ride from Stockholm to Saltsjöbaden. A municipality with beautiful views and great villas. When young, he had envisioned it was here he wanted to live out his life, after having succeeded to become a prosperous man. He had mentally pictured sailing tours in and around the archipelago in a mahogany boat with white sails. It was here he would cruise to arcadian sites, anchoring in suitable corners of the archipelago, go to pastoral little islands for splendid excursions. It was here he would bring a girlfriend, sharing the bliss of a sunset over wine and good food. Riding the train from Slussen and Marianne asked; "how was London?"

"Busy as always."

"Did you find out something?"

"Not much, met a nice chap who talked a lot about world politics."

"It wasn't worth it then?"

John didn't know how to answer her question and said vaguely, "I would say yes but he didn't tell me anything special, they can't."

She sensed he wasn't eager to discuss the matter and didn't pursue further.

They were to be picked up close to the hotel. Sitting on a bench waiting for his friend Carl to arrive, John had trouble concentrating, still bewildered after such extraordinary encounter in London with an intelligence officer of the MI6. The revelations about his father weighed heavily on him as the file on him. It was a lot to bear.

"You, okay? You seem a bit distant." Marianne asked when Carl was arriving with his boat to pick them up.

"I'm fine."

"Are you worried about how your friends will receive you after all these years?" she pressed.

"Maybe a little," he admitted. What truly weighed on his mind was what had been said in London the day before the unsettling possibility his father might have been a double agent.

"Whatever happens tonight don't consider it as a test," she said a bit harshly.

In reality, this was one of many tests, if his return to the motherland, would be positive.

"You'll be fine," she said and took his hand, which he admitted to himself he liked.

"It's kind of start again, a new beginning."

"Let's make the most of it then", she said.

Unbidden his mind wandered to his early days in Madrid flooded in with uncertainty and close to fear, as this upcoming event had a resemblance to those days.

Carl appeared with the usual smile of his and they jumped into his boat without further ado. The way to reach the island to Carl's place was a ten-minute trip by boat. Marianne was talking to Carl and appeared to enjoy the experience and share dinner with friends on an island blended with the charm of the archipelago. The boat went splendidly with a casual stride, passing sailing boats and motorboats. He heard Marianne say.

"The city suddenly seems much further away than it is."

"This is so serene, almost untouched by civilization," said Carl. Although there were red wooden cottages and bobbing yachts, riding the water between the islands. Separated the water from the land were mountain-like stones where trees were squeezed in, creating a coastline of jam-packed tree-cluster. "Look at those trees in such tricky terrain," said John.

John was fascinated by trees since Carl Sagan had written they were our cousins in the evolutionary perspective.

"I read a book about trees, they feel pain and have emotions. Look how they like to stand close to each other and cuddle and adore the company."

"I didn't know," said Carl, "but whatever they do it's a slow way." The archipelago was discovered as a resort for leisure, literally by Strindberg the famous author who made it popular. The result was a romantic affinity between the urban lifestyle in the city to the wilder habitat out on the islands. This natural space reflected a need by the wealthy upper- middle class of Stockholm in the last decades of the nineteenth century.

Carl's summerhouse was situated in a little gulf protected by harsh winds, perfectly located to benefit great sunsets. Two houses, one grandly for pompous dinners and sleepovers, the other was a rustic lake- house, simple but cozy. John had looked forward to this evening with great expectations, in the hope he would assent and come to terms with himself and his new life in Sweden. One more step towards his readjustment to his native country. He anticipated an evening with the sound of tinkering glasses and laughter and spirited chatter floating out.

When they were getting close to Carl's place two guys John knew well stood waiting.

"Hi John," said Gunnar, "sea-sick?"

"Carl still hasn't learned to drive this thing he calls a boat," said Anders, a guy with too much self-reliance.

"That's a hell of a welcoming," said Carl after he had tied up the boat safely.

A first quick look John saw the boathouse had been refurbished but maintained a rustic flavor. The main house was also re-built after a fire and looked splendid from the outset. Carl went urgently to fix the fire of the barbecue, a construction of his own. It was made with parts of wood as pillars and an old door in metal where he put the carbon for the heating.

A big table close to the water in perfect position so everybody could take in what the evening suggested to be a perfect nightfall. All looked set, with a desire to have a great time, accompanied with good food, wine and interesting conversations. Drinks were produced, rosé wine for the women and stronger stuff like the inevitable gin-tonic for the guys. The party consisted of four couples. They all knew each other since their days as youngsters, now tentatively seeking with whom to share those first moments. A slight hesitation, searching for a common theme to initiate the first stages. You lean towards someone or say something you know about, and everything gets going and as often happens in life, things just come about happenstance.

One of the couples was Gunnar and his wife Susanne. Gunnar stood out career-wise and was considered one of the best lawyers in Sweden, early on earmarked for great things. John had met him some weeks ago, for a consultation if a famous and valuable painting John thought could be his. Now a resting case. Gunnar was opiniated as most lawyers and spoke with brimming self-confidence in that peculiar language of jurisdiction and making it sound funny. He could sneeze and make a laugh. His wife was slightly timid and not noticed in a crowd.

Another couple were Anders and Birgitta. John always had problems to digest Ander's mannerism, speaking harshly with deterministic views. He gave the impression he had a poor opinion of anyone who came into his field of vision. Anders was *someone* within the Swedish Nobel Committee, therefore he behaved with superior carriage, very vocal and often belligerent.

It was rumored when Anders and Gunnar had studied at the Stockholm Business School, they had it all figured out. While other students went out to have fun, they were discussing on the health-care system or possible solutions for the United Nations.

Anders deliberately ignored John, now as in the old days. Not a person you'd like to play golf with. And there was Carl and his wife Anna as hosts.

A few overtures about the surprise to see John in Sweden and together with Marianne, wondering with undisguised curiosity if they were a couple or not. This gathering wasn't what John considered his absolute best friends, with the exception of Carl and his wife. His best buddies, he had dined with last week. They had been six buddies sharing a round table making it easy to speak to anyone. No weighty matters were treated, only uplifting jokes and tales without satirical slide-shots. Some stuff from way back was commented but they weren't trapped in telling stories of old times. They were all individualistic with a proper take on things. Characteristically they professed they hated snobs and snobbery, never went to festivals with multitudes, no charter-trips. They trotted along on their own, having been stooped for a much more exciting life than the ordinary man. Seemingly in touch with the world, looking forward to the next adventure. Mutual experiences in youth, when psyches were constructed and identity in parallel, making their relation effortless. Not the best and the brightest, no wunderkinds, no brilliant violin-players, just nice striving good blokes who had a harmless rivalry and healthy friendship. It had surprised John, in spite of the different circumstances for each and every one of them, diverse careers and at times, bad upkeep of comradeship, it still seemed to flourish after so many years. The plaster that was molded at the time still held.

As ever Carl was an excellent host, gregarious with an inborn talent for setting the tone with intelligent suggestions, making people open and chit-chat, cutting here and there if the going went wrong. He was a natural social animal, kicking around comments of good nature. It could be the simplest of themes to profound matters of the day, making people feel good. He had prepared some extravagant steaks on the grill with a salad and his wife decorated the table with detailed Swedish style. Carl fussed over the steaks for a while but it was worth it. When he finally decided they were ready, he put them on a plate, looking pretty pleased with himself. They smelled amazing. Everybody sat down and Carl's wife began to serve.

Gunnar's wife Susanne sat down beside John and said; "I'll be a terrible company tonight, I'm exhausted," to which John had no rapid reply. It only made him think how she would be when not exhausted. Carl did a toast for John with flair and ironizing about John's decisions about going from and coming back to Sweden and finished saying; "Now you are the talk of the town" and paused, "I mean the two of you." John rose visibly moved by Carl's words, wanted to give his thanks.

"To be here with all of you is what I've missed," he said with grandiosity, suddenly emotional, "I can only hope I'm worthy your friendship."

All seemed to perceive he was speaking with sincerity.

"Well spoken," said Gunnar.

"So why have you decided to come back?", asked Birgitta

"You want the short version or the long one," asked John noticing the hostility in her voice.

"Any version," said Birgitta.

"But keep it short," said Anders thinking he was funny.

John paused and gave Anders an earnest gaze. Everybody went silent, wondering if John would blast Anders after such a harsh statement. Deliberately John delayed his answer, recollected his thoughts and concluded *you are a motherfucker now as you always were.*

"You know, when I left, it was a feeling of not belonging anymore", John said with absolute honesty.

"I can understand that" said Birgitta, sitting at the far left, "it happens everyday for me." John knew how cantankerous she could be and wanted to avoid direct confrontation because whatever there was to discuss, she had a talent to stir up, creating minor havocs at any get- together. Not an easy bird to swallow. An exchange of questions and answers began.

"Why didn't you feel you belonged, because your career wasn't where you wanted it to be?", said Anders who seemed to bent to make John uncomfortable. John didn't take the comment on volley, elegantly avoided the gibe.

The woman at his left, Anne, looked seriously to John and said; "Home is not something to joke about, it's where you belong, that's why we all stayed."

"What I've noticed is, home doesn't need to be explained, it's when you have to compare the difficulties begin," said John.

"And then we lose something, by definition", said Carl, as the opportunist he was, it wasn't clear what he meant but it sounded good at this point.

"So, what's your opinion about our country?" asked Birgitta.

"Well, it's a bit early but so far, so good."

"Soon you'll be part of the furniture," said Carl and laughed to his own joke.

"My opinion is that this steak is perfect," said Anders, singing out his truth with a wish of taking the reins, mowing towards other fields. His cast-iron confidence made him speak like no other but with no empathy. "Anders, you can't tell a steak from meatballs," said Carl taking off the steam and they all laughed, even Anders had to laugh. Luckily the attention towards John disappeared, he didn't want to be the subject of the night. Words and opinions now arose like a whirl wind, it was free-for-all from this moment. The consumption of wine buttressed heartrates and boosted the speech like oil for a machine. An exchange, like a flipper-machine, of different topics whooped in mid-air, rebounded, volleyed back, virtually incoherently but you tried to stand your ground as best as you could. John, who had drunk his share was carried away and felt elated almost buoyant, ruminating that he now was where he had wanted to be for so many years. His thoughts were interrupted by a new line of topic, as the conversation was going wholesale and spiraled.

"There is no objectivity, nobody is more rightful than the other man," said Anne.

"Exactly, who am I to tell you which is good or bad," supplemented Carl.

"Kant sentenced that we can't agree but we live together in a civilized society so… and Hume said that everything is just passion," said John smiling foolishly.

"Who is Hume?"

"A guy who lived three hundred years ago and thought that all decisions are based on sentiment or passion," answered John.

"John studied history and literature, that's why he is such an intellectual snob," informed Carl and everybody laughed again, especially Carl himself. John was amazed how Carl always succeeded in conveying the right tone whatever he articulated.

"True, I say as Ted Turner; I have a limitless supply of bullshit." At which Anders seemed to agree upon, but Carl cut him short by saying; "You read too much, it's not good for you."

"Don't worry I retain only fractions, so never mind," he said laughing at himself.

"This damned iPhone has ruined my attention span, I only read the headlines," said Susanne as if she hadn't got the drift of what had been said.

"I know exactly what you mean, can't focus like I used to," said Anna as if she merely wanted to add her voice to the conversation. Susanne continued her own lane and said, "why don't we talk about something more cheerful?"

"We don't agree on anything, since everything became virtual," was said by Anders customary aggressive way, "It's the AI who has the power and those fucking algorithms, they know better," thinking he had said something witty.

"Now you are off the wall," said Gunnar but Anders continued incoherently, he was on fire and shot away more bullets. He spoke in his bent-up anger, "I think the good life makes us too anxious about everything. Look at the best-sellers list in the USA, half of them is about personal help, how to be happy, be a good father and lover bla bla."

He was known for writing articles of economic character as close to genius a man can be but the alcohol had taken hold and now his words slurred. Meanwhile his wife, Birgitta displayed a frowning face. Too much energy there, thought John. She didn't breach the right tone, speaking in C-sharp, a pure talent for polemics. The party had begun like any other, with polite conversation over appetizers, but as the wine flowed, so did the opinions. What started as a casual discussion turned into a lively debate, with everyone jumping in, each voice growing louder as new topics surfaced. Ideas clashed, and laughter punctuated the more heated moments. No one could resist putting forth their thoughts, transforming the evening into a whirlwind of perspectives, where every guest became the expert of their own passion. Argumentation was going overboard, so Carl interrupted everybody and said, "sway an opinion you do through facts, instead of hammering in arguments, therefore please don't goad Anders, he'll never stop."

"Okay okay, but before" interrupted Gunnar, "in the beginning Internet seemed fantastic, everybody could spit out their versions. Are we better off now, not knowing who is behind the algorithms?"

"Those bastards in Silicon Valley are deciding the ethics, what is their criteria and use of moral sense?" said Anders.

"Yeah, those pricks at Facebook or Twitter and their sponsors hiding behind a cloak, not accountable to anyone," agreed Gunnar.

"The problem with social media is anybody can say anything. Everything is questioned, everybody are experts, and colossal lies are coming out of the Internet."

Anders raised and left the table and there was a pause.

"I read about your speech in Brussels, I liked it," said Gunnar.

"I think it was racist," said Birgitta.

"Why, he said the truth, as Anders just said, do you live under a stone and don't see what's going on?" said Gunnar.

"It's a populist view." It was clear she was fighting with herself to not be un-polite but couldn't shut up. Many years ago, John had seen her go ballistic when someone dared to defend the American view on an issue, he had forgotten which exactly. She tended to glamorize countries in South America, after a trip over there watching women sitting in poor villages sewing in their miserable environment and bad conditions, accusing the West of all the unfair livelihoods and everything else, from the flue to Syphilis. "A populist? The moment someone says something out of the Culturati's line it's populism." "Whatever you say there is no action without feelings said Marianne, "one is a slave of one's feelings." This wasn't expected and was applauded as having said something extra-ordinary. John countered: "What moves us to action then? Passion?"

"Passion is the basic mover," said Marianne."

"Common sense?" tried John.

"Common sense only assists," sentenced Marianne.

"And the ego?"

"The ego helps and pushes those two sides of the mind."

"Your ego is the perception which creates your memory," said John.

"Accordingly, we perceive things thanks to impressions?" asked Marianne.

This looked like a duel between the two, the others were silent.

"Yes, we are just a lot of incidents, bundled together, nothing more," said John laughing.

"Meaning I'm of no real substance?" asked Marianne.

"Well, your consciousness is partly quantum mechanics."

"At what moment is my consciousness born then?"

"Consciousness is created at the proto-consciousness," said John.

"What?"

"It's the brains way of saying I'm online, like now, my neurons tell me you are a very beautiful woman," exclaimed John with vigor and got an applause as if he was a matador and finished an excellent round with the bull.

John's last remark landed like a finishing touch, bringing the discussion to a satisfying conclusion. A lot had been said and many thoughts springing around, one needed to recapture and refill the glasses.

The excitement of the bout was fading and Anna timely asked if anyone wanted coffee. They all raised in need of stretching their legs and took a moment appreciating the night with no clouds and a moon almost full perfectly seen. Marianne hadn't talk much during the dinner apart of the end. She seemed to sense how the wind went at any given moment and chose to go with the flow of the conversation when she felt comfortable. If a topic wasn't her dominion and made her unsafe she remained silent.

"What are you two talking about,?" interrupted Carl.

"We are not talking about you."

"How come I'm the only interesting person in this gathering."

"That depends on what you define as interesting."

"Until a few moments ago I was the only interesting person, now I see I have competition."

Carl left them to chat with the others. Marianne leaned towards John and took his hands.

"You were good there," she said and looked in his eyes. "You had more charm."

"Your thoughts are on a large scale."

"But incoherent, with no conclusions, I'm like twitter, only mediocrity."

Carl heard John's last words and said, "Don't rob my line here, I'm the one who self-depreciate myself," After this last remark it became evident the party had run out of steam. They had all tried to convey seriousness, talk with eloquence. No Nobel-price caliber, just ordinary people's worries. No clear winners or losers. Time was out and the party was coming to its end.

"I think we have to go back now," said Gunnar's wife.

"Yes, we ought to return to the civilization."

Before leaving Marianne took John and walked away towards a hill close to the waterside to take in the night and space they were in.

"It's beautiful."

"It is."

"Are you okay?"

"Yeah, I'm happy to be here. This is what I've missed all these years." And it was true, he meant it.

"I'm happy to be with you right now."

Carl offered John and Marianne the chance to stay for the night which they declined. A few kisses for the women and hugs between the guys to say goodbyes.

"It's so dark," she said on the ride back to the mainland.

"Can you imagine when the cities didn't have light, it was like this, starkly dark."

Maybe because John was under the influence of alcohol, he stared at the stars and with a sense of amazement, wondering how can the Church explain all that compared to what a man in sandals walking in the desert had said? And what's the astronaut's take in a little rocket circling the globe while looking down? And what about the breathtaking diversity in nature, if everything seemed to be coded, physically or mathematically, designed like a code with the DNA, surely, there must be a Coder. A thought which justifies a God of some kind.

She interrupted his thoughts by saying; "You remember when we water-skied, and the only light was a full moon?"

"I do, I did a few perfect rounds without falling came back dry. One of the best moments of my life."

"And I was impressed."

When Carl let them off the boat he said.

"I'm sorry if Anders and Birgitta were a bit hard on you. He is sometimes a jerk, and she is a forbidding lady."

"No worries. It has been a splendid evening."

They said goodbye and found a taxi close to the hotel. As it was July it was beginning to get bright at one- thirty in the night.

Sitting in the taxi Marianne back to Stockholm Marianne asked: "Did we pass the test?

"Most of it yes, there was an ugly part when that woman got angry, I tried to sit, as they say in Spain, on the balcony watching the bulls running by.

"You like bullfights?

"I did but not anymore."

John had been a bullfight-fan but lost interest, on the basis that people were shouting insults to the lonely man down there, who in his belief considered he was performing an art-form. Conscious about the implicit violence, the killing of a beast of 500 kilos with big horns, trying to survive, not having a clue of what's going on, a red mat flying over his head and what looked like a human being putting a sword in his back he had become skeptical about the whole thing.

He looked at Marianne, she had been lovely during the evening.

"I felt a competitiveness from that couple, they were over the top."

"Yeah, they seemed to corner you all the time. They are fine couple those two," she said with disgust.

"Anyways, I had a good time."

"I'm glad you like it, you fit in."

"Sometimes I think I adapt too easily."

"What do you mean?"

"Adjusting to the last speaker."

"You mean no core-beliefs or principles?"

"More a lack of personal identity."

"The higher the principles the harder the fall," she said.

"Suppose I need to find a better balance."

She shook her head slightly, a look of dismay in her face and said;

"It's not easy to find the sweet spot," she said.

Following these last words there was a moment of silence.

"John, I think you are emotionally exaggerating, go with the flow instead and enjoy things as they are," she said with a trace of pity.

"You are right, I ruminate too much."

She was dead-right, he was taking everything far too seriously, especially himself.

Marianne leaned her head against his shoulder with closed eyes, while John looked out the taxi window. His presence had seemed appreciated, his coming back might function, he felt energized.

They arrived to his flat and saw the sunrise from the balcony, but they were too tired to appreciate the beauty of it. A sunrise should be seen when you are rested and fresh, he thought and remembered the one he had seen with Jasmine in Hong Kong. The fact he hadn't entertained the notion of MI6-espionage or the existence of secret files, throughout the evening was astonishing.

CHAPTER 19

The next day John went to Sturehof to see his uncle Dennis. As ever, the restaurant was brimming with people buzzing with an urge to grab a bite, enjoy the pleasure of eating out, seeing people and to be seen. You sensed the intensity of the place by simply watching the waiters in white aprons scurrying around, with all kinds of food, drinks and taking orders, what seemed like organized chaos. The design of the restaurant wasn't refined, it was genuine; simple and pure. This matter must have come secondary in the priorities of the owners, not giving it much thought. Why bother when it was constantly crammed with people and a vibrant atmosphere.

Dennis sat at a table close to the window, looking smart in a green jacket and white shirt, which suited his white hair. John reflected on how much the way you dress sends a message what you are. At first sight, Dennis was that sort of man which exuded confidence, which he had articulated the other day with a supply of astute comments, inquiring questions, throwing any man with no self-assurance man off guard. However, after their first encounter and a more profound examination, John had grown skeptical and thought there was a sense of a façade, a frontage evading his true self.

"Everything okay?"

"Yeah, they say I'm fitting in," said John jovially.

"That's good, allow it to develop naturally, those things take time."

"You mean have the right attitude and be open-minded?" Same words he had told Marianne's son the other day.

"More or less yes, be patient with yourself and the rest will follow, it's not like when you are young, then you have the right disposition almost by definition."

"Does it get more difficult to adjust with age, is that what you are saying?"

"Well, sometimes when you realize your aren't in sync with the rest of the world and that's when problems start."

Dennis comment or maybe the way he said it, carried a sad note, hardly the upbeat start to kick off the night. Luckily a waiter arrived, and they ordered without much bothering beer and Swedish meatballs. "Not very romantic choice but it's a good treat," said Dennis.

"Do you come here often?"

"In my beginnings yes, we also went to a bar very close called Silver Bar, where the waitresses were astonishingly beautiful."

"I was thinking about what we talked about the other day, the fifties and sixties. What was it like, to be young back then?"

"In the fifties, life wasn't that sophisticated. In a way it was very simple. Things were safe, one knew what you were supposed to do in life. There was an innocent enthusiasm in Sweden after the war."

"Not so many worries, right?"

"No, we were harmless, including our parents. There was discipline and a certain order. When you were told to do something, you did it. When told to cut your hair you did it. The change appeared at the time The Beatles arrived."

The food came with a glass of beer and a basket with appetizing different sorts of Swedish bread.

"Things shifted when those guys came around?"

"You mean the Beatles, did it?"

"Yes, everything changed, not just because of the Beatles obviously. It was a cultural phenomenon, surrounding the whole society which created a profound turn, we began to protest about stuff, to teachers or our parents."

"But everybody says it was a great time?"

"All this glamorizing about the sixties, talks of social justice is horseshit, it was sex my friend sex, make love not war," he said this as if he had invented the wheel, "thanks to the pill, we did what our parents couldn't do or any previous generation."

That's quite a statement John thought while eating the meatballs. They finished their plates and ordered coffee.

"A part of the sex-thing, what did influence you?

"The social movements, student protests, the Vietnam war."

"But how did it affect you?"

"To a point only, we were dedicated to ourselves and our bubble."

"Like us then," said John laughing.

John decided to change venue. "I'll go to Hong Kong in two days."

"Because of the girl or job?"

"Job."

"But still affected by the girl or should I say woman?"

John wasn't bent on to tell his uncle about his double-trouble so he just said, "it's complicated, yes."

"Are you prepared for that?"

"What do you mean?"

"The one over there probably wouldn't come here."

"We'll see when I get there" John answered blandly, he didn't want to talk about this eventuality with Dennis.

"It's a dilemma," as if he was reading John's mind, "what's meant to be will find its way. Don't you worry too much, now tell me about London? Did you find out something of value for you?"

"Not really, small talk, not entirely waste of time," avoiding what had come out of his visit, not inferring to the file that existed on both.

"But did you meet the right person for your purpose?"

"Yeah, a man called Alistair Wellington, he invited me for lunch at White's. Talked about my father's good reputation. We also talked about Hong Kong and a bit of politics."

A nervous look appeared on Dennis face.

"Did he mention my name by coincidence?"

"No, he didn't," John lied. "Why should he?"

"Just wondering."

Again, John decided to detour the conversation again, to change the atmosphere.

"And how is the stock-market going?"

"It's hard, nobody really knows what's going on really, a part of educated guesses but if you have friends, you get a tip now and then."

"You mean insider-tips?

"Well let's say suggestions," said Dennis and doing an air quote-gesture. "And good ones lately?

Instead of answering the question, Dennis began to rant about his high-fly relations which made John ill at ease. It was the blaming-game where some idiots were the culprits and had failed him. He was a man of contradictions, at one moment he exposed charm with rapid humorous comments, others he didn't seem to be generous in mind and was envious of someone's success and saying he wasn't that impressed, and it's probably inherited money or was merely thanks to luck.

A sense of unease settled over John as Dennis rambled incoherently about his business triumphs and disasters, making him seem like a charlatan. The impression was a man who probably had wasted money without restraint when his pockets had been full. Altogether it coincided with Carl's remarks the other day.

A waitress approached their table and wondered if they wanted something else, which Dennis declined too rudely. Perhaps he is keeping a mental eye on the bill, John thought. There was a pause and John sensed Dennis wanted to ask him a telling question, something that would let him unload his problems.

"So, how are things for you?"

"John, if you think you are in a jam I'm in a fucking squeeze."

"Is it about your friends in Tallin?"

"They want me to go again"

"Is that wise, considering the article from the other day?"

"Have to, you know. I'm under pressure money-wise. Must go."

"You are aware there are investigations going on with the banks in Estonia?"

"But I have money over there, I must go and get it."

"In Swedbank?"

"How did you know?"

"Just guessing, I was there some years ago but I've closed the account." To lighten up the mood John told what had happened during his visit in Tallinn, "I was sitting in the branch- office when three guys entered the bank looking like the bad boys in a movie, unshaven, black T-shirts, wearing gold chains like rappers. Chests like oxen, black boots and military trousers. One of the guys said in rusty accent as strong as his chest; *"count the money"* and hovered up a plastic bag. An employee did what she was told. After having counted the money she said, *"it's three million."* To which the big boy sang out, *"then I took the wrong bag, thought it was two."* "Says a lot about the business he must be in," finished John with a smile.

"Perhaps they were in the same racket as my contact," said Dennis and looked down as if he was searching for something in his lap.

"I don't think you should go there."

Looking downwards Dennis said in a low set voice.

"You are right, but I'm in a tight spot, I need the money and it's taking its toll on my health."

"You don't feel well?"

"There is this pressure in the chest."

"Have you done a check-up?"

"Did a year ago."

"Do it again," suggested John.

Avoiding John's recommendation Dennis said, "you know, in my age you begin to see the up-coming residence."

"Do you know where it would be?"

"No idea," he said bitterly, "I regret so many things, all the what ifs, if you had gone that road or the other."

Like we all do, thought John. John realized Dennis distress ran deep. He was visibly nervous, fidgeting with his hands, constantly glancing at the people passing as if someone might assault him.

"Not much to do about it," said Dennis as if they didn't have enough proximity yet, to address his uncle's situation. A sense of vacuum arose between the two.

"I better go home," said Dennis.

John asked for the bill and Dennis, without even searching in his pockets, said he had forgotten his wallet, which meant John had to pay, another negative sign.

At that moment a big man approached them, the man who saw around the corners, Eric Gustavsson, almost ramming their table like a bull. "I see you have a family-meeting" he said in feisty manner. Eric wore a worn-out leather vest, not closed because of a portent stomach and a few missing buttons, his glasses were on his thick hair in the same fashion bald people wear their glasses to hide the absence of hair. John raised. "Hi Eric, nice to see you."

"Can I sit down," he asked but didn't bother for the answer.

It was obvious an introduction wasn't needed, Eric and Dennis knew each other.

"What a coincidence to see you together, " said Eric.

"You know each other?" asked Dennis nervously.

"We did a thing together," answered Eric in a low voice.

Dennis looked with suspicion at both.

"We were just leaving," said Dennis clearly distressed by this unforeseen presence of Eric.

"At least, let me invite you for a drink. Horses for courses," he said drunkenly.

"Which means?"

"What is fitting in one case may not be fitting in another" and continued, "had dinner with a friend, when a journalist I've tried to help appears, told us an outlandish story, completely misled, influenced by an unmitigated shit, instead of paying me attention."

John liked how Eric put his words and built phrases but felt confused and wondered what and who's story of things had gone wrong.

"A journalist?"

"He had issues with our late prime-minister when he discovered a governmental spy-ring."

As John hadn't lived in Sweden the last years he didn't know what he was talking about. "What spy-ring?"

Eric waived in a waiter ignoring John's question.

"Can we have three Gin tonics please" was pronounced with an accent from the tougher neighborhoods in Stockholm. "Anything you want to share with a spook like me" continued Eric, edging his elbows on the table for emphasis, followed by a worrying pause as if he had just reached a conclusion of sorts or perhaps it was the alcohol that was kicking in.

That Eric would appear suddenly after John's visit to London and meeting with Wellington seemed like a striking occurrence. If it looks like a coincidence, probably it isn't he thought.

"We were talking about adjusting to new circumstances."

"And evade bad company" said Eric looking at John avoiding Dennis, as if smelling something was going on which could be of his interest.

"And how do you know when you are in the right one," asked John.

"Intuition, first impressions are usually right." The waiter came with three gin tonics.

"Gut-feelings you mean," said John.

"More ice" demanded Eric to a waiter and continued, "gut-feelings you get through experience. Anyways, the future is to be written" he said poetically cheering them, gulping down his gin tonic.

"What about hindsight" said Dennis, "or when you know you have taken the wrong path and don't know how to fix it?

This comment for a man like Eric was a confession.

"You ponder and ask for advice," closing his eyes as if he had got his prey, "a man alone is not strong, in spite of the Swedish saying to the contrary."

The waiter interrupted them refilling the drinks with more ice.

"You seem to know each other" said John.

"We've bumped into each other a few times," said Eric not smiling.

"Are you still at it," asked Dennis with a little too high-pitched voice not pleased with this unforeseen situation.

"You mean if I'm still working as a bloodhound for tricksters?"

"Yes."

"I'm their last resort when they don't find the answers." He said this without blushing or any kind of humility.

"Good for you then, sorry but have to go now," said Dennis as if he suddenly remembered he had a train to catch.

"Do that check-up, go and see a doctor" said John when Dennis rose abruptly.

"Yeah sure, call me when you are back from Hong Kong."

He left them and the gin-tonic undrunk, hadn't even touched it.

"Bad investment of such good stuff," muttered Eric pointing at the glass.

"Definitely" said John and took a sip. "Did you call Wellington?

"Actually, I went to London and met him."

"And? Any food for thought?"

"We had lunch at White's, he didn't say much about my father, I have to admit."

"Smart fox, he is always on the go."

John hesitated whether to ask Erik about his father. "Do you work together?

"We cooperate when it benefits the case." John paused.

"I need to ask you something. An elderly man called Maxwell, said something strange. In subdued he implied my father wasn't the man I thought he was."

Eric's expression shifted, and his gaze suddenly sharpened on John.

"I think I know what you are talking about."

"You do? I'd like to hear your thoughts."

"You mean the Philby cover-up or whatever it was."

"And my father... was he a suspect?"

"There were rumors. He was in Estonia at the same time as Wennerström and people thought there was a connection after he didn't manage to catch Philby. People talked."

"So, what do you think?"

"Personally? I think he was good-maybe too good."

John went silent, the words hanging in the air. A chill ran through him what if my father really been a double agent?

"I wouldn't worry too much about it. These rumors… they come and go."

John fell silent absorbing the possibility of his father's eventual double life.

"If I find anything concrete, I'll let you know," looking at his gin tonic, "Is he ill your uncle?"

"He isn't in perfect shape no."

"He is walking a bumpy road."

Eric's mobile sounded, and he turned away and he heard him saying a few okays and cut.

"As they say, someone has to do it," like talking to himself, which was just another way of avoiding further comments.

"On the phone you mentioned you go to Hong Kong, for what reason?

"To fix a new job."

"What kind of job" asked Eric finishing his drink.

"Find suppliers in China and sell in Europe."

"Under the umbrella of the Taipan, not bad."

"Yes, I'm lucky", answered John.

"Good luck then, must go now, he said unsteadily, "there are things to do and save our little country."

Apparently, everybody seemed in need to catch trains or perhaps do the laundry thought John, sensing that Eric knew something about his uncle which he wouldn't divulge.

"You have a good relationship with your uncle?

"This is the second time in twenty-five years, can't say I know him."

"You ought to watch him, he has strange bedfellows."

"Can you be more precise?"

"He has been a few times in Tallinn, why does anybody go there? Not looking at the birds."

John wished to retort but couldn't find a valid argument in defense of his uncle, there was none.

Instead of a withering comment he suggested, "Can I be of some help?"

"Hope not but you might, someone out of the beltway could sense the shades of grey, things are not just white or black." Eric stood up.

"Saw you are in the press a lot"

Obviously, the man had read about John's speech in Brussels.

"I just said what I thought, common sense."

"But that's food for the Bollinger-left."

"You mean the divine left?

"Yes, don't underestimate them, never, they'll go after you, sure as I'm standing here, in any case must go now."

"Thanks for the drink."

Eric, a legend in Swedish Intelligence who saw around corners, went to pay rather than waiting and waived like Churchill the V-sign for victory. Eric had similar behavior or way of thinking as Wellington in that they were able or did it on purpose without hints, changed themes abruptly. Perhaps the spy-craft did this to unsettle a foe rationalized John. This craft of surveillance of anything that potentially might be dangerous and the objective of the brotherhood of intelligence for the safety of the people, wasn't an artifact you play with as an amateur. Whatever it was John was sure he didn't have the instinct for intelligence, he solely believed he had good intuition and acted upon it characteristically. He felt he had a faculty to distinguish between good or bad, perhaps visualize a trend. But not the future, he didn't possess strategic thinking, nor an analytical ability.

John walked home thinking about his uncle's plight, triggering thoughts about the long shadow of his father's past, suddenly present. The rumors and suspicion were there. Every step felt heavier. His mind spiraled as he made his way home, the familiar streets offering no comfort.

But a new adventure was calling him. Just two days, and he'd be off to Hong Kong and Jasmine!

CHAPTER 20

Marianne drove John to the airport. The last days Marianne seemed to have perceived there was something he was searching over there in Hong Kong, as he didn't explain any reason for his distant behavior despite his carefree talking in generalities. Her impression was due to moments of silence, compared to his normal behavior, a wariness had come over her. John had been kind of stiff towards Marianne and he hated himself for it. Getting close to the airport he was pumping adrenaline, but not for the right reason, only living a mental divide and feeling ashamed. Once they arrived, John took his suitcase and went to give her a goodbye kiss. She didn't move from the driving seat, she just sat and said, "are we good?"

"Something wrong?"

"You tell me."

"This is not goodbye. I'll be back."

"To me?" It was pronounced with vivid clarity, like she knew what was going on.

"It's only a few days."

"Yes, a lot can happen in a few days, you've been kind of detached lately."

"Maybe a bit tight cause of the trip," he answered blandly.

"Tight? Something you want to tell me?"

John found himself at a loss, no words came out.

"Whatever there is over there, don't lie to me."

"I won't."

"Maybe I'll wait for you," she said reluctantly and added, "my ex wants me to come back."

Being taken aback he looked at her and said, "wow we didn't see that coming did we, that's a hell of surprise."

"Tell me about it."

"Not the right moment to talk about."

"That depends, it's in your hands."

"No, I think it's your decision."

Regardless of what was said he had no choice but to leave and catch the flight. John kissed her on the chin and went inside the airport. He looked back through the windows, but she had driven away already. After the check-in and the hassle of the scanner he was in a daze and ordered a beer at the only bar there was. He was pierced because of Marianne's words and concluded women play their cards with sincerity and didn't shy away from being blunt. Finished the beer and went to the gate where the mystical words Hong- Kong via Bangkok were in big letters. He already felt guilty, he knew the inevitable would happen and texted Jasmine his arrival.

CHAPTER 21

He was on his way to Hong Kong, no business-class this time, making the trip less glamorous compared to last time, yet the anticipation to see Jasmine again captivated him so he didn't bother. The seat wasn't an uncomfortable Ryanair-seat but in view of the twelve hours expected flying-time it would be demanding. As soon as they were air-born he began to read a book about the Wellingtons, ate some food which was okay and succeeded in sleeping a few hours. There was a two-hour stop in Bangkok. John sat down in a lounge full of exhausted men, flying wrong and interminable hours. He had a look at the magazines that lay on the tables. Eying lazily publications of real estate offered in Australia, Philippines or penthouses in Hong-Kong and the like. It felt odd for John to just think of buying a home in such places. Or maybe it wasn't, I might buy a place in these places, you never know as past events had made it clear.

A man sitting close by looking like an Indian guru, with the looks as the ones you see on Instagram giving advice about life. His white hair was knotted like a rap-star, his beard had not been cut in months but had a kind of design to it, not haphazardly, to look more-guru-like. Plausibly men of guiding light have image- problem and must look credible when offering recommendations of the essentials of life. Brown face and dark brown intelligent lively eyes dressed in what could have been curtains from the fifties. A friendly smile and bearing. He looked at John with curiosity. How come all these gurus are Indians? Why are there no Gurus from Frankfurt or Oslo John thought. You can't say, with all respect, that these people have contributed to the material improvement the last many years, like inventing Penicillin or a vaccine against cholera, not having improved human conditions in practical terms but still it was they, who would tell me how to live and to be happy.

John was surprised when the guru began to converse with him, a stark contrast to the prevailing silence between passengers he had observed lately while travelling. By worry your fellow passenger might get too excited and let you know all about his big deals, a divorce, un-grateful children. Or how he, at bottom, wanted to do something different in life, raise chickens, or get lost in Africa.

"Where are you going?" the man began the conversation with that Indian accent the famous Indian Canadian Russell Peters imitated making fun of his own people.

"On my way to Hong Kong."

"Been there before?"

"Actually, a few weeks ago."

"And you like it?"

"Very much."

"The mystery for Westerners about the Orient," said the man.

"I didn't see it as a mystery, it was more of a déjà-vu-kind of gag, as if I've lived there before."

The man began to ask more questions which John answered as good as he could muster trying to keep it short. He wasn't in the mood to pour out his story. In the end the guru understood, a woman had affected his visit in Hong Kong.

"And now you are going back to see her."

"Yes."

"Let your gut-feeling decide, there are no problems, only situations in life."

"Karl Popper said that everything is about taking decisions."

"Well one is a consequence of the other, you are in a situation, and you take a decision, good or bad but you decide, you decide to have glass of water or buy stock in Apple" he said, almost with irony. "But you do it consciously, humans are the only ones on this planet who can do that, whatever we do it's consciously. The animals don't do it consciously."

John didn't want to disappoint the man and reveal what the latest the neuroscientists claimed about free will, instead he asked, "what is wisdom?"

"I think it's a capacity to balance many different things which we know of."

"A kind of intuition?"

"Yes, sometimes it's good to trust your intuition or gut feeling. It can be more helpful than just logic."

"Very interesting to talk to you, have to go, my flight is on the screen now."

"Whatever you do, enjoy, don't worry too much," said the guru with a chuckle. "There are no answers, only questions. Be pleasant to yourself, then something great might happen."

Instead of just leaving the guru, John stopped abruptly and shook the man's hand and said like De Niro in a movie; "you, you are good." John went towards the gate. Re-setting, according to the circumstances, adjust and assimilate John thought when he saw Hong Kong in big letters, in his inner vision he saw Jasmine. His brain made him imagine a field of blossoming jasmines with its sensual fragrance, revered for their purity, beauty and sensuality, he was hooked.

CHAPTER 22

During the three hskours flight from Bangkok to Hong Kong, John did read the book he had brought with him without concentration now and again, listening to a man sitting right behind him with a cough so hoarse, making it uneasy and you wonder what kind of deadly bacteria there could be in that body.

On arrival he got his old Samsonite, went towards the exit and was pleased to see his name on a plate. Having booked the Mandarin again, Hong Kong's most emblematic five-star hotel, included a limousine waiting for him. The chauffeur spoke English with such a heavy accent he barely understood when asking the standard question if the flight had been good, smiling all the time while opening the door offering him a wet towel and a newspaper.

"Yeah," John mumbled taking in the idea that he now was back in boomtown where the language was money. He was in a mixed mood, battling both butterflies of anticipation eager to see Jasmine again and exhaustion, due to the long hours in the plane. As ever the Italian concierge was at the entrance when he arrived at the hotel, his white hair combed perfectly as if he had just come out from a visit at the hair-dresser.

"Nice to see again Mr. Sherman, you are back very soon."

What do you answer to that thought John when you are a few steps from seeing the girl who you are in love with? And the guy remembered his name, astonishing.

"Hong Kong is very attractive."

"Yes, there are many attractions here," said the Italian looking straight into John's eyes as if they had a complicit understanding between the two of the definition of what is attractive and what he actually referred to. A few steps inside the entrance to the lobby he saw her from a distance, attending an older couple. For an instant he stood still in suspension, just looking at her. There are times when the body doesn't lie, this was one of those, he felt the same electric sensation as the first time he had put his eyes on her. But this time it was more complete, notions of her skin, body, her eyes, the way she used to look into his. He felt a surge of well-being engulf his whole body. In that moment Jasmine seemed to sense his presence and looked straight at John, and he froze. This must be love and what it does to two people, he thought. Meanwhile the Italian became a witness to the act, much aware of what was going between the two.

"I'll take of your luggage."

John was so distracted he had forgotten his Samsonite and said in a low croaking voice "thank you" and moved forward. Jasmine returned her attention to the old couple. Their eyes clinched. The mystique was still there. He approached the desk and the old couple who were in full conversation with Jasmine. The Italian concierge, appeared again, as ever vigilantly watching over his domain of the lobby and with his keen eye foresaw what was coming, almost interfering John's stride, seemingly with a wish to participate in this rendezvous said; "Planning to stay long this time Mr. Sherman," was expressed slightly too high-pitched, so that everybody near could hear him.

"Not sure yet."

"Hope you stay longer this time," and was off becoming aware his presence wasn't pertinent.

"Hi," said John.

The old couple looked up at John. The woman, having been interrupted, seemed to understand that John wasn't saying hello to her or the man standing close to her. She grasped immediately what was going on between Jasmine and John and said:

"Ooh, Henry, I think we should let these two talk a moment."

"What are you talking about?" asked what presumably was her husband.

"I think these people have some urgent business."

"I'm so sorry," John blurted out.

Looking at Jasmine, he felt a surge to hop over the desk and kiss her.

"You are back."

"Yes," was the only thing he could say.

Meanwhile the old couple looked first at Jasmine and then at John.

"Now I see," said the man, "yes, of course now I understand."

"Sorry to interrupt very rude of me."

The man just chuckled, "Go for it, we've all the time in the world."

"I knew you were coming."

"You saw my message."

After a thorough look John saw that Jasmine was perfectly lip-sticked and her hair impeccable, no pony- tail-fast arrangement, she was prepared and ready for him.

"Don't need your passport this time."

"I'm the same, nothing has changed."

"No, nothing has changed."

"Not for me."

"For me neither."

The manner, the way the conversation was played out and how they looked at each other. It was obvious even to a fool they were trapped together.

"When can we meet?"

"You think we should?" she asked testily.

"Yes, I only not think so, we must."

"I'll get your key for the room."

She said this fact-like and with a sad tune to it.

"Here is your key to the room."

"Wow it's the same as last time."

"It's the machine."

"But still a coincidence don't you think?"

"You mean it's a sign," she said while he observed her beautiful eyes.

"Fate or random, probably it is."

"We are very superstitious here."

"When then?"

"Send you a message."

The old couple looked at John with curiosity, while more guests arrived, Jasmine had to return to her duties.

"Sorry to have interrupted," said John with a grin.

"No, no, don't you worry I have also been young and foolishly in love," the woman said looking at her husband.

"Seize the day," said John and went to the elevator, where the Italian stood with an interrogating smile.

"You couldn't stay away from Hong Kong," with a look towards the desk.

"Yeah exactly."

"I hope you will have a good stay."

"I'll do my best."

Entering the room, he got a pang from their first night together. Almost two months filled with travels and actions of different sorts had passed but it felt like yesterday, it all vanished after having seen Jasmine again.

Her magnetism had the same effect this time as it had then. You are in an emotional mess, my friend he said to himself almost loud. The brevity of the meeting with Jasmine left him seething, he had to remind himself of his immediate plan for the evening, have dinner with Dunbar. Their cooperation was supposed to start shortly, and they had to discuss planning of what markets to attain, mark priorities and importantly, meet suppliers on the other side of the border in Shenzhen. Then after that, hopefully a rendezvous with Jasmine, this very evening.

He went into the shower and once again was impressed by the floral scent of jasmine, with dead-sexy muskiness to it, another coincidence. Afterwards he laid down and sent a message to Marianne feeling like a daredevil, saying everything was okay, histrionically short. A sudden exhaustion came over him, so he dozed off, woke up and showered again. Put on a white shirt and a jacket not the blue one this time, it was green, like his eyes. There was a knock on the door. "Yes, please come in," he said.

It was Jasmine. John drew her inside without closing the door. Enthralled they faced each other. John moved forward and took her hand and nervously kissed her on the cheek. Both stood still and watched each other with growing excitement. It was a shared desire, obvious as neon light. Her eyes said everything, thought John. Wordlessly and instinctively, they kissed, in that subtle way they had done all the other times with sensuality and tender eroticism. Nothing had changed, it was raw magnetism, they fused, again. He wanted to say something great and beautiful, use the exact wordings to tell her his feelings, to express that rare thing called love but didn't find them.

"Can't stay long, have to work" she said.

"Have a meeting with Dunbar in a moment."

"Ok."

"Same place as the first time?"

"Ok, when?"

"10.00?"

"That's fine," she said and left.

When he took the elevator, he was thriving with excitement. That short instant with Jasmine had done it and originated a hefty rush. Reminded of a poem by Frost and the road not taken, 'choose the damn path, it's better to take a road than indecision. As he passed the counter, there was a subtle interaction between John and Jasmine, veiled from any onlooker's gaze a part of the attentive Italian concierge.

"Going out for dinner?"

"Yes, can you arrange a taxi please."

"Of course," answered the Italian and went to the exit door. John cast a conspiratorial glance at Jasmine. The Italian's actions were as if he perfectly knew what was going on. Jasmine, seemingly flustered, looked at John. It was not the place or the moment for small-talk or say a simplicity, so he followed the Italian, making signs for a waiting taxi outside.

The Italian opened the door of the car to let John in.

"Are you thinking what I think you are thinking?" John asked him. The man just looked as if having been caught with the goods in his hands.

"Is it that obvious?"

"I think so," he said with a succinct smile.

CHAPTER 23

The taxi began the route to the Dunbar residence situated on Pollock's Path. A place for billionaires, not the rich, only the very rich. Historically the Peak was regarded as the most prominent location where only the Taipans could own property. Most properties in the area are townhouses along with exclusive detached houses, enjoying the exquisite harbor or South Island-sea view.

While sitting in the car it struck him how a short encounter and a kiss can affect you. A moment and it stays like glue. He looked out the window, with thoughts of no clear substance only abstract impressions of Jasmine, noticing the lights like an autist, not retrieving just watching and absorbing Hong Kong's unbelievable amounts of lanterns. Arriving to what looked like a magnificent house, he wasn't fully concentrated on the business at hand meeting Dunbar. Watching the mansion, he couldn't avoid to think of how unjust the world is in terms of money and social welfare. He wasn't impressed in the sense that this obvious opulence, would blind or alter what he believed in terms of justice and values. Only mystified how the world works, generating to a few extremely rich, and a majority of the contrary. At heart he had equalitarian views which collided with his personal strivings because of inertia, to the extent that he didn't care enough for the ill-fated, he just trolled along and did his own thing.

The story of the Tai Pans is the story of Hong Kong itself. The fortune created by Dunbar's ancestors was controversial. It began with the craving for tea in need for a balance to the opium trade. They began to sell the drug from India to the China coast. Cantonese merchants together with British interests made enormous money but the Emperor of China wanted to stop this business which led to the first opium war. China was defeated and humiliated. In 1842 Hong Kong was created and ceded for perpetuity. John was intrigued about this but thought it wasn't a theme to discuss with too much detail with Dunbar. As a matter of fact, stretching a bit, you could compare it to the more contemporary Pablo Escobar. Although it was a long time ago and you can't blame sons of what fathers had done. After passing through a security guard, he found himself inside the restricted area, he approached the front door and rang a bell, a butler appeared.

"Mr. Sherman, I presume?"

A reminder of the meeting in the African jungle between Stanley and Livingstone. Once inside the first thing to be seen was a stair as majestic as the one in *Gone with the wind* and now, John was impressed. "So nice to see you again," said Ben when he appeared, casually dressed, coming down the splendid stairs. They hugged as good friends do, which made John abandon his wonderings about the world's lack of egalitarianism. John was flattered how Ben had taken on John on a personal level. From the very first meeting he treated John like a mixture of mentor and father. Due to some tense moments mixed with pleasure Ben and John had vested a good friendship where emotions were visible but not too exposed, after all, they both had English blood in their veins where probing feelings of others were not a thing you do. The interior of the house produced an extraordinary impression of wealth and culture, proof of established power. After passing the entrance and stair, there was a passage and a library with pictures of Dunbar's ancestors in serious poses. The whole thing made you understand that you were in a place of consequence. Very different from the effect John had visiting his uncle, there it felt temporary, not a stable residence for Dennis. In this setting everything exuded permanence clearly established by Ben as the solid proprietor.

"Had a fine trip?"

"It's lengthy. A two hour stop in Bangkok where I met a guru who told me, among other things not to worry too much."

"That's a good advice. Although the worries are constant and tend to linger, what changes are the themes."

"There are short moments though, when you forget to even think, like a good golf shot, almost unconscious it seems."

"You mean when you hit an iron hundred meters and the ball stops at putting distance."

"Exactly. The definition of happiness. And what about you?"

"I got seventy-two the other day and Jane and I went to a very nice Chinese restaurant."

"I didn't know, congratulations."

"When I sat there, I ordered a whisky with a tiny bit of ice and contemplating the situation. Thinking in my vanity that I was a man in full, gave myself a few compliments, and thought it's time to relax and pick up the old clubs."

"How is your swing nowadays?"

"It's like the weather, sometimes it's sunshine and sometimes it's raining."

Ben was a man with a lot of power on his back, years of experience and a successful man's self-assurance. Born into a privileged family with a silver-spoon in his mouth, belonging to a long line of influence and affluence. President of a world-wide business. In a battle where the winner takes all, he had been forced to fight in a vicious brawl to get there. A bloody outcome for the losers where among others, a wounded brother of Ben who had longed for the station Ben now held. Having lost the battle, the brother went astray in gambling and alcohol. Yet, Ben had his own part of suffering. His father had been killed by a sniper during a business trip in Vietnam and a mother who had been more absent than the contrary. Schooled in public-schools in England, spent his holidays in Hong Kong and had learned Chinese to perfection and as a result, an attachment to both cultures. An early marriage in which two children were produced, followed by a divorce where a third party had been involved and as a result, Ben left the family nest. Never to be forgotten by his children, nor his wife, who still after twenty years had issues with him because of his breakup. The reason for the divorce was a beauty much younger than Ben with whom he had a third child, a boy. Ben had told this to John in a rare moment of transparency, "we had different issues, her perspective was beginning to blossom, whilst mine was looking towards other aspects of life. I was fifty and she was twenty-something." They parted as friends and remained so. Now he had Jane, who Ben said was the one he always wanted.

"Just to be assured," Ben continued, as the businessman he was "did you see Francois's mail about a description and his considerations about the new company?"

"Yes, I sent some notes and suggestions."

"Good, Francois will arrive tomorrow, and we can discuss it then."

"So, we meet tomorrow?"

"Yes."

"How is Jane?"

"Jane is here, she is considering leaving London and the rest, for good."

What he meant by Jane leaving London, it was a husband. In a moment of truth, dining in Paris, Ben had told John about Jane and how they had met in London and had begun an amorous relation. Jane was in a marriage void of love, now willing to begin a new life with Ben. Jane was closer to seventy than sixty. She felt she was entitled to a more replete life, including love, while there was still time. The question was if it was worth throwing away what she had in London. A bloody tough decision for that lady John concluded and as an afterthought, although Ben was fit as a fiddle, but he was seventy-two and at that age anything can happen.

"At seventy-two you begin to take notice your lifespan is max ten or twenty years," said Ben.

John was taken aback listening to Ben. This was very intimate and confidential. Last time they had spoken like this they were having dinner in Paris at the Ralph Lauren restaurant. A conversation, where themes had gone from daily strife to abstract philosophical themes, geopolitics, children and the business of love and its ramifications. Ben had admitted, he was mulling about finishing as President and CEO, just let go and let someone else take over the shop. Albeit as John knew, not any shop to step down from, more of an emporium. "Retirement isn't a bad option you know," he said with a slight seriousness. After a life in commanding positions and real heights, perhaps he wanted to enjoy what there was still left for him. He had become aware of the exit door turning seventy, thoughts about how many more years he had in him.

"I know it's a depressive thought I can't evade. I've travelled and done business all over the world, at times with excellent results but now, I'm not that thrilled anymore."

During this unexpected outpouring, John remained silent, unsure of how to respond.

"A sign is, I prefer old movies, they capture the essences of my life and times. Now I have a sense of not belonging to this new world. Ben paused and seemed to shift and apologized, saying, "sorry I got carried away."

"Are you happy with the idea of the company we are setting up? I ask you as I've been thinking there is another thing you might be of help."

"Me?

"John, you know we have different companies spread around the world. It's a wide portfolio not always with a clear or defined core business. We receive offers as participants in many places. It's not easy to decipher if we should participate in or not. Perhaps you would be interested in being a kind of ambassador for me. Kind of pre-due- diligence, avoid business we shouldn't touch. Would that be of your interest?"

"You mean go and see the prospects before it starts?"

"Yeah, the other day I got in my hands a project in Punta Cana, have you heard about the place?"

"Have actually been there a few days."

At that moment Jane arrived, his new life-companion, charming with corporal gestures of empathy, beguiling and a feline elegance, easily fascinated by. She gave the impression she knew the art of getting along with everybody. A perfect woman for a man like Ben.

"So nice to see you again."

"The pleasure is mine," said John.

"Just arrived? What can I bring for you? The usual gin tonic?"

"Yes please, indeed", answered John with a linkage of Englishness.

While Jane fixed the drinks John looked around and saw on the walls were filled with books of ancient tract and wondered how many of them Ben had read.

"Here is your drink," said Jane.

Having been interrupted Ben changed to a more social line.

"How was Stockholm?"

"As always but kind of better I would say."

"Maybe it's you, seeing things in a new light?"

"That's a possibility."

Ben was right, John's take on Stockholm had changed, since he lived there.

"And you have a social life there?" asked Jane, "that's important."

"Despite all years abroad it seems so."

"And they have received you well?"

"Apparently yes."

"Maybe you offer them a fresh take on things," said Ben, "Not like me, I'm not sure I still have things to offer the world." His tone was disenchanted.

"I think the world needs you," said Jane

Ben's discontent was too evident. Which reminded John of Ben's son Stewart, who had tried to cheat him, a deceit which probably was lingering like a cancer. Out of delicacy John wasn't sure to ask about his son. Stewart had misled his father, which had become evident at an encounter in Wimbledon. Even worse, his son had been involved in a money-laundering scheme and dumb enough trying to unsettle his own father as the President and Taipan of the company and John had been instrumental of the disclosure of all this.

At that fateful moment in Wimbledon, a Spanish businessman had punched Stewart in the face and some blood was spilled, and John had succeeded to buttress the relation between father and son. This episode must have been a big blow for Ben and might have triggered the idea of quitting. If your too enterprising son, tries to betray you, something is utterly wrong.

"Like my son," he said as if knowing what John was thinking.

"How is he? Everything settled?"

"Stewart has been charged by the Spanish authorities and we are waiting a date for his trial, we'll see how it ends. Seems he hasn't understood the lesson he was given in Wimbledon."

"You'll fix that," intervened Jane.

"Not so sure about that," said Ben.

"Let's hope for the best," said John copying Jane's intention of optimism.

"It's a tricky one, not easy to avoid if there is an order to extradite him."

"If that would happen you have good lawyers, they'll know how to handle it," said Jane insisting in a positive venue.

"Lawyers, they are all bloodsuckers," said Ben in a thrust of anger.

"You mean ambivalent," said Jane, "in that I agree."

"They think the world functions thanks to them, when it's the other way around. We give them issues so they can live carefree, without taking risks. They are like carpetbaggers."

"You need a good old holiday."

"The problem is, lately I've noticed my experience isn't always the most cherished."

"But you have a new CEO now."

"Yeah, so far so good, we'll see with time."

"You need rest, play golf and walk the streets in Paris with me," said Jane, offering encouragement. "Ben is recessionary today."

"Meaning?" asked Ben grunting.

"Let's say not expansive, I'll take him to a beach somewhere, a bit of sun and he becomes the charming man he really is."

"Or was," said Ben raising his hands in desperation.

"Come on darling, John didn't come here to listen to your discontent." Ben rose to serve himself a second drink.

"We might go to the Bahamas soon, our business is moving away from here, it's getting tight and it will be worse. Lot of pressure from China now, limiting free speech and relocating business from Hong Kong."

"I saw there is a movement among young people protesting Beijing's politics," said John.

"Yes, things are on fire. There will be trouble if they suffocate any resistance the autocratic way."

What Ben was saying out loud was what many had foreseen in 1997 when China took over the city and it was proclaimed one nation two systems. In John's perspective, that comment made his new up-coming job, fragile and could be in danger. There were worrying signs, which even John had become aware of and began to feel a tremor of doubt, maybe Hong Kong wasn't the future for him.

"Where will they go, to Singapore?"

"Probably but we can't go all of us, England has promised to take big numbers but how big is the question. We are over seven million and they can't take that."

The pearl of the Far East might be doomed, thought John. Ben drank a bit of his gin tonic and steered the conversation to another direction.

"Met some guys the other day, kids under thirty, trying to sell me the idea of bitcoin, explaining to me crypto-money, block-chain etc. I don't get it. Who is behind bitcoin?"

"It's a mystery surrounding all that."

"All that talk about mining, I'm too old for this."

"What happens to bitcoin if internet fails," asked John.

"Easy money with new methods it sounds to me," said Ben. "In Hong-Kong the official language is Cantonese, but the unofficial one is money, not bitcoins."

"It's called greed or playing the casino to me," said Jane.

"I've tried to understand bitcoin and failed, impossible to grasp," said John.

"I think it's Ponzi-game, sooner or later it will disappear," sentenced Ben.

This was said by a giant in finance during the last 40-50 years John thought. On the other hand, he might have lost his touch for new pastures. Ben was probably a classical entrepreneur where you took risks with things you could see and touch, concrete products.

"Crypto? It's all Chinese to me," John said sparkling a laughter from Jane. Ben, however, just shook his head and sighed.

"Tell me about it, maybe it's a sign. Time to get out while I still can, before it gets too complicated,"

"You are well and kicking," said Jane.

"For me aging is not a problem it's automatic, the difficulty is to get used not being young anymore."

"I agree on that," said Jane as if she had also perceived that feeling.

"Those guys are like an unwelcome message, telling you to stop. I can't mutate and force myself, something I don't get," said Ben, "the world has changed and I haven't noticed it."

Was Ben losing the grip due to age and lack of enthusiasm? At seventy is quite an age to run like a hungry Usain Bolt when new businesses opportunities are thrown at you. At seventy-two, what drives you to get going in the morning, wondered John.

"You watch too many old films and listen to old fashioned music,." intervened Jane.

"Seems there is a shift at seventy, the world isn't mine anymore, I can't flounder around and try to be modern, it's not natural."

"You must rejuvenate, do new things, go to the gym, read books go to the theater with me," said Jane.

Raising he said, "you know she is right," now smiling.

"Of course, I'm right, but with so much data and so many responsibilities, slowing down might actually help you see things more clearly." said Jane wisely.

"Indeed," said Ben with a sigh.

"Let's see what the kitchen has prepared," said Jane and they finished their drinks and went into a dining- room.

A Chinese woman appeared pushing a silver-trolley. She looked very old and had trouble with the plates, but her smile showed a desire to please. John had long since resolved to treat servants with dignity and be nice to them and discovered that it was appreciated. In contrast, some people treated them as air, something you need but don't really care about.

"I thought you needed something simple as chicken and rice," said Jane, "hope you'll like it."

"John and I have many things in common, we are chicken-freaks."

"Absolutely," said John when the old servant wondered, "like peanut-sauce?

"Love it."

With shaky hands they were served a light claret by the old lady which accompanied the chicken well. They talked away about the current Hong Kong, without going too deep into what was now an open secret, the rough screws from Beijing were coming into effect. Jane talked about her change, after her escape from London, avoiding too many personal details after what looked like a flight from her husband. For John it was odd to sit in this luxurious house in Hong-Kong, listening to intimate details of a couple who had decided to have a go at the future. They were both in an age where time is vital before any undesirable phenomenon occurs. John was surprised how private the conversation was, and at the same time friendly between the three of them, it was like old friendship, being in the same boat with similar issues to tackle in much the same veins. There were moments when John got the impression that he was the son Ben always wanted to have, compared to Stewart, who had a knack of choosing tricksters as company. As for John, Ben had become in a very short space of time something of the missing father and a mentor-figure.

Ben excused himself for a moment, which Jane profited from and said to John.

"You know he really likes you."

"It's mutual."

After a splendid dinner, John let Ben know he had a date with Jasmine.

"When do I see you again?" asked Jane.

"Why don't you two come to the Chinese Club tomorrow, there is gala of some sort."

"The two of you?" asked Jane.

"There is a woman," Ben explained.

"In Hong Kong? That's fantastic. Either you are a very brave man or very bad one," she said with a smile.

"Great see you tomorrow then" and John began to leave. Ben led John to the door and said:

"Be careful with that girl."

John looked at Ben surprised.

"Don't let her down."

"What do you mean?

"You come and go. She is young, you might mislead her if you don't have real intentions."

John felt embarrassed and didn't know what to say.

"Have a good night, see you tomorrow in my office."

CHAPTER 24

Stepping into the Stockton bar was like staying in a 19th-century classical hall, a reminder of a Victorian-era home. At any moment Prince Albert could walk in. Mounted animal heads and cabinets filled with books reveal themselves while your eyes adjust to the low lighting. Decorated with antique artwork, vintage leather furniture, small tables. Soft lights and soft music in the background. Jasmine was already there, her long black side-swept hair, crossed legs in black skirt and black high heels, sheer beauty in the open at play. It was a picture he would remember, not an act of voyeurism just magnificently dazzling.

"Hi," he said.

"Everything okay?" she wondered.

"Yes of course, no clouds when you are around."

A banal phrase but that's how he felt. She wore a grey jacket of Ralph Lauren style, the rest all in black, a combination which gave her a dignified look. At the same time, distinctly sexy in John's eyes, a man who observed these matters with keen eyes.

"I've missed you", said John.

"Me too."

"It feels like I never left Hong Kong."

They had been separated almost two months, unsure of how to act at these first instants. If in doubt no good, act according to your gut feelings, John thought. But this time, it was Jasmine who acted first, she put her hands in his, which felt like he had been given a drug. Her touch had that effect on his nerve system. All those little cells working, billions of them, marching in unison towards the higher sublime sensation of well-being with another person.

"I'm happy to see you again," she said.

"Me too," he answered. "You look stunning."

She looked down a bit and asked;

"Are we doing the right thing?"

"It depends on what you mean by the right thing?"

"When I saw you enter the lobby, I felt something very strong inside."

"That's what I feel now."

They were scenting, insecure how to express the raw essence of emotion with the right words and lay out their feelings as there were so much unpronounced. He was captivated utterly transfixed just being with her and the way her eyes looked straight into his. This was combined with a lingering anxiety arose wondering could this affair prevail. Would it be possible?

"Don't look like at me like that."

"I'm not going to ask you what you mean saying that."

She put her hands in her lap looking down.

"It might sound simple but you make me feel so alive with energy, like a breath of fresh air ."

"What a comparison," she said laughing but something emerged in her face, like sorrow.

"Okay it's not Shakespeare."

"Did you have a good time where you have been?"

"Let's say it was hectic."

John gave her a summary of what he has been up to, from New York and his daughter, Wimbledon to Stockholm.

"You sure have been busy."

"The truth is most of it turned out well."

A waiter interrupted them.

"Would you like to drink something? White wine?"

They had only been at Stockton's a few times and the waiter recognized them, remembering what they used to drink. Obviously, he remembered Jasmine, who wouldn't.

"Yes please."

The waiter gave a nod of confirmation and withdrew.

"Isn't it bizarre? Here I am with you, after flying a long night's sleep, to another world."

"Yeah, it's difficult to grasp you are here."

"And yet, nothing feels out of place, everything is familiar but wrong somehow."

"Maybe that's because part of you is still there, where you came from." She touched a point there.

"Humans were used to the savanna, not flying in planes around the world, it's difficult to come to terms with and then, just like that, all my doubts are gone."

"You dance with words."

"What do you mean?"

"I don't know if you are playing with me."

"I'm not playing, can't you see what I feel right now?"

"I see you here now, but I also see you far away, a world I have nothing to do with."

Despite everything their inner doubts, and how to take hold of the situation, passion drew them closer. Looking at her, John found a rare equilibrium of mind and body. He felt so attracted to her and was overcome with euphoria, as if a surge of high levels of dopamine was released and flooded his brain. Still, he was in control and not nervous in her presence. It was pure excitement combined with well-being. All the same, what might be going on, he wondered, in a woman, half his age, from a very different part of the world and such a contrasting background? He didn't find an answer to the thought. They drank a bit of wine as in need of doing something with their hands. John moved closer and they kissed with a sensitivity that surprised both.

They hadn't been together more than maybe thirty minutes and still, both evoked the same strong emotions. He sensed a sensation as if their relation had been mapped out long ago.

"What do you want John?"

"I'm just happy to be here with you, this is real, sort of thankful that we both feel the same."

"You say this now then you leave me again."

"What can I say? I've been here a few hours and now here with you, it feels like where I was yesterday doesn't exist."

"How long will you stay?"

"Don't know yet."

He took her hand and just looked. Then he waived and made a sign to the waiter to refill their glasses.

The waiter appeared with the bottle of wine.

After this interlude and when the waiter had left them, they were pulled together in a passionate kiss. A couple sat down close to them, so they distanced themselves from each other realizing their actions were probably over the top, exceeding what is appropriate in a public setting.

"I had dinner with Ben."

"I see him almost every day at the hotel."

"He invited us tomorrow with his new friend to the Chinese Club, hoped you would come with me?"

"The two of us?"

"Yes."

"That would be fun, never been there, you must be a member."

"Suppose Ben is."

In the way their rendezvous was running, he dared think they might spend the night together, John ventured; "Are you free for the night?"

"No, my grandmother needs me, I ought to go home."

"Is she sick?"

"Well not exactly, she lives alone, I sleep there at times."

When they left the bar and walked a bit, the kisses became more passionate and as natural as ever, proof of their needs and their feelings.

"This is amazing."

"It's your fault," she said.

"No no, it's our fault" he said.

Outside Stockton's a fortune-teller approached them and before they could react declared the difficulties they would pass but predicted great love. Jasmine liked what the woman said and looked warmly at John, making him feel chosen. Perhaps she is the one, he thought. A taxi came, a rapid goodbye and she left. He decided to walk to the hotel, a good idea for a good night's sleep. Once inside the hotel, got his key and took the elevator to the 19th floor. He was so smitten by her he didn't see things with normal spectacles and thought even an elevator has its charm. In the room he relaxed, put on the TV and watched the news on CNN, changed to the more tranquil BBC before he slept. Inevitably he began to do comparisons between his two girlfriends; Jasmine had him jolting instantly. Her beauty was undeniable, a harmonious blend of physical grace and inner serenity. She wasn't one for grand pronouncements on roof-tops, preferring to express her affection through actions rather than words.

Her introverted nature manifested not as shyness, but as a quiet confidence, the almost imperceptible touch of her hand, a subtle language of love spoken in shared glances and small acts of kindness. Adaptable and serene with a constant source of unspoken support. With Marianne it was different, she was good and likeable with a basic understanding of things. Obviously, there was a common cultural base but she didn't make him exhilarated. In most things she was the perfect partner, well-to-do, liked what he liked, similar tastes. If you had a hard look at them, they were alike in features with the difference of twenty-five years and what that means. What do I have in common with a woman from Hong Kong? Live in Hong Kong? Would she be willing to leave everything for him? Doubtful. Before sleeping his thoughts came and went, wary of his duality and concluded again it was a character flaw. Straight men do straight things and what you are doing is playing around as if you were a Casanova-charmer and could do whatever you want according to your whims.

Guessing the jet lag would set in or a possible headache he took an ibuprofen with a glass of water, amazed how these things function. He put Spotify on and searched his list of tranquil music and lied down on the bed and enjoyed the moment. It was late night outside yet all the lights in the skyscrapers altered the darkness. Strangely enough Stockholm felt close and at the same time far away. The music he listened to was so beautiful it made him sentimental, better sleep now.

CHAPTER 25

After a good night's sleep he went down for breakfast. It was a great upper to absorb the spread the Mandarin offered. For John breakfast was important. He began with a mix of delicious fruits and then strong coffee, continued with scones and slices of ham and cheese.

Walked to McKinnon's office, that is Ben Dunbar's company, in a good mood, the jetlag hadn't set in yet. He was more lagged by Jasmine and his own actions. The sounds of the streets of Hong Kong were as strong as ever. He wondered if the recent protests he had read about were impacting people's everyday lives.

Francois was waiting for him in the entrance, as ever elegant, greeted John with his usual French flair.

Briefly looking around John found the McKinnon's building remarkably large and impressive. As John had known Ben on a personal level, he hadn't heeded how major player Ben really was. At any moment he could be on the first page of Forbes. After a few initials and small talk with Francois about flying and how- is-the-family, Ben appeared and led them into his office. A big enough wood-paneled room to have a board meeting in, a mahogany desk, leather chairs, walls filled with photos of important people together with Ben which gave the visitor a clear indication of who you were talking to. This was Ben the Taipan, not the melancholy one from yesterday. He ran an empire in and from Hong Kong. Without hesitation they addressed the matter at hand, the creation of the company. Francois made a presentation of a pragmatic plan with Gallic charm of how the new company would get going, both in the short term and strategic thinking. He spoke with eloquence, articulating the project without being pompous, making it sound refined thanks to his French accent.

"What do you think John?"

"Sounds great to me."

John had been somewhat distracted as he just had seen a drawing which said:

To join corporations like ours there are two kinds of people the ones who works a lot and the other who wants to take credit of what they do, stay with the ones who works.

"You are looking at that drawing I see," said Ben.

"Yes."

"Well, it's one of those things," he said, as if it didn't have importance but it sent a shining message.

"To begin with, let's put this boat in the water. Francois and John you go to meet Chen in Shendi and meet the suppliers we already are in contact with. Explore their interest, close deals and make binding contracts." Francois's phone rang. He answered it, looking suddenly stressed. "Excuse me it's my wife's doctor, she is in labor. I must go back to Paris."

This unforeseen news took them by surprise as nobody seemed to have known his wife was pregnant.

"You better fly back," said Ben.

"Wasn't supposed to be now, it's a month early."

"You take care of your wife, get yourself a flight back. No worries, we get going anyway, John goes alone and meet Chen."

Chen was Ben's partner since a lifetime.

"Is she okay," asked John.

"So far so good it seems," said Francois looking worried and made a phonecall.

Ben turned to John.

"There is a ferry which takes you to Shendi and Chen is already there and he'll pick you up."

"She broke water and is at the hospital."

"Well let's hope for the best," said Ben and crossed his fingers. Francois made a few nervous phone calls.

"My secretary can fix a flight for you," said Ben and lifted his phone.

"Is she okay," asked John again.

"I shouldn't have gone."

"It will be fine for sure," said John to say something soothing.

"We'll see."

"John here can do the visits with Chen, and they report to us all what they find. Overall, this doesn't change our project," said Ben

"Fine with me," said Francois.

Ben's secretary appeared and got the message to search possible flights. Meanwhile they discussed pregnancies and related topics until Ben's secretary returned. She must have been very efficient because she had arranged a flight to Paris four hours later. Once this was arranged Francois seemed to feel more at ease.

"Everything settled then?" asked Ben.

"It's what it is," said Francois looking on a newspaper that lay on the table, the China News, with screaming headlines about the yellow umbrellas that lay on the table.

"How is it going with the protests?" asked Francois.

"It's tense. People are being squashed, the government in Beijing is limiting rights of freedom."

"You think one-country two-systems are in danger?"

"After the Tiananmen square-business we were chocked, this time it might be worse."

"But what about the theory trade creates freedom and mercantilism fixes?"

"Not yet but with time it will," said Ben. "Patten, the last governor, tried to fix democracy during his time which worried Beijing. At the foreign ministry in the UK, they are worried because the growing Chinese market is a huge potential for English business, and they don't want to mess it up with their leaders. So far, the success was based on the relationship between free movement of capital, freedom of speech and the rule of law," said Ben.

"What options are there if they take charge completely?"

"Tricky, our assets are overwhelmingly in greater China and growing in mainland China as well."

The story of Hong Kong aside of the colonial interest from the British empire heavily concentrated on commercial power in a few hands; run by descendants of the founders for 150 years. It involved two conglomerates that have influenced Hong Kong's business life and one of them was Ben's, that is McKinnon and the other Sands, two family-run empires, represented by men known as Taipan or "grand-manager". Both houses were heirs to the swashbuckling, globalist version of British colonialism commercial bravery, unfettered capitalism and owed their success to China and in general in broader Asia. For two centuries, McKinnon and Sands have been central to Hong Kong's economy. In 1949, Mao Zedong won the Civil War and people fled to Hong Kong. They came in millions, and they brought their connections from the mainland to trade. People worked in their homes manufacturing cheap products. They became entrepreneurial and Hong Kong became a boomtown. Made in Hong Kong was sold all over the world and with that, financial power. Some years ago, Hong Kong stood for about 25 % of China's GDP with over a billion people, compared to seven million, living in an area same as London. However, there were worrying signs, the last years there had been protests by the umbrella-movement which took fire when the bill of extraction was born and a million of them took to the streets because they wanted democracy.

"You are worried I understand," said Francois.

"Well, it's controlled by our Lords, the Mandarins in Beijing," said Ben.

"You really think they will take away this freedom?"

"The Chinese have their own distinct ways of approaching things, when a Chinese dissident gets the Nobel peace price by Norway, the Chinese then ban their salmon import and suddenly Norway is selling huge amounts to Vietnam. Where do you think that salmon goes to?"

"It's just show then?"

"Very much so."

"I talked to a person the other day who thinks they are afraid of Western values, the force of the Internet," said Francois.

"They are frightened they might lose the grip of power. We'll see if the Joint Declaration of two countries two systems of 1997 will be followed. Maybe you have read that recently the president at the Ming Ching Bank was abducted to China. Now he is back but resigned for "personal reasons". Top bankers have been detained, disappeared, or died of unnatural causes in the past year. Under President Xi Jinping, China has become tougher with regards to us in Hong Kong."

The meeting was concluded in a spirit of mixed optimism and a concern Hong Kong might lose its strength. Francois and John left Ben. While they walked together John watched the magnificent offices in the building with a certain awe and recognizing its importance

John asked, "what do you need to be on a board like Ben's," asked John, "what kind of talent is needed?"

"You must talk in numbers, not just in words? Know financial gearing, stuff like cash flows."

"How to interpret a balance-sheet?"

"Yes, not the technical aspects of accounting. Key is how to interpret an income statement and understand what is going on in the business. What may be going well and not so well, know the company's health not wealth."

"What about strategic thinking like trends and building relationships?"

"Of course, nevertheless, if you get there, observe the behavior of the older board-members. Check who is the data junkie and who is financially fluent."

"What strikes me is how the guys who started Google or Spotify for example, can stay. One thing is to have a good idea and get it going but to maintain yourself up there."

"Relations, and once you are a board-member, if asked an opinion, you say things like a doubtful oracle, there are pros and cons, we have to give it a serious look before we decide, which is to say nothing but doesn't irritate anyone."

"And now and then crack a funny comment," added John.

"That's basic," said Francois and laughed.

Hearing about the issues Hong Kong was facing their concern grew. John didn't want to dwell on these worries but felt the need to hear Francois thoughts.

"Is this a good thing, our project?" asked John.

"Ben is a vital and weighty man here," said Francois not sounding convincing.

"Hong Kong is a great financial hub it would be tragic to let it go."

"Suppose it's a balancing act and we are lucky to be with a man like Ben."

"Yes that's right, you leave now?"

"I'm just going to get my luggage at the Peninsula and then to the airport." "I'll inform you after my meetings on the other side."

"Ok, see you in Paris and we have a good French meal, no Chinese cooking" said Francois with a grin.

When they were outside the building Francois hailed in a taxi and they shook hands.

"Let's go to a French garlic-smelling place with quarrelling waiters only speaking French."

"*Exactement,*" said Francois.

"Good luck with the baby."

John continued to walk, once again struck by the sheer enormity of Hong Kong as he took in the sights around him. He texted a message to Jasmine about the reception at the China Club. It took her ten minutes to answer.

"*At 20 hours; where?*"

"*I pick you up the Mandarin.*"

Rapidly appeared "*Okay*" on his screen.

CHAPTER 26

John went back to the Mandarin, checked out as Ben had offered the apartment he stayed in the last time. No Jasmine was in sight and was given an envelope with a key inside. The Italian concierge was talking to a crowd of what John thoughts were Chinese guests and excused himself and came forward to John.

"You are leaving again, so fast?"

"Not Hong Kong, have an apartment."

"It's more convenient," he said with a smile as if understanding John's situation.

"Take care and be good."

"As you said the other day, Hong Kong is very attractive."

"It is, I was supposed to stay for three months and here I am."

Once in the apartment he read his mail and searched news from Sweden.

There was an intriguing message on John's mobile from Eric Gustavsson. He let know in a crypto language there were troubles ahead with regards to his uncle. John answered back asking what he could do about it.

The answer came immediately; *can I call you?*

The phone rang.

"Everything okay where you are?"

"It's different."

"Different? I'm calling you cause a coronel has disappeared and later found drowned. He was an intelligence officer at KSI."

KSI the most secret Swedish organization of them all. "But what does this have to do with my uncle?"

As ever Eric didn't answer John's question.

"It's supposed to be suicide, I don't think so. Anyhow, I happen to know your uncle had some kind of relation with the man."

"This means he is in danger," said John.

"Probably, do you know where he is?"

"The other day he told me he might go to Tallinn."

"Have been investigating bank accounts related to the missing man and found unintentionally your uncle's name on two bank accounts in an Estonian bank, here."

"Here?

"I'm in Tallinn."

"I didn't know my uncle had money there," lied John.

"It turns out that you're named as the sole beneficiary of the accounts if something happens to him." And he continued;

"John, there are two accounts in your name. It seems, one is tied up in money laundering, which puts you in a dangerous position. But the other… well, that one contains documents stolen from the Stasi after the fall of East Germany.

"If you can't open the account, how do you know there is even a document inside?"

Erik paused, measuring his words. "Sometimes, information surfaces through… unusual channels. Let's say we have reason to believe it's there. And we need you to confirm it."

"Me?" said John perplexed.

"Those documents could reveal the truth about how Philby escaped and might even clear your father's name. You could either be a pawn in someone's game, or you could finally get the answers you've been searching for."

John didn't know what to say or think.

"Listen, only you or your uncle can access them. Probably he's hoping you'd open it, not just to save his skin from prison, but maybe to help you too. Plus, those papers could explain how Philby slipped away to Moscow and as I said, might even clear your father's name. So, you're caught in a choice: protect your uncle, clear your family's legacy, or risk getting dragged even deeper into this mess."

Erik continued telling John about how they had received the information from a source in the MI6 and that the rumor was that the documents were stolen from the Stasi archives after East Germany's collapse. These documents reportedly reveal information on the Cold War espionage networks, including details about who helped Kim Philby escape to Moscow. They might exonerate John's father, potentially proving he was not a double agent but a scapegoat in a Soviet scheme to protect their real collaborators. John went numb.

"So, let me get this straight again," John said, "You're saying I'm the beneficiary of some bank accounts set up by my uncle?

"Yes, the account is entirely illicit functioning as a front for money-laundering scheme, created under layers of secrecy, involving offshore shell companies, false names, and encrypted transactions. Whoever was behind this has been careful and methodical. Since your name showing up means you're tied up in a way we don't fully understand."

"I don't know what to say."

"Hmmm" grunted Erik softly, as if he didn't quite believe it.

"I mean it."

"Hmmm", Erik grunted again, making John irritated.

"So what do you want from me?"

"You go there and unlock it."

"You want me to walk into a bank and claim it?"

Erik, a man whose calm demeanor rarely wavered, let out a small sigh.

"Yes, the accounts are flagged by several intelligence agencies. You are the only one who can unlock it."

John stayed silent for a moment, letting that sink in. The implications were chilling.

"From what date is this account?"

"Seems three days ago."

"Did my uncle open the account?"

"Probably."

John leaned back, shaking his head. "Why me? Why not let the intelligence guys crack it open? You've got the tech, the resources,"

"We tried."

"How did you try to open it if it's not your account?

"Let's just say certain doors open for those who know the right people."

John couldn't even begin to imagine what that really meant.

"Believe me, they've thrown everything at this account. Encryption, surveillance, infiltration. But whoever set this up anticipated every move. The system's rigged. It only responds to your identity. If anyone else tries, it's set to wipe itself clean."

Jack felt a cold sweat prickling the back of his neck. "And you're sure this isn't a setup?"

Erik said slowly. "It could be a trap. But our agency analysts think it's more than that. Your uncle or whoever put your name on the accounts didn't just do it to lure you in—they did it because they need you. They need you to access something in that bank. Something only you can retrieve. Why exactly is not clear to us. Your uncle might be smarter than we thought."

"Or someone wants to make me look like I'm involved," John muttered, rubbing his temples.

"Exactly," Erik agreed. "The agency's best guess is that if villains are behind these accounts they are trying to use you. As a scapegoat or to unlock something they can't or don't want to appear".

John stood and paced the room. "And there's no way for you or anyone else to get into it without me?"

"No. You're the only one who can do this. The account and the stolen documents could be the key to expose them."

"Who?

"We are not sure yet, but this might be the key to expose whoever they are, and you're the only one who can open that door. It's a risk, but it's also an opportunity."

John exhaled sharply. He hated feeling like a pawn, but the more he thought about it, the more it made sense. If this account was linked to money-laundering, it could expose their network, he couldn't just walk away.

"But you're not going blind," Erik added, "We will provide support. You'll have eyes on you the whole time, and we'll track every move once you enter the bank. But only you can initiate the process."

John's mind raced through the possibilities. If villains were after this account, accessing it might reveal more than just their identities. But that didn't make it any less dangerous.

Finally, he said to Erik. "I'll do it. But I want guarantees. Full surveillance, backup on standby. If this is a trap, I'm not going alone."

John heard what seemed like laughter. "Understood. Everything will be in place."

This changes everything and it has to be settled the sooner the better John thought.

"We would arrange the flight for you."

"Are there flights from Hong Kong to Tallinn?

"I doubt it, you would first go to Helsinki and from there to Tallinn."

"But before I go, I have to do a few things there."

"How long would it take?"

"A few days," he said without enthusiasm.

"Ok send me a message when you know."

After the line was cut John threw his mobile on the bed and felt the weight of the decision. Someone had laid a bait. The agencies have tried and failed and now want to use him, but they'll be watching his every move, ready to intervene, he's not alone.

John never imagined when he left Madrid that a family member might turn up and be a trickster with dangerous relations. John had a knack for attracting risks but within limits, his uncle, however, played in an entirely different league. John now understood why his uncle had been so nervous, this is a high-stakes situation. He sent a message to his uncle, no answer. An associate was dead, possibly murdered, and his uncle apparently vanished. On the other hand, the two accounts were a chance to redeem his father's honor.

CHAPTER 27

John went back to the Mandarin, to pick up Jasmine reflecting on the conversation with Eric and its meaning. However, the closer he got to the hotel and Jasmine, those thoughts were diminishing, converting to a desire to see her again. The two months separation hadn't limited their affection, evident the night before. No reluctance or hesitance, nor unnerving silences. They had merged with an innate understanding and a sense of a shared destiny. She stood waiting on the staircase, as beautiful as ever outside the hotel when he arrived. Their salute was a bit shy or reserved-like as if the world was observing on them, which it wasn't, a part of the Italian concierge, who might be nearby checking his domains. They found a cab and sat silent in tensed anticipation of the immediate future, reluctant to say meaningless words as their love affair was surging back to life again. Ben and Jane were at the entrance of the China Club where there would be held a promotion of a brand of some sort. It was the first time John and Jasmine went out socially as a couple. Jane kissed Jasmine with a smile and a blink.

"Nice to meet you, I've heard so much about you," said Jane.

Jasmine looked surprised at John.

"You are perfect together."

Outside this notorious place the impression was it could be London or Paris. Boisterous men arriving in Rolls-Royce's made their way like stately galleons under sail. Comparable to "the Bonfire of Vanities" with rented luxurious cars for the last track to show off, giving the impression of wealth at work. Beautiful bolstered boobed sirens came out of the cars in high heels with curved dresses and short skirts displaying their thighs, knockouts following where the money goes. Sirens of the night with a craving for adventure. It was alluring and seductive.

"Yes, you look great," said John to Jasmine while thinking if the way you dress is proof of your mindset. Jasmine got the attention by both men and women when they entered the Club. She didn't have to be envious of other women, who looked at them with both curiosity and disdain wondering, who is this guy with such a beauty. He took her hand and squeezed it a bit and she answered with a gentle smile. Tonight, the owner of the club, the flamboyant David Chang, was promoting his own brand. Chinese oriented designs, with tall oriental women going around like an open catwalk, showing the latest of his creations. This was *the* place for the ultra-rich. It smelled of lust and excessive respect for money and its prizes. An odor of extreme desire for luxury, extracting emptiness despite the very beautiful, contracted in such a small space. Some men seemed too old to be there in the first place, especially with these Ferrari-bimbos. The feast was in full swing with strained and raucous laughter all around.

"I feel old in places like this," said Jane.

"We *are* old", said Ben with a smile.

Drinks were offered and they had a glass of champagne in their hands without ordering it. A man approached their little party accompanied by two bombshells of women, very tall and very glamorous with enticing features including filled bosoms and alluring lips among other notable attributes.

"What are you doing here Ben you should be working out new deals."

"This is my new lifestyle."

The man was Ling Who, a tycoon in Kowloon. They were all presented in an awkward way, the bombshells more as prizes and exhibited as fine racehorses, apparently not speaking English and only smiling foolishly. "These are my deals," he said eying what looked like two Russian sirens.

"A very substantial deal," said Ben with a fatuous look on the women. Ling Who was one of the prominent players in Hong Kong, frequently mentioned when there were substantial investments in financial spheres.

"Power is the ultimate aphrodisiac as Henry Kissinger said," whispered Ben only John could hear.

"Nice friends Ben has," said Jane laughing.

"Their bodies work as heating missiles, right on", said Ben.

"Oh please Ben," said Jane, looking unpleasantly as if he had said something inappropriate.

At that moment two men came forward forcefully.

"Dunbar," shouted aggressively one of them.

"Hi Tom, courteous as usual," said Ben.

"Oh, sorry my name is Tom McNally introducing himself and here is my Russian friend Vladimir Nabokov. The Russian looked like a Slavic version of Daniel Craig, hardwired and effective in his movements in a black jacket looking fit, no extra fat there, trimmed like an athlete.

Ben said to all.

"Tom is my eternal competitor, he is Sands."

"No, we are not," said Tom, which seemed too definitive in John's taste.

Proper presentations were made and Dunbar asked:

"Any worries on the other side of the hill, I heard you were in Beijing."

"Just some small talk about Cathay Airways as you might expect, and Coca-Cola."

"Are we good?"

"We have excellent relations in Beijing."

"Good for you," said Ben not looking pleased. John noticed an aggressive and almost vulgar manner in the man called Tom.

The Russian didn't say a word just listening and watching the hard tone things were taking.

"You are as beautiful as ever," said Tom first looking at Jasmine's bosom and then at John.

"Are you the thief of our crown jewel at the Mandarin?"

Everybody sensed a sudden tension. John hadn't time to answer as a waiter passed in need of space with a tray full of glasses which Tom profited from and took Jasmine aside. John could see a worried look in Jasmine.

"I imagine you know him well," said Jane in a low voice to Ben.

"Not really, business-wise yes but we are not on intimate terms."

Jasmine turned up again. Tom had vanished in the crowd together with the Russian.

"I think he wanted a conversation with those," said Jane pointing at Jasmine's bosom.

This comment made the four of them laugh out loud.

"Did these or those answer him?" asked Jane.

"These," she said pointing at her bosom, "I couldn't hear what they answered, too angry to listen to myself, his eyes were just too much."

Ben looked at John and said;

"He is quite offensive, in everything."

"And who was the Russian," asked Jane.

"I've seen him now and then, not sure."

Jane took Jasmine in her arms and showed her the sight from the rooftop, which gave Ben an opportunity to talk to John.

"Lately many Russians here in Hong Kong, smells money-laundering." John was reminded of his conversation in London with the MI6-man and wanted to say this to Ben. It might ruin his trust as a friend if he didn't tell Ben about the MI6 interest in John's eventual inside information doing deals with a Tai Pan in Hong Kong. After a few seconds of mental squeeze, he decided to keep his mouth shut about it.

"It's okay for you to go alone to see Chen on the other side, that is inside China?"

"That's what I'm here for."

"You'll meet the companies Chen already talked to and hopefully close some kind of collaboration for our purposes."

"How much check-up of possible suppliers do you do in cases like these," asked John thinking of what Wellington had told him about strategically bad deals.

"We do the usual stuff and trust our experience."

"My experience is they seem so eager, repeatedly ask me what's my target-price as if there was a cushion to make discounts."

"That's their idiosyncrasy. Anyways, the ferry takes you to Shendi in an hour, Chen is there and pick you up."

"Great."

"Why don't we go somewhere else," said Jane when they came back.

"I think it's a good idea," said Ben.

"I think we have seen enough of this."

At that moment Tom and the Russian appeared again.

"Already leaving?

"We have another party," said Jane looking innocent.

Tom gave an unpleasant smile at John.

"And what are you doing here in Hong Kong? Apart of stealing from us this lady."

"I'm just enjoying the evening as everybody else." John's frustration was visible.

"By the way, you don't steal a person, maybe their time, if they let you," said John.

"What's that supposed to mean?" said Tom.

"Just that I'm not stealing yours, time is the real thief here."

Ben stepped forward, his voice calm but firm.

"Maybe you should worry less about John, no need to throw accusations around, Tom, try to be nice for once, John works with us."

"I'm always nice."

"You make me think of a psychiatrist I once met," said John.

"And?

"Let's say you have some issues to take care of."

"Is that all," Tom answered not so tough this time.

"For the moment it is."

"Is that a threat?"

"How could I be threatening you?"

"You just did."

"Well, then we have distinct versions of what a threat is."

"So let's call it a day and cheerio to you," said Ben.

"Let's go now," said the Russian and took Tom by the arm.

After this incident the four of them began to leave the club. Being the man he was, Ben was stopped the whole way till the entrance saying hellos to anyone who passed them. They let him pass as if he was a Rolls-Royce in a roundabout giving way instead of continuing. Suppose a Rolls has more respect than a Kia John thought, obviously in Hong Kong, Ben was *the* Rolls-Royce.

A man looking splendid in his white suit approached them.

"Hi Ben, you out with beautiful women?"

"David good to see you."

It was David Chang, owner of the China Club.

"We were just leaving, Tom McNally did it."

"Again? He is sour shit," and looked at Jane. "You are Jane Fox; we met in London I gather."

"You have a good memory."

"This is Jasmine and John Sherman," said Ben making it sound as if they were married.

"You are a lucky man with good taste," he said looking at Jasmine.

"Luck is something you work on," said John.

"Luck is an attitude."

"And in business?" asked Jane.

"In my humble opinion there is no luck or magic formula for success, not in business nor in love for that matter," he said jovially.

"Diligence is the mother of good luck," sentenced Ben with a smile.

"We must meet and talk," said Chang, directed to Ben, "there are clouds in the horizon. Arrests of prominent voices, I feel a visible pressure on Hong Kong and our way of life."

"I agree, there are subtle threats to our executives," said Ben.

These two must know each other thought John as this type of conversations weren't "come-il-faut" in Hong Kong anymore.

"The boys in Beijing have signaled they are unhappy with our banks and businesses because of the compliance with US sanctions."

"And the international banking industry is concerned, lots of talks to move elsewhere, like Singapore and Tokyo."

"And we are unhappy because of that new bill, allowing extraditions of criminals to the mainland, I think there will be protests," Chang said, with a melancholic tone in his voice, his usual smile absent.

"We have made some movements," said Ben without mentioning where or how much.

"I can't do that, only if they confiscate all I have, I'll have to leave."

"If they strangle free speech and the rule of law, that means the beginning of the end for seven million people."

"And don't forget most of the people in Hong Kong are born after 1997 and they want a say in all this, they want democracy."

"We are boring the ladies and your friend, what do you think of what is going on?" asked David looking at John.

"It's not easy to have an opinion, only impressions, I don't have the facts," said John.

"David nice to see you as always," said Ben and added to wrap it up, "nobody knows what will happen."

With that they sensed this impromptu discussion of the pros and contras of what was going on in Hong- Kong had come to an end and decided to be in contact.

Once they had left the place and were out on the street Jane said.

"That was awful, I mean the assault the man from Sands made."

"Usually, he is not such an ass, he is a son of a bitch for sure but why taking it out on John," said Ben.

"I'm sorry if I stirred it up but he was too thick."

"You made a good point though."

"And these women, what do you call them, bimbos?" asked Jane in disgust.

"Here we call them concubines. Very prestigious to have."

"Do you agree?"

"Well, there is a story about a man who had five of them and a wife. He decided to build a house with seven levels, one flat for each, on the top he lived by himself. During the week he worked himself upwards, one concubine for Monday, one for Tuesday and so on. On Sundays he stayed alone in his own flat at the top."

"He must have been exhausted," said Jasmine.

"When do you take the boat tomorrow?" asked Ben.

"There is one at 09.15."

"Maybe we shall call it a day then," said Ben.

"Yes Ben, I think we ought to leave this young couple on their own."
Ben assented.

"Call me when you are back" shaking his hand with what John perceived as affectivity.

John and Jasmine walked a few undecisive steps.

"What just happened is horrible, men kind of attack me," said Jasmine, "they think I can be treated like merchandise."

"I understand."

"No, you don't, it's horrible. They think they can treat me like a piece of meat."

"I'm sorry, what can I do to make you feel better?"

"Hold me hard and say you like me for what I am."

John did with great emphasis what she had asked for.

"There is cold bottle of Prosecco in my refrigerator, shall we try it?"
Both knew what this implied and without too many words they went to John's apartment in mutual consent. Once inside they acted out their impulses. They didn't finish the bottle because there were other basic instincts to take care of. Afterwards they sat down on the balcony watching the harbor, sipping the rest of the Prosecco.

John knew her intimately as a lover, but as a person, he knew close to nothing, which led him, ask about her years in the UK. Jasmine had studied tourism with marketing at the Regents University, which according to her wasn't among the best or high-profiled ones academically but had cleared her for a job at the Mandarin. There had been a boyfriend during four five years, which had ended when she went back to Hong Kong, not exactly why wasn't clear. A new one had appeared, an English soldier, the very same one who had picked a fight with John a few weeks ago and because of that incident her relationship with the man had ended brusquely. She was now free. For the rest she talked about her family and her friends, where the majority didn't live in Hong Kong, they were spread around the world, especially the ones from the university years. John saw in her a woman with a clear path, determined when she wanted something. If she had decided, it was one direction, and one goal. She wasn't an open book or talkative about sentiments, not disinterested only that she wasn't effusive with words. She was like a good dance partner who adapted to his choice of movements and actions and never negative about any of his proposals nor resisted his physical approaches only an amiable response.

"I go tomorrow to Shendi to see Chen, Ben's man."

"You must be careful."

"What do you mean?"

"I hear that things are changing on the other side."

"I'll be back sound and safe. Stay the night?

"No, have to sleep with my grandmother again must go now, next time I'll stay with you."

"I come with you."

They left the apartment in an ecstatic silence. At the same time there were many thoughts to handle and consider, the immediate future or any kind of future were scuffling their minds. A taxi took them to Jasmine's grandmother's place, a rapid kiss and John told the driver to wait until she would be inside the building. He watched from a distance inside the taxi as she reached the portal searching for the keys in her bag. Thanks to a lamp-post close by, gave clarity to her shapely figure and formidably shaped legs while she swiftly climbed the few stairs with a straight pose, a picture even Reubens would be excited about. For John it wasn't a fetish-like obsession objectifying the female body, it was a naturally appreciation inscribed in his DNA. But it wasn't just her physical perfection that affected him, he was also sensitive to the nuances of each of her gestures, at times he couldn't read, as she didn't express herself so much with words. She expressed her affection wholeheartedly by her actions and presence. Once she was inside, John told the driver to go back where they came from. Were men too fixated of women's bodies? The simple answer is yes. On the one hand they are to be blamed themselves. Nowadays it is so common with plastic surgeons improving something you didn't like of your features, breasts, lips or bottoms. Influencers were paid big money showing off their perfections, creating anxiety among the many who weren't. "Love your body and yourself", sponsored by beauty-clinics to refurbish the fat to the right place, which is ultra-sexualizing women's bodies. And women do create this superficiality themselves and crave reinforcement. There are studies, indicating women feel worse than ever, especially young ones, probably because of Instagram and the like making it happen.

Back in the apartment, he became very much aware it was time to face his dilemma, being torn between two lovers. The weight of his un-decision was unbearable and whatever path he would choose would reshape his future. But as Aristoteles had said about the past and the future, none of them existed now. A thought which didn't help him much. Would it be wise to leave his life in Stockholm for all the uncertainties a life with Jasmine might bring? Probably not he concluded, and I have things to solve the ever-present worry of the Tallinn-account and his father's past.

CHAPTER 28

The day after John went to the harbor to take a ferry to Shendi. He was told it should be a ride of an hour. Bought his ticket and saw no foreigners like him, they were all ordinary Chinese, this was humble people and didn't care about John. He found his seat and began looking idly out of the window. The boat began its route, and he found it strange there was no control when they must have passed the frontier.

I can only hope Chen is there because I have no idea where this is leading were his thoughts. Of course, Jasmine appeared in his mind while the boat was moving. And Marianne. I can't fix my own wishes or is this an addiction to be unfaithful they say many people have? The man from the MI6 had mentioned that once you get the feeling of misleading or have a double life, it's not easy to brush it away. An hour later the boat arrived to a little port and people started to get off the boat. He took his baggage and didn't see Chen. A few Chinese guys looking tired and wily observed him. They understood he was alone and that there was no one to pick him up. Ten or fifteen minutes passed, and all other passengers had been picked up and John was the only passenger still there, with no Chen in sight, he began to feel nervous. He called Chen on the mobile but there was no answer. It took him a few minutes to decide he must do something.

He approached a man standing picking his teeth with a toothpick. "Do you speak English? He didn't obviously. "Hotel? Nearby?" The man just looked with no ambition of understanding. Again, John said the magic word hotel? The man opened his mouth slightly and uttered guttural sounds which wasn't understandable. A little bit more of this when another man came forward and said something which might have been close to the word hotel, took John's baggage, made signs with his hands meaning come with me, which John did. A car stood close by so John followed the man trying to act assured and spoke, in his effort to make the man believe he was in control which he wasn't. Some aha intonations sound, and the man started the car. Once on the road, the man began to speak, even smiling and said the word hotel, now definitely. After a ten-minute ride, they arrived to what looked like a hotel and John felt alleviated. A young guy made his way to the car, dressed like a piccolo from yesterday times. Paid the taxi, went into a hotel with the tranquilizing sign of a four-star hotel.

"Excuse me, do you have a room?" The man in the lobby spoke some basic English and made it clear the price would be 15 Euros.

"I'll take it."

Once in the room he immediately phoned Chen's mobile. A man he didn't recognize answered the phone.

"Who are you?"

"I'm a friend of Chen."

"What? Can I speak to Chen please?"

"Give the address where you are, and we pick you up."

This didn't seem normal and bothering thoughts began to appear in John's mind. John gave the name of the hotel and after a nervous wait there was a knock on the door. Two men looking as any Chinese but with hard faces and an unwelcoming watchful gaze. One small with dark eyes, the other more like a wrestler and a size which gave you a hint to resist any ideas of violence.

"You better come with us."

His English was fair with typical Oriental sing-song sounds.

"Who are you?"

"We are from the police."

"Have something happened to Chen?"

"Not that we know of," said the small man.

"Where is Chen?"

"You come with us," was now pronounced rudely in a threatening tone.

"Why?"

The man's only response was a subtle movement towards the giant looming at his side. The next instant, John's shoulder was seized in an iron grip. The raw power told him everything. This wasn't the police. This was serious trouble. In the lobby the man who had signed in John looked with a scared expression when they left the hotel John hadn't paid. They entered a parked car and a short ride to what didn't look like a police-station. Leading John inside and without further ado John was left alone in a dimly lit sinister small room, the paint long gone. The only furniture two rusted chairs and a scarred table the only silent witness. A single bulb illuminating a forbidding and secluded place where only bad things happen. It reminded him of a movie from a Nazi-prison where there was a sign, "everything is forbidden". After what seemed an eternity, the little Chinese appeared and sat down with a menacing expression.

"You know Chen, don't you?

"Y-yes, I do, not much. We were supposed to meet. I was supposed to be doing business with him."

"Business? What kind of business?" he said scoffing.

"Find suppliers."

Leaning forward towards John he said.

"Do you know why you are here?"

"I'm the one to ask that question," said John while observing the man's black eyes, even his clothes were black from top to bottom. There was a tiny tattoo, two pyramids on the man's right hand, a badge, showcasing the group he belonged. The man looked at John with an exaggerated composure, as if he wanted to convey his self-assuredness, making it clear who was the boss. He gave an appearance of a man dull as dishwater who had seen too much and had concluded that human nature was despicable.

"Answer the question."

"No idea why I'm here."

"What's your business with Chen?"

"Chen was going to pick me up in Shendi. We were supposed to visit a few companies to do business with."

"I think you are lying, Chen is a traitor."

"What, come on, he is a respected businessman."

"I'm also doing business," he said.

The man began to ramble about China's rights to defend itself against the enemy, hinting they were everywhere, at all moments, finishing off by saying that "Chen is corrupt."

"Okay but why am I here?"

The man gave a hint of a smile. His manners suggested a theatrical rightness of what he was doing, as if he was the only one who knew the answers to everything. The unravelling situation was what weren't supposed to happen in real life, only what you read about. Wellington had told John if you are in scrap, be calm don't get angry, don't show lack of strength, don't show feelings, that's the way to defeat intimidation.

Clearly the man in front wasn't likely to be trifled with, obviated by what looked like a knife in his trousers. To use a knife it needs a man, a trigger is for anyone he had read somewhere.

"There are many useful idiots in this game," he said with narrowed eyes.

"What game? Why am I here? "Why do you interrogate me?"

Despite Wellington's recommendations, John was getting angry, like a slow burning fuse. John was indolent at moments but now he was angry, an anger he didn't really know he had in him, or it could be his nerves going havoc? Sitting in a room with a shit like this, his frustration was mounting. He felt a strong temptation to hit the guy in front of him, he was just waiting for the ignition. The situation was so bizarre and freaking him out. He felt he was caught in something far bigger and more dangerous than he ever imagined. Despite his fear now gnawing at his inside, decided to play tough: "You can go to hell." He spat, a desperate attempt to regain some shred of control.

The man curled his lips into almost amused smile:

"There is no hell," he said calmly.

"Because of?"

"We have Buddha or nothing, progressive thinking."

"What about Chen?"

"Don't you worry about him," he said in an ominous tone, one that only crooks would use thought John.

Although looking like a Chinese from the films of thugs in Sean Connery's Bond-films he seemed to have mellowed a bit thanks to John's outburst of wishing him a one-way ticket to hell.

"And how do you dare to talk to me like that in the position you are?" was said in a menacing tone.

John calmed down, it wasn't in his interests to show defiance.

"I'm sorry, in what position am I?"

"You are in my custody, and you will spend the night like a prisoner to cool off until we decide what we do with you. The problem with you people, you, think you are above us you don't respect us. You treat us like dogs. But that will change."

The man stood up, pacing in front of John.

"We have Chen."

"What? What do you mean?"

Smiling coldly, he said; "We have him. And we want you to tell the Tai Pan."

"Tell him what?"

"You will tell him that we have Chen. And you will tell him that if he wants to see Chen again, he will do as we say."

John was led into a room which without a doubt looked like a real prison cell. He didn't say a word, closed the door from the outside and John was alone. John was numbed and didn't react first and just stood looking at the walls, a tiny window with bars and a bench. It began to dawn on him what was going on. They had taken his mobile, he was *incommunicado*. He lay down on the bunk and thought now we'll see how tough you are John. Was this because of reckless acting, he wondered. The situation was what you read in the papers and now it had happened to him. His thoughts went randomly without a pattern. Is this the effect of being jailed, you lose the ability to think coherently and slowly you get mad and desperate? During his military service he had slept one night in a cell like this. But that time he knew it was limited in time; he was castigated because he had said something stupid to his sergeant. Now this was another ballgame in a very different environment, this was hard-core China, where people could be abducted for weeks, months or even years. What if this was the end and he would perish here. The world was full of tales of people who disappeared in godforsaken places, and this might be one. He was railing off due to fear. He needed to recapitulate and not let his mind wander off. Breath and focus. It began to function after intense concentration. He found he was adapting and beginning to comply to the circumstance. Oddly, he found himself drifting, lost in thought, contemplating the course of his life.

Unexpectedly thoughts appeared of people, assorted episodes in his life. It didn't come in bursts, just passages, haphazardly moments pouring his brain. The astonishing thing was how vividly memories seemed to soar through his mind, each one appearing with startling precision. He remembered when he had taken his daughter in his arms when she couldn't sleep, his mother when they would meet up somewhere in Stockholm, swimming in the sea, a few scattered points won in tennis, a good cigar he had smoked in a restaurant in Barcelona after a good contract had been signed and of course, Jasmine. Should we really go on? Was it conceivable for them? Somberly he concluded it wouldn't be possible. But first you must get out of this my friend. He looked at the window as the symbol of freedom. Despite the dire situation a thought of being grateful arose, how lucky he had been where he had been born and what it withholds of privilege and possibilities. He closed his eyes, heard voices of people talking in a room close by his cell. He wasn't sure but it seemed they played ping-pong. Is that what they do to spend the time as guards? After an undefined time, the door opened. It was his interviewer, smiling.

"You can come out now."

John raised and they went into the room they had been before.

"Sit down. "Have you read any Chinese authors?"

"Not much."

"It looks like you've read The Art of War by Sun Tzu."

"You mean attacking is the best defense.?"

"Not exactly, your position depends of your environment." He pronounced the sentence as if reading a text.

"You mean you adapt to circumstances?"

"It all depends on the moment and the forces you face you must adapt to different scenarios."

Wow and I thought he was a simple raptor. The man has another side to him maybe he isn't that brutish.

"You surprise me," said John.

"What's your relationship with Chen?

"I have only met him briefly. Listen, I'm here to do business with him and you interrogate me as if I was some kind of thug."

"Chen is a traitor to China."

"Sorry but I've no idea what you are talking about. Check me out, go to your lords of intelligence and check me."

Probably he didn't buy a word or didn't care what John was saying, he only expressed a self-satisfied smugness. There was a silence and then the Chinese said as if John's words seemed to have an effect on him.

"Have done that already."

"And?"

"Your father was a spy."

"What?"

This came as a chock to John and the Chinese saw it.

"Not any spy your father. He worked for the MI6, maybe it's in the genes," he suggested.

"Sure, like Nadal's future son's will win Roland Garros hundred times."

How would this man know this? He must be involved in some way in Chinese Intelligence or perhaps the rumors were true- that the police were monitoring citizens and foreigners all over the globe. And it was true what he had said, didn't make him feel better, nor safe. This might get ugly. This little shit might know about Jasmine, I should leave China, do my own thing, be a tennis-coach for older less talented people, sit in the archipelago and drink beer. Suddenly a man entered the room, the Russian John had met at the China club came in through the door. Was there a hidden plot and I'm being conned, maybe Dunbar and even Jasmine aren't what they say they are? What looked like a friend to Dunbar's competitor is now here. Who would be the next man to enter the room, Federer or Lady Gaga, anything was possible it seemed. John felt the air-pressure in the room was getting tight in disbelief of what was happening.

"It's possible you work for the Swiss Intelligence."

John almost smiled.

"You mean Swedish Intelligence."

"That's what I said," a bit less aggressive in tone and manner.

The mode had changed since the Russian's entrance and the Chinese seemed somewhat more toned down. Nabokov said something in Chinese. The Russian gave the impression being somehow superior to the Chinese. His looks and body-language were of a man with a faculty. In John's nervous perception, by now, he looked definitely like Daniel Craig, underlined with a potential of a threat including physical violence. It seemed this guy could kick the Chinese to sawdust if there was any need. After what seemed a muted conversation between the two, the Chinese changed attitude by the second and had lost his brutal security and apparently had played his cards too much.

"I think there is has been a mistake," said the Russian. The Chinese looked at John and said:

"You are lucky man you have good friends," he said with beatific smile.

"We can go now, I'll take you to the airport," said Nabokov also smiling.

"Mistake? Is this what you call Ping-Pong diplomacy you come and go?" John referred to the Nixon administration forty years ago with the Secretary of State Henry Kissinger had extracted a peaceful relation with Deng Chiao Ping and travelled back and forth to China called Ping-Pong diplomacy.

"You play ping-pong?"

"Fairly good yes."

The Chinese smiled and said;

"We have a table and rackets here."

"Haven't played much lately but okay if you want."

The Chinese smiled and the Russian looked at John with appreciation and made the thumbs up.

They left the room and entered a room with a ping-pong-table, the Chinese gave John what looked like a good racket.

"You want to warm up?"

They began to hit forehands, and John sensed the guy was a natural forehander, I must test his backhand, might be his weakness. After hitting a few balls back and forth the Chinese said, "let's start now." No time for a real warm-up to check if the man's backhand was good or not. The man had a terrible screwed serve and John began losing 0-2. John tried to serve on his backhand with an under-screw and it functioned. 2-2. It went on like that until they were even at 9-9. The Chinese served and John netted the ball, 10-9 for the Chinese. It's now or never. A new serve on John's forehand which he succeeded to deflect far out, way on his opponent's forehand who returned it too high and John made his best shot, smashed a no-doubter in the wrong corner on the man's backhand. 10-10. A smash in ping-pong is not like a slap-shot in ice-hockey which is like AK-47 Kalashnikov, or a hard hit in Fronton, it's not like being hit by a truck, it's a feeling being outsmarted. A smash in ping-pong is light, fast and lethal and at the same time subtle. A new serve which John returned a short backhand just above the net which the Chinese netted, now the tables had turned match-point for John, 11-10. John went to the right side of the table and made a backhand side serve without screwing which surprised the Chinese who lifted the ball too high. John just smashed it down, it was over, 12-10. The Chinese wasn't happy when acknowledging his loss. The Russian was standing just smiling.

"Let's go now, I'll explain to you in the car."

The Russian began to explain his mission or job. He knew about Marbella and the Gang-of-Four and John's role in the story. He behaved in a very friendly way which surprised John.

"Who are you," asked John when they approached the car alleviated.

"I fix things."

"Like a fireman in a fire?"

"Yes, something like that."

"But who do you work for?"

"I work as private investigator for a company."

"Which has a name?

John's mind turned to the famous science-fiction novelist Nabokov.

"It's an insurance company," answered Nabokov.

"And a restaurant in London."

"Didn't know."

"Wow an insurance company, who takes care of imprisoned people in China?"

"To a point yes, we do."

"Whatever you do, I thank you for what you just did. What about Chen, do you know what has happened to him?"

"Nothing for the moment."

"The guy who interrogated me said he has Chen and has his mobile."

As John had met Nabokov with Ben's competitor he didn't think it would be wise to say more of the possible blackmail.

"Yeah. I'll investigate that. I'll be back in Hong Kong in a few days."

"How did you get me free?"

"I'll tell you next time," he said smiling.

Maybe he was working for the infamous group Little Green Men Wellington had mentioned in London. The Wagner Group, a Russian private military company, which appears to be a conventional business company. Their management and operations deeply intertwined with the Russian military and intelligence community. The Russian government used private military companies to extend its influence overseas without the visibility and intrusiveness of a state military forces. More flexible, cheaper, less accountable. Nabokov left John outside the Guangzhou airport. Once inside the airport he bought a flight to Hong Kong, a distance that could be done biking almost. Tilting towards the usual greed or need for companies to cover their costs, the flight was over-booked creating a hassle at the gate, everybody scrambling with elbows on the desk, letting the woman who attended them know, in a gruff way they mustn't miss the flight. John behaved as a gentleman and stood at the desk a few meters, to not overwhelm the woman. He would been seen anyhow being a much taller figure than these guys, making her willing to give a ticket to him instead of the guys shouting desperately at her. He put on the Berlusconi-smile, which isn't authentic but can be used as a weapon of seduction, a white grin devoid of emotion. After a while he heard, "Sheeemann". She made it sound like a new gender and gave him a ticket with a smile, "you can go now", while the rest of the bunch was yelling recklessly. Cleared and having passed security, he went to a bar, ordered whiskey on the rocks, as if alcohol would act as a mechanism to reduce his stress level. He had a second one, shuddering and thinking if one was good maybe two would be twice as good. Must call Ben and let him know about Chen's disappearance. And who was the Russian? Maybe it was the whiskey playing tricks on him, but a sudden paranoid thought crept in, had he been followed? He looked around and saw people apparently with no interest in him. I'll buy a mobile in Hong Kong and send a message to Wellington and let him know. On the plane a Chinese woman of older tract sat to his left burping with an odor that was intolerable. A thing which wasn't uplifting considering the state he was in. Suddenly he was up to his eyeballs of China and everything it meant. He was exhausted in body and mind.

CHAPTER 29

Once he arrived in Hong Kong airport, he took a bus to downtown. Slightly suspicious after the stunt as a jailbird he decided to walk and see if any of the passengers were following him. Not an easy task, as they all looked the same in his eyes. He wasn't even capable of distinguishing if they were Japanese or Chinese. He thought the Japanese had wider and longer faces and bigger eyes compared to the Chinese. He realized the Orientals had very black hair and no bald men, that was strange. Is it in the food? Saw a bar, went in and ordered his third whisky of the day. He was slipping into that blurred space between sobriety and intoxication where everything felt just a little more vivid and carefree. Before calling Ben, he wrote him a short summary of what had happened. Ben called after five minutes.

"As I wrote, Chen is missing," John said agitated and effusively, as if he was reporting a positive matter, when it was the exact contrary, intoxicated by the day's events and the whisky.

"I see," said Ben calmly, "we should meet, are you okay, you sound strange?"

"No, it's fine."

He was getting drunk.

"How did you manage to come back?"

"The Russian guy we met at the China Club arranged it."

There was a pause.

"Where are you now?"

"In a bar in Hong Kong."

"We better not talk on the phone, come to the hotel," said Ben.

"I would prefer we meet close at Stockton's, it's close. He was thinking of Jasmine who might be in the lobby and it wasn't the perfect moment to have a chat with Ben in the state he was in.

"Am in a meeting right now, so let's make it here, give me two hours."

Having agreed to see Ben he called his daughter in New York.

"Hi dad, can't speak right now I'm in class."

"I love you," he said a bit too slurry."

"Are you drunk dad?"

"Not yet," trying to make it sound like laughter.

"Everything ok?"

"Yes, everything ok, call you later then" and they hang up.

He was thirsty and he ordered a beer instead of more whisky, revealing a degree of self-control. It's funny habit your mind plays with you as if the beer and whisky will fix the drama I'm involved in. It wasn't just a sensation being afraid, it was frustration and daunting. Three whiskies and a beer, what am I doing? After the stunt as a prisoner, he was on the edge and felt adrift and lost. Scrutinizing the last weeks he had been roaming like a crazed animal. Involved in matters he didn't control and now he felt defeat, as a sheer fear of his future, probably for the first time in his life. A sensation of an opposite epiphany, like not being his own man, led to his confusion and a feeling of being lost, unsure which path to take with his life. This self-analysis was prompted by the stress he had experienced having been interrogated by a jerk in a prison- like situation, inside China. Clearly it had released a fear-factor, creating strained emotions of all sorts. And there was Jasmine, Marianne and his daughter, in that order. Obviously the wrong and not rightful order. Looking steadily at his glass of beer and seeing the bubbles gracefully dancing and shifting with no apparent order, he realized, he had to straighten up, he had a responsibility towards his daughter, be a man, confront the challenges instead of sulking. And thanks to his psyche, a change of heart and a thought arose. It wasn't his fault he had been under arrest and the embroiling business of Chen's disappearance. Don't blame yourself and he almost began to smile when thinking how lucky he was, being freed from the skirmish in a prison in China, who would believe that. He drowned the beer and left in a better mood.

When he arrived at the Mandarin fortunately, Jasmine wasn't to be seen when John entered the lobby. The Italian concierge ushered John into what must have been Ben's private office in the hotel.

There were four people and Ben in a splendid office, with a fantastic view of Hong Kong.

"Let me just finish off with these gentlemen," he said. "You might learn something," he said as if everything was normal.

"As I was saying, we are excited about the future, our portfolio is headway into China, Hong Kong-land, we have large investments in South-East Asia, like Vietnam, Indonesia. We put a lot of emphasis on innovation and of course sustainability, we must think ahead. From now on I'll dedicate my time with regulators, relationship with government and new partners. As you know we've been here for generations and offer stability but we also need to adapt. We must know what customers need, you need to know what you are good at is key," Ben concluded sounding a bit over-reaching John thought, he might be distressed due to Chen's disappearance. The session Ben ended, and the visitors left, they were alone. "Journalists, tell me what's happened. You look, what shall I say, tipsy?" It was said with Ben's gentle tone Ben always conveyed.

"I know, had a few stiff whiskeys."

"I see," and he began to laugh.

"Did they help?"

"Who?"

"The whiskeys."

"I would say yes, perhaps not a cleansing but definitely alleviated." John told Ben the whole story as good as he could, from the start when Chen didn't show up in Shendi and the interrogation with the Chinese, who came to fetch him at the hotel and the Russian, Nabokov.

They discussed this new situation for a while and after some and pros and cons. It was decided to postpone the business of the packaging company and see how things would evolve before initiating anything. For John this was a serious setback, in an instant the job had evaporated due to external forces. John was on his own again. Once again, random was weaving its unpredictable threads through his life. He would have to re-think his situation.

"In any case there are a lot of opportunities here in Hong Kong for a man like you, we'll find you something."

Ben stood up and went for a glass of water close to his desk and after a long pause and deep thought he finally spoke.

"Chen must have been abducted," said Ben.

Absorbed in his own thoughts John was reminded of his stunt in prison

"My guardian was a strange man, at one moment just a simple thug ranting about Chen being a traitor then he transformed and displayed glimpses of culture."

"Chen isn't a traitor."

John understood the disappearance of Chen was a big blow when his closest business aide was lifted of the scene mysteriously and wondered if Ben at bottom trusted Chen. He must be calculating the implications in the case Chen had gone astray by his own, or that he was simply kidnapped. Ben being a master of the business universe, probably seeing the problem in hundred dimensions and must have sailed in previous fuckups and learned, therefore must have resources.

"How long have you been working together?"

"Since the very beginning, he is my man."

"By the way, why is a Russian, with enough power to fix me out? That is strange," said Ben looking out.

"And apparently he was a friend with the man from Sands we met at the China Club."

"Yeah, you are right, what do they have in common?"

"You could call your friend Tom and see if he knows something," John said innocently.

"That I will not do."

Ben saw that John was dazed having discovered there was no job any longer, at least for the moment.

"About your job we'll figure out something."

In a moment of rare display of pouring out his thoughts John said: "I came here full of illusions about the job and bang everything is upside down, you are put into a cell, and you are interrogated as if you were a thug."

"The thing I mentioned the other day about the project in Punta Cana, maybe it might interest you?"

Big turns John thought melancholy.

"There is a project in the Dominican Republic, we are considering participating in. You could go there and see the people we are dealing with, before we do due diligence see how it looks and more importantly, the people involved. The proposal is to construct a hotel close to the beach, a five-star resort." He said this as if John was into five-star projects every day.

"Did this come up just like that?"

"No, I've been considering it a long time, since we played golf together and you told me your life-story. And you speak Spanish."

"I do."

"I understand your feelings but first we must see what has happened to Chen. As I said we'll come up with something, we only postpone for a while."

Ben got a call.

"Have to go now, have an extraordinary boardmeeting today, seems they can't proceed without me."

"Because of Chen's disappearance?"

"They don't know about it yet. Anyways I'll let you know stuff." Lately everybody will "let me know" John thought. It's time to send a message to Wellington and inform of the interrogation. They had agreed in that poised idiom of English understatements to do so if something *came up* and this was something coming up. He also considered he ought to tell Ben about Wellington.

"When I was in London just before I arrived in Hong Kong, I met a man who knew about my father."

"That's great," said Ben while raising.

"He is at MI6."

Ben sat down again.

"You surprise me."

"I didn't think it would be necessary, but this man let me know if I could call him if I had something of interest and I think we have."

"But why would he be interested in a possible kidnapping?"

"Among other things he wondered how much research we do when we pick up a Chinese supplier for the very reason many of them work for the Chinese state."

"I've always been reluctant towards those fellows at the MI6, and their secluded world of secrets, coming to think of it, intelligence is what we are all doing in one form or the other," said Ben. "Fine with me, perhaps he could give some light to all this."

"I'll send him a message if ok for you, I mean mentioning this thing about Chen?"

Ben raised, "yeah perhaps he could be of help, at least he is on our side of the fence, by definition."

They said goodbye in an uneasy fashion. It was visible that Ben wasn't happy having his "camp de aide" of thirty years being eviscerated to China.

"I'll call you, go do things with Jasmine."

"That's exactly what I will do."

"I can fix you an invitation to the Jockey Club if you want, my secretary will fix it."

John left the Mandarin with no Jasmine in sight. I'll call my daughter again he thought, when a message came up on his mobile. It was Marianne. "Are we good? Tell me you are okay M."

Fine timing, it was like being sternly screwed in long-distance. John self-pitying himself went to the apartment and almost fell on the bed, looked at the ceiling. The effect of alcohol was diminishing, and he began to drivel about what had happened. Here I am in Hong-Kong, making things more difficult than a reasonable man would ever consider, you lose your job, you stir up your love-life like an extravagant vainglorious lover. Marianne's message made him feel the squeeze, a grip on his mind a tight unpleasant empty feeling of falling, not knowing where he would land, or how or crash. The whole situation reminded him of a song by Queen; *too much love will kill you, if can't make up your mind, impossible to choose, you are the victim of your crime.* His confidence was leaving him. He was engulfed with a sense of loss beyond his control. Exhausted and haunted he slept. He woke up in a haze an hour later. The only thing that was certain was he didn't have a job. An opening not specified had appeared in Punta Cana. The project Ben had talked about was a momentary thing not a strategic choice. Again, it was providence and thought the best would be not decide too much ahead, just take what there is and we'll see.

CHAPTER 30

After this extended powernap, he took a cold shower, shaved, dressed, put on a white shirt as if that color would put in in a better mood and it worked, either thanks the shower or a vanity-look in the mirror made it happen. Instead of texting Jasmine, he called her up.

"You are back what happened?"

"It didn't go as expected."

"What do you mean?"

"I'll tell you if you have dinner with me."

"Chinese food?"

"You choose place."

They met and hour later in Kowloon outside the restaurant she had indicated. She was dressed in a typical Chinese outfit.

"Now, that is sexy."

"Not supposed to be, it's traditional."

It was a tight Cheongsam-dress in red with dragons and a phoenix embroidered in silk fabric. Her shapely figure perfectly reflected and in full view of the world.

"How do you get into that?"

She just smiled and said, "it's a secret. You said Chinese and dressed accordingly."

"And these dragons? Does it mean something?"

"Dragons is a symbol of great power the red color symbolizes good luck and happiness."

"I doubt those high heels are typical Chinese dressing-codes," he said with a grin.

"They are for you."

She knew he had a thing for high heels, not an obsession, but it added up to the rest he liked to say. Her figure with that tight dress and high heels was a strong combination to be watched, not only by John, but also obvious for passersby who happened to be in their pathway.

This part of Kowloon was another ballgame compared to the financial district John usually walked around. It made him feel as an alien and in hostile territory, unwished for, making it worse by stealing a local beauty. The restaurant was pure Chinese, red lanterns, decorated with bamboo and artwork depicting scenes from Chinese culture and soothing Chinese music. A waiter approached them with an admiring glance at Jasmine and led them to a table.

"Everything here is in Chinese".

"You better do the ordering then."

The waiter came back and took Jasmine's order.

"What have you ordered?"

"A little bit of this and a little bit of that."

"That sounds good."

"So why did you come back so fast?"

John told the story factual-like, without too much drama. When he had finished, she took his hands.

"That's terrible John."

"It made me think a lot, being a captive has a special effect on your thoughts."

"And what did you think?"

"About us and a few memories arose, didn't get to the future."

He didn't tell her that the job had gone dry.

"Weren't you scared?"

"At first, I wasn't but when it began to sink in, yes."

"But they didn't hurt you?"

"No, but little by little my thoughts were going mad and whacky, I was in the middle of nowhere."

"So, what were you thinking?"

"It was bizarre and became like a documentary-film, you were in it, a leading role," he said teasingly and smiled.

"Who were the others?"

John didn't mention all details in that feature. Luckily the food arrived so he didn't have to answer her question and managed to put it behind. Endless plates in colors were put on their table. Bewildered John understood that it really was a little bit of everything.

"I serve you," she said and handed out something in grey and pink, difficult to determine what kind of food it was.

Jasmine laughed when John tried to eat a pinkish thing, which must be an ancestral species from the Cambrian explosion.

"You have a good chop-sticktechnique , she said with a smile.

"I try, what are we eating?"

"It's krill, a shrimp. Do you want me to show how to use them "Dim song?"

"Which means?"

"From the heart."

John struggled with both with the chopsticks and without great success, gulping down whatever he ate with glasses of wine.

After many unsuccessful attempts he said, "I give up," he said, "or I eat them without peeling the shrimps."

"Those you do by hand."

Because of John's faltering technique, he needed something more solid, asked for the menu and found what he needed, Chinese grilled chicken with jasmine rice, instead of the colored stuff they had been served.

"Is this jasmine rice? Didn't know there was one."

"It's supposed to be sweet and delicate," she said, "like me."

"Another coincidence, Jasmine all over the place, how could I forget you. I'm bound to be with you."

John regretted immediately what he had said, it sounded as a bad premonition.

"Do you want a desert?"

"Something digestive".

The waiter came and cleared the table, and they ordered sorbet. Eventually John asked for the bill, paid and they departed.

"Let's have a drink somewhere," suggested John.

A taxi took them to a deserted bar, the same one he had gone to after having a fight with her ex-boyfriend. The music in the background was Chinese which he had begun to appreciate.

"What's music? Seven notes and some half-notes but what is it?"

"I don't bother but I like it."

They sat down in the bar and ordered two glasses of rosé.

"It's extraordinary to think that a simple combination of vibrations, not seen by the human eye can make such emotions. What's the process?"

"Don't think about it and enjoy it."

"You are right, one shouldn't insist on defining things, it loses its charm, like love," he said while looking at her innocently.

John noticed Jasmine wasn't as talkative as usual.

"Everything okay? "

"John, have to tell you something, I'm having threats," she said with a haggard face looking into her down hands.

"What threats?"

"This morning when I went to the hotel, two guys stopped me and said they knew about my grandmother's past and threatened to tell the Chinese authorities if I didn't pay them."

"What guys?"

"The looked like criminals, like the Triads."

"You were black mailed, why?"

"They said they would relieve my grandmother's past if I didn't pay and cooperate."

"Cooperate how?"

"Give information of certain guests that stay in the hotel."

"But what kind of guests?"

"Give names of Russians and Americans, an upcoming IT-event at the hotel of what we are told are high-ranking people in different industries."

"And what exactly should you do? Tell them a guy in his fifties working for General Electric is staying at the hotel? There is no value in that."

"I don't know."

"And the event will be at the Mandarin?

"Yes, it's an IT-computer thing with people from Silicon Valley etc."

"Doesn't sound very specific for black mailing."

"Yes, but what surprises me checking the reservations at the hotel, there are a lot of Russians the days of the event."

What she was telling John coincided with what Wellington had mentioned, about existing Russian organizations tempting prospects with money to get information about a new project everybody was talking about, the quantum-computers, which would create a huge shift technologically as data could be provided in a revolutionary way and that meant power.

"But what did your grandmother do? It doesn't sound credible."

"After the Chinese civil-war she worked as an informant for the USA smuggling people from the mainland to Hong Kong or Taiwan. The authorities would send her to China in jail if they knew." It was blurted it out nervously.

After John's last visit John had read a lot about the history of Hong Kong and the Chinese civil war. After the war massive exodus begun towards Hong Kong from mainland China after Mao had taken over in 1949. A severe famine during spring 1957 led to a wave of refugees from Guangdong. Thousands of hungry civilians gathered at the border claiming to seek *"relatives"*. Some of the refugees were capitalists, some were farmers and criminals. The criminals who came established the infamous Triads in Hong-Kong. Many dived into the deep and dirty Da Peng and Shenzhen bays, swimming the deadly four-kilometers journey to Hong Kong, braving choppy, treacherous seas, tied together by ropes. Others drowned or were attacked by sharks. They were known as freedom swimmers. All in all, hundreds of thousands of young men and women f led mainland China and risked their lives in search of freedom in the British colony. Some were shot dead by border guards, or arrested and sent to labor camps as the act of defection was considered treason. More recently China had imposed a national security law on the region of Hong Kong in response to months of pro-democracy protests. The change had been swift and brutal. Dozens of activists and dissenters were arrested, raiding any opposition newspaper office. Outspoken media outlets were censured. Books pulled from public libraries. Schools and universities have been ordered to promote *national security education*, banning scholars and journalists and thus everyday citizens suddenly find themselves afraid to speak out about politics. Prominent pro-democracy figures have been forced to flee overseas or face prison on the mainland.

"If I don't cooperate my grandmother can be sent to prison in China, they told me."

"These guys appear out of the blue and threatens you with prison if you don't pitch in?"

"Yes."

"Have you talked to your parents about this?"

"They are not here they are in England."

"Maybe it's a bluff and they just want to black-mail you and get money?"

"I don't know."

"There is a guy I met in London who could be of help," said John.

"What guy?"

"Actually, he is an intelligence officer."

"And why does John go to London and meet a spy?" she asked him making a wry face.

"To learn about my father."

"He was a spy also or?"

"Yes, I didn't know until a few weeks ago."

John took a sip of the wine looking at the wall in front, smartly lit to enhance the sight of all the whiskies, gins and rums.

"And who were they, the people you met?

"No idea, they looked like Triads."

"Do you think the Triads collaborate with the Chinese police?

"That's what we hear every day."

"What do they want from you?

"$250,000."

John made a whistling sound.

"Giving names of hotel-guests can't be worth that, it must be a bluff."

"They seemed pretty serious."

"And how much time do you have?"

"Don't know, they said they would come back."

"You have family in the mainland?"

"Yes, aunts and uncles."

If she was black-mailed because what her grandmother had done and with family on the other side of the mountain, the ruthless Chinese wouldn't bulge to get what they wanted. A scary thought came to his mind. A few hours ago, he had wondered if he was being played and now this idea surfaced again, was he in a surrealistic play and he was somehow the protagonist? There seemed to be too many random coincidences. His world had become spooky and treacherous at every point. Especially considering what had happened a few weeks ago when he tried to tail intelligence, he had realized he wasn't made of the right stuff. Too hazy for him. No value in me as a supplier of spy-craft, only a useful idiot as that dreadful Chinese had said. Or was he caught in the famous honey-trap by Jasmine? But for what reason? What could I possibly offer? Literally nothing. After reflecting of this eventuality, he reached the conclusion she wouldn't spend days and nights together playing him. This last consideration got traction thus he decided to contact Wellington.

"Let's go and buy a mobile with a SIM card. I imagine the intelligence guy I met in London doesn't like open lines." He surprised himself by his cunning detail of an untraceable phone.

They went into one of the thousand shops with the latest in mobiles and in a nick of time, he had a new mobile and SIM-card. John texted Wellington; *would like to speak at the soonest, Jack Sherman's son.* He wrote thinking it sounded effective. It didn't take long and a short message appeared on the screen. "Call you in half an hour, this phone is in the breeze."

Jasmine didn't question what John was doing she seemed puzzled and silent. Changing theme while waiting for the call from Wellington he said:

"I would like to meet your grandmother."

"She thinks she already knows you."

"You have told her about us?"

"A bit."

They talked about how and where they should meet her and when the half-hour was gone the mobile rang.

"Hi"

"Alistair here, I gather something has happened?"

"More than that," said John and gave a short count of Chen's disappearance and his event in a prison cell and Jasmine's tale.

"Ok fine, John, I fly tomorrow to Hong Kong, big wheels are moving," was said in the characteristic tranquil way of the master-spy. No exaggerated timbres or excitement just leveled words as if talking about the possibility it might rain tomorrow.

"What?"

"Can't tell you."

"As always then."

"I'll let you know when and how we meet."

And the line was cut. Strangely, this made John feel better, which he tried to convey to Jasmine who looked miserable.

"Who are you talking to?"

"The man I met in London, a spy."

"A spy? Who are you John, are you a spy? You come and go, are you honest to me, are you a spy as your father?"

"Wait, wait whatever is going on, I might be in a mess for different reasons but not playing with you, maybe the world is playing with me or that fucking destiny or random but no, not with you."

She looked confused.

"Why should I trust you?"

"Because I'm telling the truth." What he wanted to say was that he loved her but this wasn't the moment. After this emotional eruption they stayed in telling silence. After a while he took her hands and kissed her and as it turns out, when two people are in love, passion takes over and they felt better and decided to go to his apartment. This time she would stay for the night. Once inside the apartment, with the door firmly closed, the outer world and its problems disappeared momentarily, the external felt irrelevant. From a state of worry, they switched to a state of passion. He enjoyed her exceptional beauty instead. The whole package from bottom and up, stirring and stimulating his being. It wasn't a question of comparing she was simply magnificent. Their kisses were instinctive and urgent, their bodies yielding in harmony eliminating any thresholds of their feelings. It was natural and wordlessly. Afterwards Jasmine fell asleep, and John went out onto the balcony and called his daughter.

"Are you okay dad?"

"Yes, I got a bit emotional when we talked, being so far away and all that." As always it made him happy to talk to her and calmed his nerves and took away his turmoil.

"I would like to see you I could go to Hong Kong."

"That would be great."

They talked a long time, and it was agreed it was a better idea she would come to Stockholm instead of Hong Kong as soon as he was back. Then she changed her tone and said,

"I've been meaning to tell you, the guy you presented to me."

"Douglas?"

"Yeah it's going well, I mean, really well."

"Oh yeah? What does well mean?"

"I don't know. We've been seeing each other regularly, he is nice, you know. He isn't like anyone else I've met. He listens and he is just… easy to be around."

"Okay, alright if you are happy fine with me but go slowly anyhow," he said with a grin she couldn't see. Well that's complicated. The son of Ben of all people. But at the same time, so what, if they are good together I'm not the one to judge anything here. She knows what she is doing.

"You know what, I told him about you."

A beat of silence, a little surprised John said, "what do you mean?"

"We sat there in Soho in a nice winebar and I realized how much I need you dad."

John didn't know what to say.

"And told him how much you have given, always does and listen to my stuff."

A small chuckle in his voice, "I'm your dad, I have to," he said with a warm grin she can almost hear.

"Well… I just wanted you to know."

"That's good. And I also need you."

After these words a silence hang in the air for a moment. They ended the call, feeling an unspoken warmth and connection.

Looking out, watching hundreds of skyscrapers that were alight, he deduced they were filled with people making deals thanks to the Internet 24/7. Whilst taking in the immensity of Hong Kong he wondered if the Chinese would take over completely, eliminating freedom of speech and what the English called the Order of the Law. The people of Hong Kong were obviously aware that dark days might come. This place will be very different when the Chinese steamroller takes over in a more definite way. Those mandarins in Beijing are afraid that the freedom of Hong Kong might spread to the whole of

China. What was astonishing, was how China thanks to the reforms carried out by Deng Xiaoping had gradually led China away from a planned economy and Maoist ideologies, opened it up to foreign investment and technology, turning China into one of the world's fastest-growing economies. Deng had instituted decentralized economic management and flexible long-term planning to achieve efficient and controlled economic growth. Freed industrial enterprises from the control and supervision of the central government and gave factory managers the authority to determine production levels and to pursue profits for their enterprises with an astonishing result.

Standing on the balcony he had a sense an epiphany was emerging, not a lightning bolt of clairvoyance, more a scrap of an unexpected insight came about, an intuitive perception he hadn't recognized before, like identifying and old friend he hadn't given due consideration and now identified. Previously when he had made efforts for a personal introspection, he didn't come up with a satisfactory rational and not captured an answer that hold water. Perhaps watching the immensity of Hong Kong being so far away from his own shores, provided the means and created the condition to a conclusion. This inspiration of sorts, clarified he had been a lone wolf for many years and carried out his undertakings according to the wind without a clear direction, nor defined goals. At the same time, on the positive side, he didn't fudge the obstacles, believing that by sheer strength and positivism he could climb whatever mountain there was to mount. But evidently it requires more than that to succeed and have a satisfactory life. Yes, he had made friends, had good jobs but there was no integrity in his acts, he was running in the dark, not a fixed objective. And more importantly, it explained why he had left Sweden that fateful time in his life. He had been unanchored. A young man without a family, friends yes but no girlfriend. In dogs-land, no collar. By and large no girlfriend had been by his side, just a few flings, no real hook-up grounding him before going to Madrid. Nothing had held him back. He knew he was more complete when with someone, which didn't mean he couldn't be alone. For him it was like playing golf alone which he had done but not to be compared to share the days with a playmate, which was his natural element to swim in. He went back to Jasmine who was awake.

"Who did you talk to?"

"My daughter."

"How old is she?"

"Nineteen."

"We could be friends."

"That would be nice."

"Are you a good dad?"

"We are very close."

"Do you have a photo of her?"

He took his mobile and showed her.

"She looks like you."

"We are a bit alike yeah."

"You miss her?"

"Always."

She understood he meant it.

"I read that book you mentioned about a Chinese woman and an American journalist," said Jasmine.

"Did you like it?"

"Very much but not the ending. There are some similarities to the heroine's life's and us."

"I know," said John.

The tale in the book was a beautiful love-story with a sad ending. John thought that the only ones who would really like a story like that were those who had been in a similar situation. It was for those who had felt the big one and who had sacrificed their love for reasons they couldn't dominate.

"Is this, I mean us, a Hugh Grant-film where they end up together in spite of everything?" she said.

"Everything?"

"You know what I mean."

"I don't know," John answered, conscious that there were decisions to be made in the very near future. There was a new stone in his shoe, the mysterious bank account in Tallinn, and that was a challenge which demanded his attention.

CHAPTER 31

Waking up after a good night's sleep, they had breakfast in a coffee bar nearby. They shared a sandwich of ham and cheese.

Jasmine had tea and John strong black coffee. Their conversation from the night before hung over them like a menacing cloud but they didn't let it show.

"Are we good?"

"I'm good," she answered looking in his eyes.

"It was nice last night."

"You make me happy," she said not offering a detailed wordings of how and why, more of a factual confirmation.

"As all the other times, it was perfect."

"No news from your spy-friend?"

"Not yet, but he is supposed to be here in Hong Kong at any moment." She took his hand, gave him a short kiss and raised, "have to work now, give me a call," and she was off to the hotel. While walking back to the apartment, he concluded that after yesterday's stint in a prisoncell inside China, losing his future job and that Jasmine was black-mailed by what might be thugs from the Triads anything could happen. Back in the apartment John lay down and tried to sleep but couldn't. The fear to face his karma and its ending robbed him the peace of slumbering.

In the afternoon John picked up Jasmine to go and see his grandmother in Kowloon. They would meet her at a place called the Pacific coffee-bar. Jasmine's grandmother stood outside waiting when they arrived, found a table in the shade, a typical warm humid day in Hong Kong and they sat down. She was gray-haired, combed in classical way but an unmistakable vanity was perceptible in the dress and the bag she had under her arm. She spoke good English mixed with Chinese. She had penetrating intelligent eyes which took aim at John, measuring him up. Meeting a Chinese grandmother who had once worked for the CIA was intriguing and could perhaps offer notions of his lover's nature. John noticed the respect and love Jasmine had towards her grandmother. It said a lot about Jasmine and her care towards her people.

"Nice to meet you" John began.

The woman just looked at John and then at Jasmine and said, "you like her?"

Dumbfounded by this very direct question, John fumbled with what to answer but recovered and openly smiled, "Of course I do."

"I can see it,"

Her grandmother said something in Chinese.

"She likes your eyes and wonder if they are green."

"You like Hong Kong?" asked Jasmine's grandmother.

"Very much."

"What are your plans here in Hong Kong?"

"I'm trying to close a deal for a job."

"Here in Hong Kong?

"No, it's for Europe."

With a worried look she looked at Jasmine.

"Whatever you do, don't lie to her," which reminded John of another woman who had expressed the same a few days ago.

"I won't," he said.

"Jasmine has told me a lot about you and what you did after the war."

"And what do you think about it?"

"It sounds fascinating," he said this without thinking, sounding stupid qualifying her heroic interventions as fascinating helping refugees over the border from China.

"You can't imagine, it was horrible and hard."

"I would like to know more about it."

"That's forgotten now."

Although not forgotten by everybody, John thought. Clearly Jasmine's grandmother wasn't aware of the danger she was in. They talked about everyday things for a while but eventually it was obvious the old woman was tired and wanted to retire.

"We'll go with you," said John.

"Don't you worry it's just a few blocks to my apartment. I've walked a lot of in my life."

"Hope to see you again soon."

"You are not a gambler no, you don't look like one?"

John wondered where she got that idea.

"Actually, we are now going to the Jockey Club and the horse-racing" said John

"Be careful what you got, don't waste it," she said with a glance on Jasmine. "Be a good man and take care of her."

"I'll do my best."

"Maybe we meet again," she said resting her hand on Jasmine's forearm with a touch of care then she turned and left them walking slowly but steadily.

"She likes you."

"How do you know?"

"I just know."

"If the eyes tell a person's character, she seems intelligent and penetrating, she almost looked through you," said John.

"She is astute and tough I couldn't do what she did."

"In extraordinary situations one's true character come to light, like golf," John said laughing.

"You always know how to turn a coin."

"Golf is in many ways like life, it gets the best or the worst out of you."

CHAPTER 32

After this encounter they went to the Jockey Club to watch the horse races as Ben had provided two invitations, if not it would be impossible to enter due to strict rules of membership. The Jockey Club is one of the oldest institutions in Hong Kong for racing and betting, this evening it was crowded to the hilt. They went out to the terrace when David Lang appeared and smiled to Jasmine in recognition of beauty.

"You like gambling John?"

As ever John was amazed how some people were able to remember names.

"No, I'm not a gambler," answered John.

"You should try it perhaps tonight is your lucky night."

"Any inside advice of which horse?"

"Put your money in race number three, my horse is running, his name is Random Fast."

"I like the name."

"Thinking of staying long in Hong Kong?"

"No idea to be honest."

"But you work with Dunbar?"

"Yeah, that's what it seems."

"With this beautiful lady you should stay forever, there are a lot of opportunities in this city for a man with ambition."

"But things are changing here I believe." John said it as a question.

"They can't quash seven million people is my view."

"I hear it depends on who will govern in Beijing."

"True, that's the big question and if they would take over everything many of us would move."

"Like Singapore or Taiwan?"

"Or Canada," said Lang with his perpetual smile.

At that moment a man approached them, dressed in grey flannels and blazer, smoothly silver-haired, self- confident and slick. Clearly a British specimen from the empire. He exuded the confidence that goes with the entitled classes and public-school education.

"What are you talking about David," he asked with typical upper-crust accent that said it all.

"The future."

"Forget that, enjoy, Carpe Diem. Spend your money while you can."

"I'm worried about it."

"As long as this institution is safe nothing will happen," the man spoke sentence-like.

"I'm worried about the seven million living here, what will happen to them, I'm not worried about the billionaires or the cronies, they will take their money and go elsewhere."

"Hong Kong is too important, too big. Sorry I haven't presented myself, my name is Christopher McFarlane." It seemed he believed John and Jasmine would know who he was.

"I'm the man in charge here let's say." His mobile sounded and he excused himself and left them.

"Those British, lots of education but no manners. He is the director of the Jockey Club."

"I'm going to bet on your horse, I'll be back in a minute," said John. It took some time to fix the betting and while he was walking back to Jasmine after having followed Lang's advice and for a second, he observed Jasmine from a distance and was raptured.

"I've followed your advice and put my money on the one you mentioned."

"Never trust the owner of the horse."

"Betting is considered more serious than the lottery in Hong Kong," said Jasmine.

"Lottery is too risky," added David and laughed, the charm personified, perfectly dressed in a Chinese outfit

"Nice to meet you, hopefully we meet again," he said and left.

They stood from a distance watching the race and it was impossible to know who was in the lead or not. The sound level was enormous, everybody shouting in the hope their horse they had bet on was in the lead. When the riders and horses finally arrived at the finish, Jasmine saw Random Fast in the lead.

"You won," she said laughing out loudly.

She was right, Random Fast won and they went to collect his bets.

"Luck with the help of inside information, I should come every day."

"How much did you win?"

"Five times what I spent."

"You are a lucky guy."

"Not always, I was once in Monte Carlo, found a table of roulette, nervously put my bet on number fourteen, three times, with a Carré and lost everything."

"Was it much?"

"Not really, I played where the poor tourists played, no big deal."

"Are you a gambler?"

"No, never buy Lotto's or gamble really."

He cashed almost 1,000 Hong Kong Dollars.

"What do you want to do?"

"Shall we go and see the Peak?"

"Yes, in the night it's beautiful, let's go."

Another cab and off they went to Peak Tower station. At that point they took a tram to reach the Peak. The journey uphill was a visual experience, skyscrapers glided past at what appear to be impossible angles while the tram makes its ascent. The angle upwards was very steep so when John tried to stand straight, he almost fell which made all the other passengers laugh at him. Once they reached the top the view was astonishing, an enormous number of skyscrapers, all lit up it seemed, it was overwhelming.

"It's unbelievable what they have done here, they must have rather good architects."

"Lots of people have contributed."

"It's the most amazing view I've ever seen."

"And with me."

"What makes it so wonderful is thanks to you," he said looking into her eyes.

"Don't look at me like that."

"I'm not playing with words, not playing at all, it's damn serious."

"But you will leave soon, again."

"Do you believe in this, in us?"

"I don't know, I only know I want to be with you."

"I'm too old for you," he said with unusual sincerity.

"I don't care about your age, I care about other things."

"Like what?"

"Your good humor for example."

"Would you consider moving from Hong Kong?"

"I have already thought about it, even before you came into my life."

"London?"

"New York maybe, if I would get a visa. I could work at the Mandarin in New York."

With her attributes she would get a visa wherever she applied, John thought.

"I could but will you love me wherever it would be?"

"Why would I love you here and not there?"

"Because it's different, me in Sweden?"

"Of course, when there is intention," and he stopped.

"I'm not so sure, I'd miss my family."

They spent a while up at the Peak and decided to go down again.

"Sleeping with your grandmother or with me," John suggested with a smile.

"Tonight? With you."

They arrived at the apartment with an urge to be together physically. John went directly to the refrigerator and opened a bottle of champagne. When turning, she stood in front of the lamp creating a silhouette effect of her body, the sensuality of her legs, seemingly without nothing on a part of her high heels. John just looked, fumbling with the bottle. He interpreted her act as an implied invitation, she knew how much he liked what he saw. It was a sexual display so natural they were surprised how instinctive it had become. The attraction was complete and therefore love-making was the catalyst for their way of expression.

CHAPTER 33

Invariably aware a decision about their relationship needed to be made soon, they spent the days tightly together disconnected from the world. There was no word from Ben nor Wellington. No plans, improvising in and around Hong Kong, stopping here and there, going to the bars for a drink or a bite. If a cloud appeared in their mood, they brushed it off with a drink at the first bar or intimate stuff, keeping the real world at distance. As a city it was a theatre of perfection but it wasn't Paris in John's opinion. They felt on top of people they happen to come across, listening to conversations about trivialities like buying refrigerators or a dog. They didn't have such mundane banalities, they were in an invisible cloud of romance and passionate love. Jasmine's unconditional commitment made their time together so complacent and relaxed, never a rejection or reluctance. The more he saw her, the more beautiful she became. Despite her extraordinary attraction, it didn't make him undeterred and he hadn't lost his senses, but it stupefied him how beauty affects and a bust line alter spirits and your frame of mind. It surprised him she didn't seem to be aware of her female charms.

The next day Jasmine suggested they should take a boat-trip around the Hong Kong islands and have a picnic. They found a shop and bought bread, cheese, ham and brought a bottle of wine from the refrigerator in his flat. Went to Victoria Harbor, where there were announcements of ferry trips to the nearby islands. They decided on a ferry called the Shining Star, hopped on the boat and found seats on the open deck. The route began taking them eastwards under giant bridges, indicating heavy traffic and movements of merchandise. After all Hong Kong was one of the biggest seaports in the world. The trip would take a bit over an hour, so John lied down in Jasmine's knees and rested his worried mind and succeeded to doze off. They arrived at a little port and began to search for a place for their picknick. Finally, they saw what could suit their interest; a little hill which gave a view over the sea close to a tree giving shade. A tranquil place and they sat down with their improvised in-handled stuff. It was as hot and humid as ever. She took the stuff they had bought, made a sandwich while he opened the bottle in traditional manner where men open the wine-bottle and women fixed the food.

"This is like a painting of Monet," said John.
"I prefer Renoir's, his paintings are livelier, more realistic."
"I was once in Paris at Jeu de Paume and saw when all the impressionist paintings were in one place."
"We could go to Paris together."
John brushed away a thought about his last time in Paris with Marianne. There was too many Paris in his life.
"Do you think that you can love in different ways," she asked.
"You mean different kinds of love?"
"Or that you really love only once in life?"
"I think there are different kinds."
"You mean passionate or practical love."
"Yeah."
"And which one do you prefer?"
"Passionate."
"And for how long time is it passionate? With time love flies away."

"Time makes it less intense, less hanky-panky."

"Like all men you are obsessed with that."

"Are you good in the kitchen?"

"Are you checking me if I would be a good wife?"

"No, just wondering."

"If I can cook?"

"Yes."

"I do Chinese mostly and what about you, do you cook?"

Not answering her question, he said.

"With time it becomes harder to be impressed."

"I don't know, I'm more easily impressed now, I appreciate the little things more."

"I'm impressed that I'm so impressed by you, but seriously, when I was young, I was by far more excited by things."

"John is being serious, wow."

"And what about you?"

"I'm not so profound as you are but I like the way you talk and express yourself."

That wasn't a profound declaration of sincerity but she seemed to mean what she said and exhibited herself frankly, which was one of the things he liked with her.

"What do you believe in?"

"You mean in God?"

"Yes."

"For me the institutional religion, well I don't know, it's a bit like science fiction when you read the bible very closely."

"You should read Buddha, a lot of wisdom there."

"You tell me what to read and I'll do it."

As all lovers go through with underlined uncertainties, superficial signs are taken seriously therefore when dark clouds began to appear as they were under pressure both internally and in the atmosphere, they decided to go back to Hong Kong. They had talked well but they circled around their fire and the doubts of the future. There was a rising awareness of the impossibility of their union, filled with nuanced sadness, not spoken out. Back in Victoria Harbor leaving the boat, it was beginning to rain tempestuously. At that moment three men approached them. Immediately John sensed it wasn't good. He recognized the smallest of them. It was the man from the Triad he had met in that club with Stewart, Ben Dunbar's trouble-making son, in his last trip to Hong Kong. The other two had typical predatory looks, a Triad preferred company. From a distance the man shouted. "Have you seen Stewart?" snapped the Chinese rudely.

"I know you, we've met."

"Yeah,"

John saw the tattoo on the man's right hand, the very same as his guardian in the prison from the other day, as the one who okayed his passport in Stockholm. There was also a tattoo on his face which looked like a way of hiding a scar. This is not coincidence. They are from the same Triad.

"I want to speak to Stewart."

"And why is that, he owes you money?"

"How did you know?"

"You have the look of someone who might be willing to lend money," lied John.

"Don't fuck with me."

"That I won't do."

Passengers from the boat became aware that this gathering wasn't a friendly one. John saw the guy was excited. He seemed to have an internal fight, getting more nervous by the second.

"Stewart owes me money, big money, you tell him to pay not later than tomorrow," now completely wired up.

"I have no idea where he is."

"But you can find him."

"How much money?

"A lot, $250,000."

"Don't think I'll see him."

"But through his father. You are a good friend to the Taipan. "Here is my card and my number, call me or you come with the money to my Club, you know where it is."

John took the card and didn't say anything.

"You understand?"

"Understand what?"

"What might happen if we don't get the money."

"Honestly? I don't."

John understood the menace in case he wouldn't call or appear.

"This isn't my thing" John tried.

"But now it is" he said smiling for the first time and gave Jasmine an appreciated look, "you could work at my place, need a job?"

That last comment made Jasmine look away. It was obvious the man had information and John shouldn't affront the man and said, "I'll see what I can do."

When they left the port hastily wonder-stricken after this incidence John got a message from Wellington;

"Be at the Mandarin at 18.00 hours today."

"What was that all about?" asked Jasmine.

"I imagine Ben's son has undealt business with the guy."

John hadn't met Stewart since the debacle at Wimbledon and he only knew there was a pending judicial matter against him and knowledge of his whereabouts. John sent a message to Ben saying they ought to meet.

"This looks like a conspiracy did you see his tattoo?" said John.

"Yes, he had two small pyramids, same as the ones who came to the hotel."

"If this guy claiming money from Stewart relates to the one who kidnapped Chen and held me captive and with the one who threatened you there is a scheme at play.

"What do you mean?"

"It's rather coincidental, don't you think?"

CHAPTER 34

John met Wellington at the Mandarin. Despite having met just once in London over lunch, they greeted each other as there was a common bond between the two.

"Suppose you don't come to Hong Kong solely to have a chat with me," said John.

"No, there is an English delegation coming for a congress regarding quantum computers, AI and assuring future relations with the mainland."

"And you participate as MI6?"

"To a point, I do travel where things happen, quirks here and there. Now tell me what's going on."

"Maybe because I'm confused by all this but I have a theory."

"Or being clairvoyant."

"There seem to exist too many coincidences."

"You mean random don't the workout?"

"I mean these recent events don't seem to occur accidentally."

"Welcome to my world."

"Do you believe in random?"

"The short answer is no."

"I'm not saying there is guiding hand but too many factors are somehow interlocked."

"Usually they are intertwined, and that's for a reason but yeah, things appear quirky at times."

"That's one way to put it."

"Okay tell me about your adventures."

John made a transcription about the interrogation how it had developed and even brought up the ping-pong match.

"You let the Chinese win?"

"No, I beat him but there is more to this mess I find myself in, Stewart, Ben's son, who was involved in that ugly affair cheating his father, the history of the Gang-of four you know about, might be in a trouble owing money to a Triad-member."

"Go on."

"Well, the man who ran into us, well he rammed us, claims Ben's son is owes him $250,000 and now he wants Ben Dunbar to know about the debt and make him pay it."

"What kind of tattoo was it? Like two pyramids on triangle on his hand?"

"Yes, how did you know?"

"It's my job, it's the Triad version of the trinity, mind, body and spirit, a sign of gang affiliation."

"The same tattoo as my prison guardian and ping-pong partner, they might be related?"

"Probably there is a connection."

"Using me as messenger towards Ben. Perhaps they are linked to Jasmine's threat of Jasmine and the kidnapping of Chen."

"Jasmine?"

"My girlfriend, she works at the Mandarin."

"What about your girlfriend, why is she black-mailed?"

After John told Wellington how Jasmine's grandmother had been assisting the CIA smuggling of refugees to Hong Kong they sat in silence pondering about these events, when a waiter came by and they ordered two beers.

"I'll look into that". In MI6-parlance John assumed that meant something.

"Think about it, you appear spending time with a prominent Tai Pan, who has a partner called Chen. And there is a son with doubtful bedfellows, who apparently is no genius and a gambler. Add to this, you go out with an employee of Dunbar, who's grandmother smuggled refugees from China to Hong Kong. Someone has come up with the conclusion they have leverage kidnapping the partner, black mailing Ben Dunbar while using you as the postman."

"That's it, exactly."

"Summing it up, we are facing distinct scenarios; one is the disappearance of Chen and your interrogation, then you are pursued by a Triad-gang-member which has nothing to do with you personally, more Ben's problematic son and then, the girl and her grandmother, my friend you are immersed in the midst of it."

"Seems I attract danger."

"Maybe they are after the Taipan?"

"That's stretching it or?"

"Considering, Chen has useful information about Dunbar's emporium, years of high-level-connections business-wise in China and Hong Kong."

"Incidentally, what do you make of this guy Nabokov who helped me out."

"Better you should know it, he is our guy."

"He is MI6?"

"Yes."

Now it dawned on him, he had treated John as a friend and warned him about the Russians.

"But he is Russian, he is not supposed to be on our side."

"He changed sides."

"And you trust him?"

"Completely, he has family in England, wife and two beautiful girls living the perfect life in Chelsea."

"Maybe he has a double life."

"People change, Nabokov was a convinced communist but began to see another side when he was on missions in the west."

"Isn't it always like that?"

"More often than you would imagine. In the end it's either money or the honey-trap that make some change sides, the exception of the rule is for higher reasons."

"Honey-trap?"

"Sex, you use a relation to get information, perfect for extortion and black mail."

Wellington looked at his papers and one more time changed venue. "Hong Kong has become a spying hub. If you look around, who are the ones spying on whom? That woman sitting over there looking innocently in her magazine? Or the two gentlemen having small talk? The waiter arrived with the beers, and they cheered without a word. "Perhaps the waiter is a spy" he said laughing.

"Are you a known figure so to speak? I mean do they know you are MI6?"

By the word *they*, John meant the enemies whoever they were. He imagined the enemies consisted of the Russians or the Chinese, sometimes added with some crazed over-zealous populist regime, before they went the whole way and became dictators and completely corrupted and afraid of their shadows spied on anything that moved. "Probably, anyone sitting here could be a spy, FBI or GRU. And if they don't who I am, they are incompetent" said Wellington.

If it was what he had just heard and they see me with this guy, I'm a marked man, thought John getting nervous by the minute.

"The influence of Russian money, through oligarchs here in Hong-Kong, due to a large extent American sanctions have turned the tables, and we must safeguard the citizens of Hong Kong and our own interests" said Wellington.

"Looks contradictionary."

"It's morally and effectively an impossible situation."

"You mean these Hong Kongers trusted you and now they feel abandoned."

"In a nutshell yes."

"Wow," said John suddenly laughing. "I go from one crazy thing to another. I come here for a job, lose it in a jiffy cause of a kidnapping, while I have encounters and friendly chats with spies."

"What happened to your job?"

"This thing with Chen led to Dunbar think we must postpone it for the moment. Buddha was right, in the end, I lose everything."

"Are you talking about his search for two chickens at the time?"

"Exactly," said John sipping on his beer.

Wellington changed his position took away his papers and leaned forward as men often do when they are to say a confidential big truth or advice.

"So, what shall we do with the drunken sailor and that girl of yours?

"You mean I'm the sailor?"

"If it's the one in the lobby, she is a fine piece, shamefully beautiful I must say."

"She is."

"We'll find out something, I better get going and do some check-ups."

"And if the Chinese put pressure on her?"

"She could always go to England, she wouldn't have problems there."

"But if something happens to her now or her family?"

"We must work fast on it."

"Meaning?"

"We always do our best to protect our citizens."

What that meant exactly wasn't clear.

"Could you be more specific?"

"We have friends here, don't forget this was ours for 150 years."

John looked around the room they were sitting in.

"As the Chinese say, one should live in interesting times."

"The disappearance of Chen is big for Dunbar."

"We don't know yet if he ran away or on his own."

"They have worked together over decades."

"Doesn't mean anything, I've seen men turn sides in the most incredible ways."

"One never knows," said John, as his own dilemma suddenly popped up in his mind of how to find a solution of his own affairs.

"Give it time to absorb all this, don't forget you are your father's son. I think you have sound instincts."

This simple comment without any concrete content or solution fell into fertile ground in the ruminating vineyard of John's mind. When they had met in London and John was asked to be a supporting kind of agent or as he had called it, a pigeon stool for the MI6, his vanity has jumped a bit but he didn't feel secure if a relation with a hefty spy- organization like the MI6 was a good choice. Watching Wellington's calm manner and the ease he carried himself and seemingly in control John wondered how he would behave in a more physical situation.

"Are you trained in physical activities like fights?", asked John

"I have black belt in karate."

"Guns?"

"I've done my bit," he answered with the typical English understatement. Like when you ask a Brit, do you sail? And the answer; I've done a bit yes, after having sailed around the world, alone. "I've only been fighting with rackets", murmured John wistfully. After all this was a man of the secret world, a high-level representant of the old empire's secret world with their style and manners. He wore a casual jacket like John's with a white shirt no tie. Ties were out. John didn't see him dressed in the oriental black-arts-pyjama used for fighting. John took a second look at the man and discovered he was well trimmed, and movements more like a cat's, a thing he had taken for servile at first. He had charm, helped being steeped in wealth and privilege. A man exacerbating so much charm it became a peril. Would be interesting to see him getting annoyed. His eyes had a determination you felt absorbed by.

"Then we are safe then," said John smiling.

"Your father knew how to handle himself in a fistfight I've heard."

"Until you are in the thick of it you never know I suppose."

"Some run some fight."

"And you?"

"I stay."

"And fight?"

"Without doubt, I say as old boxers, it's easier to take a hit when you see it coming, therefore I plan."

This thought of a constant war-like situation was absolutely unknown to John. He had never been truly tested in a real crisis.

"John let me know if anything turns up, I'll be watching you," he said with his smile showing perfect white teeth. "Can you take of the bill, I have to run now."

"I'll put it on the expense account," said John.

"Can't agree more," he said.

John wrestled with the decision to tell Wellington what Erik had asked him to do. The strain had gnawed him ever since, leaving restless and in desperate need of release. Finally, he told Wellington about the mysterious bank account in Estonia and his need to go there. Wellington raised an eyebrow and said, "That same information has just reached us, and we were thinking of acting. The rumor is there's a document tied to the old spy ring your father was chasing—something that could shake the foundations of the English establishment."

"And if it's a set-up?"

"I shouldn't tell you this but there could be a cover-up."

"What do you mean?"

"It's possible certain persons within our community are complicit in this and want the document to be destroyed. They knew what your father was looking for."

"And

"It's possible but if the document is real, it could blow the lid off the Cambridge five-scandal."

"And if it's not? I walk into Tallinn and never walk out."

"That's the risk, John. The MI6 wants that document… badly, And your father's reputation, hinges on it."

Hearing this John felt a surge of emotion, his throat tightening as he struggled to find the right words.

"I can understand what you are going through," he said quietly. "Your father's legacy is a heavy weight to carry but this might be the chance to set things right."

"I'd like that."

"I'll come back to you again about all this."

They stood up, a manly handshake and Wellington went down the stairs where John saw Jasmine in the lobby at a distance. Wellington passed her without stopping, made an informal military salute which Jasmine saw without understanding the meaning of. She then looked up and saw John. She made a sign like what-was-that-all-about, and John just smiled.

After fixing the bill John sent a text message to Jasmine.

"Let's go and do something."

"You want to see the Big Buddha?"

"If you want, yes," he wrote unenthusiastically.

"Give me an hour."

John decided for a refreshing walk without a clear ambition just to clear his mind as the saying goes. No mobile-watching just allowing your legs and thoughts to wander and see where they take you and where they lead you. His creed that sheer optimism could mend life's obstacles but now he discovered it requires more. Life isn't just pedaling on a bicycle. If you stop, you fall which is true, but you need a plan and John didn't have one.

Whatever his stance, as he understood things, it was a Hemingwayesque take, or Kiplingesque angle, in that you need courage, stand up for your beliefs and act with coherence as close to the truth as possible. His conclusion, though simplistic, was that if life was a kind of battle, you fought for the good and must win.

CHAPTER 35

John and Jasmine met on the backside of the Mandarin, a place which looks like Times Square in the HongKong version. A sensory overload, a constant hum of vehicles, buses and trams fill the air, a raw energy and vibrant chaos of Hoing Kongs-urban life. They were trying to figure out how to go, she suggested, "We can take the ferry and then catch a bus."

They found what they needed and after a five-minute brisk walk boarded the ferry. While they rode together, she turned to him and asked.

"Who was that man you met in the hotel?"

John gave Jasmine a short version of what had been said, skipping any delicacy that could be negatively understood. His answer seemed to reassure her and they relaxed and enjoyed the quiet trip, hand in hand. It took them an hour to reach the Big Buddha monument and the adjoining monastery. It's one of the biggest bronze Buddha statutes in the world, thirty-four meters high situated almost 500 meters above sea level. They were in no mood to climb the 268 steps taking instead a scary cable car. The view over the ocean and its islands was magnificent. Although John preferred much more the view from the Peak taking in the enormity of Hong Kong than this one. The monument meant to symbolize the harmony between man, nature and his faith. They saw an inscription; *Do not dwell in the past, do not dream of the future, concentrate the mind on the present moment.*

"That's what we all should do," said John.

"Easy to say."

"The view is good, but I prefer the peak."

They went to a bar close to the place where tourists were busy taking photos.

"Hey, we have to leave, now, the ones that threatened me, they are here" said Jasmine nervously when John was ordering a beer.

"What?"

"Trust me," and took his hand firmly, "Look over there to the right." John saw the two men she meant. They stood out among the tourists looking like heavy-weight boxers, one with a tiny tattoo of triangles on the forehead, broad-casting the allegiance. A permanent statement, visually declaring where your loyalties are without saying a word. John got it and avoided making too big movements, acknowledging that they had seen them.

"Let's take the cable back."

He grasped her hand firmly and skillfully navigated through the crowd, determined to reach the cable car and return swiftly. The men that apparently were chasing Jasmine were nowhere to be seen, allowing John and Jasmine to board the cable car without their followers. Inside the cable John tried to fix an Uber, which was difficult being in the air. They didn't need one, a taxi stood by waiting for tourists who had gotten tired of the views. Well inside the cab John said,

"Wow that was lucky."

"I told you, I'm afraid" said Jasmine looking shaken.

Wellington had told John to inform him of any foreboding events and decidedly this was one. John texted a to the point message to Wellington; *"Have a situation, being followed."*

"Where do we go?"

"Let's go to Kowloon."

"Hungry?"

"Not much but you are as you ask me."

"This guy Wellington will help us."

"Is he the real MI6?"

"Yes, and he has resources I'm sure."

When they arrived and left the taxi John noticed how different from the Finance district this was, here every neon-light was in Chinese. The area was boisterous, buzzed with energy of restaurants, the chatter of the crowds and the calls of street-vendors and the aroma of Chinese cooking with smells of spices and grilled meats.

"It's the umbrella movement," said Jasmine.

The crowd was not any crowd, it was huge, with megaphones chanting excitedly slogans in Chinese and horns blaring.

"What do they say?"

"It's about freedom, they want democracy."

"Maybe we should join them," said John with a grin.

Concerned about the possibility of the demonstration turning dangerous, Jasmine decided to find a place to eat, escaping the potential of violence

"No no, we better find a place and go inside."

John watched Jasmine exam the various nouns with curiosity: He had no idea what they symbolized or represented.

"Let's try this one, it says Happy and long life."

"Then this is it."

The restaurant was almost as rowdy as the protesters outside. Well inside having found a table and sat down. John began to give a bigger account about his talks with the MI6-man, after all she might be in real danger.

Again, she relaxed seemingly reassured by this. She began to do the ordering knowing John's tastes by now. They were served wine and John watched how she took her glass and drank. Her hands were as delicate as her way of approaching her lips partaking in a few drops of wine with grace.

"This means I might have to leave Hong Kong, and I don't want that" she said in a matter of fact-way.

"That's' a bit early to conclude, Wellington might be of help."

"How come you know these people?

"I told you, just before I went to Hong Kong, I met him in London. He is, as it seems, quite high up in the MI6."

"Do you trust him?"

"Actually, I met his Swedish colleague or more exact a collaborator of sorts who was the one who recommended me to call him."

"But is he trustable?"

"For the moment yes."

"Wait a minute, you meet spies in London and Stockholm?

"Strangely enough yes."

"Are you the one I think you are or are you using me?"

"Why would I do that? I'm as surprised as you are."

"How come, a Swede out of nowhere is so friendly with a Taipan in no time?"

"You don't mean that."

"No I don't," she said smiling with a little smile, as if embarrassed. The food came in and they dug in at the plates but not as usual or with hunger. A disturbing conclusion crystalized in his thoughts. I should leave Hong Kong and start anything in calm Stockholm. Forget the whole thing, Hong Kong, Ben and Jasmine. Further, Hong Kong was losing its strength. China was taking over in all spheres and the tycoons and friends would leave when things would get ugly. I'm in the wrong place at the wrong time.

They sat in silence, inevitably absorbed in thoughts of the recent events, caught in whirlwinds of what ifs, their future together hung in the balance. The picture was dire. She, a young woman from Hong-Kong, harassed by the Triads. John, a man from Stockholm, without a job since that opportunity had faded. Two worlds utterly disparate that wanted to be fused but couldn't.

"Is it possible for us" she asked. "I can't leave just like that, I have family here."

It was the very first time she showed a sign of hesitation or was it an excuse of some kind?

"I just can't leave, where to? What about my grandmother?"

"What about coming with me to Stockholm?"

John noticed an alarming look in her eyes.

"What you are saying is you are going back to Stockholm."

"Probably, would you consider it?"

"Seems very far from here."

"Madrid?"

"Sounds warmer at least."

"We ought to try something."

"Try is not enough."

"I mean, seek an option."

"Do you know what you are saying? It could be a mistake."

"We shouldn't worry making a mistake before you have a chance to make one," he said earnestly.

"You always find the right words," she said and took his hand.

There had been a tiny reluctance a moment ago but now she seemed to be her normal self again.

"I'm trying to figure this out and it's not easy."

"It wasn't meant to be easy" said John which sounded too cliché-like.

"John I really would like to, but I see too many obstacles."

So far Jasmine hadn't at any point hidden her feelings, even if no wordings of bombastic romanticism but at every moment, she had been committed in body and spirit, perhaps factual-like but no obtrusive side-comments. Until now.

"I think we could do it."

"You say this, when you are with me, what happens when you are in Stockholm, and I begin to long for Hong Kong?

"Why would I change?"

"You might prefer a Swede instead of a little Chinese woman with lots of baggage?"

"Jasmine, you aren't any little woman."

"You are an attractive man and you'll find your way without me."

"Me attractive, what about you? You are the definition of an attractive woman." Suddenly, he was jealous,

"There would be a long queue of predators to take my place".

"Don't say those things."

"And if I stay here?"

"Do you really mean what you are saying?"

"One takes decisions and live by them, so far, we have been let's say physical with no barriers in mind or body, I could go on doing what we are doing."

"Meaning?

He didn't have to answer as his mobile vibrated.

"Hi," it was Ben.

"Hi Ben,"

"You said we ought to meet, would you mind come by my house,"
said Ben

John hesitated, "I'm with Jasmine, we are in Kowloon right now,"

"Great why don't you both come?"

"Okay, come to your house," he said looking inquiringly at Jasmine
who made signs of a confirmation, we can do that.

CHAPTER 36

After this brief telephone conversation John fixed the bill and they went out looking for a cab.

"What does he want?"

"Don't know, but this might be good a moment to tell him about the tattooed guy and Stewart."

"I think he likes you a lot and trusts you."

"And do you?"

"I do but not sure I should."

They couldn't say when it started but there had been a shift in their minds during the last hours. Even though more mesmerized of her than ever, a thought had been growing in John's mind, it became evident, their affair was doomed. In the taxi they sat in thoughtful silence. There were too many incognitos, so many unknown charters, added with a possible danger for Jasmine of being taken away to a scrubby place behind the hills in deep China. They arrived at Bens' magnificent house and saw it in almost daylight this time and it was outrageously beautiful, surrounded by what appeared as haphazardly planted trees but if you looked keenly there must have been a plan. They were led through the heavy iron portals by a security-guard to the residence. John noticed the discreet cameras of vigilance on the walls, probably much needed for unwelcome intruders. The absurdity of being a Taipan meant you lived in a bastion hiding behind a bulwark of fences. Jane opened the door once, no butler this time.

"You look like a Hollywood-couple, said Jane, which John didn't understand what it meant.

Ben was struggling to get out of a chair and muttered, "we must change these bloody low seats it makes me feel like an old boxer who lost and tries to fight when it's useless."

"You need to go to a gym and get yourself a PT," said Jane.

"You wanted to see me I understand but before I want to clarify one thing." Again, John noticed Ben's deference towards him. "Listen I've been unfair to you. I've dragged you to Hong Kong and now we might have to stop our joint-venture, at least for the moment and I don't want to let down a friend," said Ben looking at John.

"That's nice of you to say," said John as he wasn't sure what to answer.

"I want you to know we'll find a solution of some sort."

Jane took Jasmine by the arm and said, "let the boys talk and I'll show you around. I'll fix a drink for you, what do you want?"

"Yes, anything," said Ben, "champagne, whisky."

"Anything? Well, a glass of champagne would be fine."

Ben opened a bottle of Taittinger and gave a filled glass to John. "You remember that Wellington I told you about, he is here in Hong Kong."

"And what does this gentleman think about our situation?

"He says, the Russian who fixed me out and we met at the Chinese Club is working for MI6."

"Wow, you see, I'm surprised because I'm too old. Lately everything surprises me. I'm surprised that I don't care so much about working anymore, surprised I want to wind down and pass the baton."

"Well, perhaps now it's the time to enjoy, take out the prize of what you have done," said John trying to be convivial, seeing the state Ben was in. "Anyways, this man might be of help to the case."

Ben was oblivious to what John had said.

"You see, in my age you are conscious of the finish line, a constant evaluation of what was done or not has been done. When I left my wife, I lost my kids for years, their mother hid them and the result is this, a corrupt son going out with a stripper, trying to cheat his own father and now my daughter in Paris having doubts again. All that crap about finding herself, instead of act upon what you are given, as good as you can."

Not easy to comment on decided John and stayed silent.

"My daughter is lukewarm. She is not a part of my life and that hurts." John knew perfectly well about those things he had been there himself with his daughter.

"What's her argument?"

"Don't know really. "Probably, in her view, I'm callous."

Ben sat in silence for a while.

Once more John sensed Ben had a strong confidence in John and needed to talk away with someone. Likely when you are at the top of the pole, managing a vast business you can't talk like this to anyone. Perhaps he had lost the illusion of the jolts of ups and downs in business, the jarring of the rough and tumble as the leader of his emporium. At seventy-two, with a son who had betrayed him, a daughter who didn't talk to him, an important player in a business where there were sharks swimming around waiting to see you tired and get a bite of you must be a tough one. The situation reminded John of what he had studied during University and about Aristotle, about men in power. The responsibility makes them more serious. Older men with long experiences of good and bad, discern and accept that life is too often a bad business, cynically anticipating danger compared to the young, who trusts everybody as they haven't yet been cheated when time is not spent in memory but in expectations.

Seeing a giant in business like Ben in this melancholy state in his palace is a stark contrast to how is portrayed to the outside world. Regularly he was seen as a big brass smiling to the camera dressed in black-tie or sitting in a hefty sailing boat at the rudder, a man in full but when for some strange concoctions, if you see the very same man in another context, outside a court having been accused of felony or a tax- evasive, your view shifts John thought.

"Everything is so many years ago nowadays."

As if from reverie, Ben was back returning to their original topic.

"This Wellington is he here because of this damn quantum-computer thing?"

"That's what he says, people coming from the Government with the idea of saving future investments in China and Hong Kong at the same time." "Yeah, as a matter of fact we'll have a reception for the bigwigs at the Mandarin tomorrow 17 o'clock, you should come and present this gentleman to me."

"He is a nice fellow and a smart cat or whatever you call them in spy's argot."

John was pondering what to say to Ben about his son and decided to spread it out.

"There is another thing. We got a visit or more exact, an encounter with two Chinese guys a few hours ago."

"And?"

"It's about Stewart."

"They want money?"

"A Chinese guy, I met on my last trip who owns the strip-club *The Boss*, says Stewart owes him money, $250,000 . His name is Koo Long."

Ben didn't look surprised, neither of the fact nor the amount of money.

"What has this to do with you?"

"Basically nothing, he told me to say out the word, that is to you."

"Smells blackmailing and then he added; "I might be old, but I don't take blackmailing. "We should go and see this guy and see what he wants" he said with a sudden vigor as if the fighting-spirit had returned to him.

"Are you sure? These guys are no choirboys."

"Me neither," said Ben. "Let's get going."

The blackmail news put Ben in a fighting mood, almost a relief to John and he saw a hint of what Ben must have been like.

"Okay, what about the girls?"

"They'll come with us."

They finished their drinks and told Jane and Jasmine what they were up to.

"You follow us downtown and wait for us outside or nearby somewhere, I'll think of something while we drive."

Ben's chauffeur arrived in a discreet Kia.

"Can't go in a Bentley to those places," was Ben's comment with a chuckle.

They arrived at the same Club John once visited with Stewart and John had met his stripper-girlfriend. "Take them to *the Old Man*. It's a famous bar inspired on Hemingway and exquisite cocktails." We'll be there in a jiffy."

"Where are you going in the middle of the night?"

"I'll explain later afterwards."

"You better," said Jane.

After some initial doubts from the bouncer hunks outside of the Club, they were let in. Ben took the lead and went to the bar to ask for Koo Long. The club was full of men of all ages dealing in the mating- business involving money. The girls were dressed in outfits where much of their figures were in the open. Ben and John were approached by two girls of the night catching prey for the evening. Faster than expected the tattoo-man came towards Ben and John.

"This is nice surprise," said the Chinese. "What can I do for you?"

"Let's skip the gibberish, tell me what you want."

"What does that mean?"

"Another word for crap."

"If you say so, your son owes me money. I suppose Steward is your son," he uttered with a smirk. Ben let it pass.

"How much?"

"A lot."

"How much is a lot?"

"Around $250,000."

"And for what reason?"

"I borrowed him money."

"Gambling on horses," said Ben mutely.

"I don't know, probably."

"And you want *me* to pay you?"

"I don't' care who pays me."

"Well, you should, it's not my debt."

Ben hunkered down in silence looking at his shoes, in what seemed a long while, finally, he raised his head scouted the man in front of him and the place and said with half-closed eyes.

"Listen son, I have a deal for you."

"What deal?"

"I can make this club shut."

"I doubt that."

"Don't," said Ben with a firm voice. "First you must prove this is true about my son's debt and if it is, I propose we make a deal. If we then agree, I'll help you to not get caught in dealing with drugs and other stuff we both know about."

The Chinese took in this information and wasn't that tough anymore.

"You have no right to talk to me like that."

"Save it Koo. I need proof."

"I have notes with Steward's signature on."

"Lending money is castigated according to us Christians," said Ben now smiling.

"Shall you say, you are like a bank."

"Trafficking with guns is not well seen by your people."

"I have friends," he said blandly trying to maintain a good composure.

"The question is, who has the strongest friends, you or I? Are yours the ones that decide and strong enough? Hong Kong is changing, I doubt the ones that now governs will tolerate this."

The tattooed man was losing face, a Chinese sin.

"I've tried to reach Stewart without success and I haven't seen him lately."

"Have you asked his girlfriend," intervened John.

"Yes, but she says she doesn't know."

"Is she working here, tonight?"

"I don't know, I'll check," he said with a stupid smile. He left them and came back with the girlfriend stripper dressed according to her job. "Hi," said Ben with a smile trying to be nice.

"You are Stewart's father," she said.

"I certainly am, seen him lately?"

"No, haven't seen him in a week."

"Any idea where he might be? It could be of help if you let us know his whereabouts," said Ben. Meanwhile the Chinese was just looking with harsh eyes.

"He has been talking about Macao lately," she said after what looked like an inner debate.

This piece of news mentioning Macao made Ben look at John as he would understand what it meant.

"Let's go, thank you for your help. I'll come back to you" he said to Chinese, and they were on their way out.

"For sure he is at the Casino, and I know people who can inform me," said Ben while began to leave the place. "Those Triads, I know some from the *We Group*."

Ben quickened his pace and John struggled to keep up.

"They are like Freemason's or the Mafia. A racketing in the shadows, involved in the opium trade since my ancestors. Mao forced them to leave the mainland and so they went to Hong Kong."

Once outside the club, John asked Ben:

"Is it true what you said in there?"

"No, but it seems what I hinted must be true."

"You rammed him like a rugby-player."

They hooked a cab and went to the *Old Man*.

"That was fast, what have you been doing where you didn't want us?" said Jane.

Ben gave a brief account of what had happened and a few details of the place.

"You know those places?" Jasmine asked with dismay.

"I've told you why I was there," said John.

"You didn't call me that night."

"Men," said Jane, "you can't trust them," not looking angry only smiling.

"And what about women are they to be trusted?" asked Ben smilingly.

"More often than men," said Jane.

"Can we order something," said Ben looking out for a waiter.

A man presenting himself as Vladimir. Russians all over the place thought John.

"What can I do for you sir?"

"What do you want," Ben asked Jane and Jasmine, adding "I'll have a whiskey on the rocks."

"Which one please?"

"Whatever you suggest."

"I'll give you a Jura ten years old."

"What do say about two negronis," said Jane looking at Jasmine.

"Okay never had it before."

"It's a bittersweet cocktail, a mix of joy and the sourness of a challenge," said the waiter.

"And you?" without mentioning the sir.

"Whiskey sour."

The drinks arrived and the four of them talked about the sudden turn of events.

"I have some contacts in Macao, tough guys from the old Triads, we kind of respect and trust each other." The visit to the strip-club and what ensued there despite the problem at heart and the problem with his son had put Ben in a good mood. When they were leaving Ben said to John.

"Tomorrow some people from Whitehall are coming to our hotel for a chat. The secretary and a few bigwigs from the government. You should come John and see how these high enders deal with the problem of Hong Kong. 17 o'clock, okay?

"Perfect I'll be there," said John also now more upbeat.

"Your man from the MI6 is coming, will be interesting to hear his thoughts, privately that is."

CHAPTER 37

John and Jasmine went to his apartment with a foreboding feeling and sat down on the terrace. In silence looking over the harbor and its harbor splendor. It was a warm night, you could hear the thrum of the city, a vibrant counterpoint to the quiet intimacy between the two. Below, Hong Kong's dazzling panorama unfolded, lights mirrored in the still water of the harbor. The city had a unique blend of East and West and seemed to infuse the air they breathed, making the moment, this place feel suspended in time.

John had a sudden look on his mobile, read a few mails and a rapid look of the news about Sweden and was struck by a wave of yearning. He longed for listening and speaking in Swedish, the taste of the food and just being there. By all accounts Hong Kong was an amazing place, especially with Jasmine but it wasn't his dominion. John went for the wine and filled two glasses. They sat like two birds on a birch watching something unspecified. It wasn't easy to find the right words for anything.

"What are you thinking?" she asked.

"We have started something without knowing the end."

"It's always like that."

"But it feels so right, to be with you."

"Maybe this is just a wonderful dream and now it's blowing away."

"How can I be so happy with you and still a feeling we won't make it together?"

"When are you going back to Stockholm?"

"Soon, my daughter wants to come".

"Why did this happen to us?"

"I don't have the answer to that," and instead of talking, he took her in his hand, and they went inside. They made love in the most subtle people can do. It had become their natural way of transmitting their love. She was silent afterwards, apparently in her thoughts. He laid without moving, only touched her thigh, doing circling movements with his left hand, a desire to express his love. He was at peace, no doubts, it was perfect, an arcadian stillness you only find when you are fulfilled, a moment you shouldn't forget.

"I love you," she said.

"Me too," he said deeply touched.

CHAPTER 38

At 5 pm the next day, John arrived at the hotel and was led to a secluded area for a gathering hosted by Ben, the Taipan of Hong Kong, to welcome the British delegation. The group consisted of MPs and civil servants, all in pin-striped suits, who viewed this event as a minor inconvenience compared to their real goal: securing lucrative contracts with Beijing. The Secretary, their sharp-eyed leader, greeted Ben with thinly veiled indifference. Ben opened the discussion, emphasizing the importance of strategic investments that would benefit both China and international players. The Secretary, however, seemed focused on mainland opportunities, brushing off concerns about Hong Kong. Ben voiced apprehension about China's increasing control and questioned whether the 1997 Treaty of Joint Declaration, which guarantees Hong Kong's autonomy under the "one country, two systems" principle, would be honored. The Secretary's dismissive attitude suggested that these concerns were of little importance to the delegation. Wellington, sensing the shift in power, raised the issue of China's artificial islands in the South China Sea, warning of their impact on international trade and military dominance. His words made the delegation uncomfortable but didn't sway their priorities. Their focus remained on the potential profits from Beijing, not Hong Kong's autonomy or human rights. As the meeting ended, it became clear that the British delegation saw Hong Kong as a secondary concern, overshadowed by their pursuit of favorable relations with Beijing. Ben and Wellington reflected on the short-sightedness of this approach, recognizing the delicate balance between profit and principle.

"Short-term opportunistic thinking," said Wellington after the reunion.

"A Chinese proverb says two tigers can't share one mountain. Whitehall can't have it both ways," said Ben angrily. "Anyways can we talk a bit?"

"Of course."

They sat down again. A waiter came by and took their orders.

"Can I go the point without going around?"

"Fine with me, I prefer that," said Wellington.

"John told me about you and your line of work which I suppose is needed, do have you any information I'm not aware of and you want to share with me?"

"We are talking about your man Chen I suppose?"

"Yes."

"We are trying to assess what has happened and despite having our man in place, Nabokov, who helped John to get out, we are not sure yet. I'm confident we'll know soon about Chen's whereabouts."

"This Nabokov, the man we met the other day at the China Club," asked Ben, "is MI6?"

"He is ours," said Wellington.

"And he is the one to find out?"

"Among others."

"Why are you so sure you'll find out?"

"We have some leverage to be exercised and to be utilized," answered Wellington.

"I can't even imagine what that can be, or your methods but I'm quite interested in knowing if he has been abducted or ran away by his own will."

"Never any suspicions about his loyalty?"

"You never know a man's motive until it's too late. I know he has family on the other side, but he has come and gone before without trouble."

"How long has he been with you?"

"Over forty years."

"There might be blackmail involved, usually that's the way they operate or one of their methods. When I say they, I mean it could be the Triads."

"What are we to do then?"

"Just wait a few days."

"John, have you informed the gentleman about the threats your girlfriend is receiving?", looking towards John.

"Yes,"

"Actually, we think there is a connection between her and Chen. As it seems, Chen is most probably Jasmine's grandfather," said Wellington.

"What?" said Ben and John in chorus.

"We've found a birth-certificate, which proves he is the father of her mother." This was a bombshell of news.

"Now I see, that's why he always been so nice to her. Chen recommended her for the job at the Mandarin," said Ben.

John didn't know what to think or what to say, this will come as a huge surprise to Jasmine.

"Are you sure? What proofs do you have?"

"The man you met in Shendi, who held you a while had a birth-certificate. Nabokov stole it, how I don't know. I have it here," and took out of his pocket a yellowed paper and gave it to John.

"We have checked and re-checked in our outlet here in Hong Kong and it appears clear. As you know, Chen went to the UK frequently and was under surveillance, seems he made the payments for Jasmine's college. Certain businessmen come under our radar as you might understand."

"Are we all under your surveillance?"

"It depends," replied Wellington. "By all accounts it's pretty obvious Chen and Jasmine's grandmother had an affair."

John looked at the paper, didn't understand a word and gave it to Ben, who read it with an astonished look.

"It looks right. How do we know it's not a fake?"

"We checked and it seems water-tight," said Wellington.

"Now I remember," said Ben, "many years ago he told me about a romance, an affair that couldn't be but I never understood there was more to it. He was miserable for a while but that was it."

"We all have our secrets," said Wellington in a rare moment of sincerity.

Now you are talking, thought John. A waitress came and served three beers.

"Has his kidnapping something to do with Jasmine's grandmother helping refugees over the border?" asked John

"That's what I'm beginning to think. The man who held you is a Triad-member."

"Not a policeman, as he presented himself?"

"For certain no, although they cooperate with the authorities if they will benefit from it. Very commonplace method getting ransom-money harassing and extortion."

"That is why we have been threatened by them."

"My hunch-feeling is there is a design here; Your girlfriend is threatened by what all accounts look like a Triad guy, and thanks to their cooperation with the authorities and by accident or not, he learned about her grandmother and now blackmails her, putting two and two together they kidnap Chen, getting more leverage. Not to forget the man who rammed John yesterday and claimed money your son borrowed, allegedly."

"This whole mess is getting worse by the minute," said John.

"You might have been what triggered it," said Wellington.

"That's plausible," said Ben, they combine Jasmine working at the Mandarin, she is Chen's grand daughter, who helped refugees come to Hong Kong and my genius of a son.

"Both had this tattoo of two pyramids on their right hand."

"Same Triad."

"The only thing I can say, I'm sorry."

"Or maybe it's a blessing in disguise," said Wellington, "as I said, Nabokov is trying to locate Chen."

"What shall we do then?"

"First, we have to find the man, until then nothing is my advice," said Wellington. "We've lost the trail, for the moment."

They finished their drinks and agreed they would be in communication if anything surfaced.

CHAPTER 39

John went to his apartment in need of a nap. He was woken up by the sound of his mobile. There were two messages on his mobile. The first from his daughter; announcing, to his surprise she had found a cheap flight to Stockholm in three days. The second; "come to the Peninsula's rooftop at seven this evening, it's about Chen and Jasmine."

Who the hell is this and how come they have my number? Must have been when he was in that cell in Shendi, and they took his mobile. First things first, so he sent a short message confirming to his daughter. Very much aware he had to leave Hong Kong and Jasmine in just two or three days. This raised his stress level to a maximum level. To the unknown second message he wrote: *who are you and why should I go?*

Short answer: *It's in your interest, come alone.*

John's first reaction was he must inform Wellington but hesitated. The rooftop at the Peninsula is not isolated of people so no danger in that. Nonetheless it would be irresponsible to not let Wellington know. The situation was harrowing.

Okay will be there, he answered after giving it some thoughts of all places they can't abduct at me the Peninsula.

At that moment Wellington called:

"Don't do anything stupid," he said tersely.

"Do what?"

"We have your phone tapped I saw the messages."

John took this in silence, how could he be so utterly stupid and thoughtless.

"I was going to call you", he lied.

"You were? This is no time for heroic stuff, you go and we cover you." Realizing his error John was lost for words. How he would be covered he hadn't a clue but this is MI6, they know these things by now intensely distressed by what was happening. It was 18.00 hours, a cab to the Peninsula with the traffic at this hour would take at least thirty minutes. Left his apartment in a rush and found a cab. After half an hour's drive he entered this legendary hotel and asked for the roof top. Shuddering with excitement he wondered how he was protected. Took the elevator sweating, the adrenaline was at full throttle. Not like when he was going to see Jasmine, this was of another kind, he was scared and bordering on being drunk by his own audacity. The more you sweat the more you get he said to himself observing his own image in the mirrors of the elevator. Just when the doors to the elevator was closing a fat man tried to get in and they almost touched due to the man's girth. He stared at John as if saying, "yeah, I know, I'm fat, so what". Maybe he was from MI6, thought John.

To John's surprise the man from Shendi who had put him in confinement a few hours sat in the bar waiting, now smartly dressed not like a communist caretaker.

"Hi," he said pretty near a smile.

That it was the same man from Shendi calmed John.

"Wow it's you," said John bewildered.

"Does it surprise you?"

"It sure does. You aren't a communist after all."

"At bottom who is?"

"I'm not, never been."

"I didn't tell you but I belong to an old society and we have our own way of doing things."

"And what is that you do?"

"That depends who is asking."

"You mean you belong to a Triad."

"That's none of your business," the man said harshly, "we've got Chen and for your information, he is the grandfather of your girlfriend. We want money and I think you could fix that since we know about her grandmother's interventions with refugees, you pay us, and you get Chen back and we forget."

"I know about her grandfather," which surprised the man.

"How?"

"I just know it."

"Anyway, we want $500,000 ."

"And where do I get that?"

"You talk to your boss?"

"And if he refuses?"

"No Chen, and we might tip the police about the grandmother," he said with a calm expression.

"Do you by any chance know the guy with the strip-club *the Boss*?

"Why do ask?"

"Sorry wrong question, I see what I can do and come back to you." He wondered if Ben wouldn't mind pay the money to get his wingman back sound and safe aware of extremely brutal these Triads were known to be.

"I'll give two days."

"And how are you planning to deliver Chen?"

"Here at the roof-top with a helicopter if not, at an address I'll give you."

"A helicopter?"

"Avoid interference by the police."

"Give me a contact in case I don't succeed or whatever."

"Here is my number," and showed it to John, "copy it, see you later, alligator," he said and left John. The waiter appeared with a friendly smile, John asked for a cold beer. Suddenly Wellington was there, Nabokov was with him.

"We heard everything are you good?"

"Heard, how?"

"Remember the guy in the elevator? Your pocket."

"Wow," said John searching in his pocket and yes, there was a little device there.

"You were good," said Wellington showing all his white teeth, of course being a member of White's.

"Nice to meet again," said Nabokov.

"Say hello to Ling, the waiter," said Wellington.

John understood, the waiter was Wellington's man.

"You didn't think going alone I gather? Or"?

"Of course not."

"You go and trail the man," Wellington said to Nabokov, "the fat guy will know where he is by now."

"He is obviously yours," inquired John.

"Even the taxi you went in is ours."

"Is this real?"

"This is what I do for a living."

"Damn it, I'm impressed."

"Never go barefoot."

"What do you mean?"

"In our trade it's a cover."

"You are monitoring me."

"Until this business is finished, yes."

Now they know all my steps, it is exactly as he had said, there is an imprint whatever you do in this digital world.

"Have I disappointed you?"

"Well, you should have informed before saying yes to this meeting, a mistake."

"I'm sorry."

"Don't you worry, I'll contact as soon as we got things clear." John left the hotel feeling foolish.

CHAPTER 40

He met Jasmine at Stockton's and John broke the news to Jasmine:

"A few hours ago, Wellington presented a birth-certificate to Ben and me, previously checked through their channels and claims it's legitimate. Chen is your grandfather."

The revelation hit her like a wave, leaving her completely speechless. Her heart raced as a whirlwind of emotions took over—shock, confusion, and an overwhelming sense of worry. How could she not have known? Questions flooded her mind, but she couldn't find the words to voice them. As the weight of the truth settled in, fear crept in alongside the unease—what did this mean for her, for her family? She felt as if her world had shifted in an instant, leaving her unsteady and anxious about what came next.

"I had no idea."

"Maybe you should talk to your grandmother about it," he offered.

"That changes everything."

"But there is more, Chen is sequestered and a man I just met, the very same that who had me in prison a few hours say will deliver Chen but with a ransom of $500,000."

"Who are you, John? Is this really happening?"

"The man from MI6 is trying to find a solution to solve it."

He then told her about his meeting at the Peninsula. Jasmine began to cry.

"You went alone? Those Triads are dangerous."

"I had no choice," he said almost defensively but truthfully.

She calmed down a bit and said, "That's why Chen always was so nice to me. Now I remember a few years ago my grandmother told me she had once a romance that couldn't be. Like us," she added.

Not the moment to tell her that Chen had financed her studies in the UK.

"Maybe they made a kind of agreement and lived through it."

"I have to go and see my grandmother."

"Do you want me to come?"

"No, I need to do it alone."

"Speaking of things, my daughter is going to Stockholm in three days.

"Good for you, you must go then."

"Yes."

"You'll leave me again."

John was silent, she stood up, John also raised, grappled her and draw her into his chest, lamely she let him hold her.

"I'll call you later," and she left him standing and began to walk away.

"I'll let you know how all this works out with Ben I mean the money part," he said but she didn't hear it. He stood like that for a while indecisively, hoping she might return. He began to walk to his apartment. Suddenly he was hungry and went for a burger, entered an outlet stating they had the best burger in Hong Kong, quite a statement to assert. He wolfed it down, like a car in need of gasoline. Despite all the stress hunger had set in. It wasn't the best burger in his life but barely all right. Well inside the apartment and computer in his hands he had many things to juggle. Absolutely not let down his daughter. He sent two messages, one to Erik about Tallinn, that he was ready to go to Tallinn tomorrow so he could arrange whatever there was to arrange, another to Marianne about a possible arrival. He also called Dennis but no answer.

CHAPTER 41

John went to the Mandarin. There they were, Ben, Wellington and Nabokov.

"All for one and one for all, said Wellington, "here comes D'Artagnan.

"It's one for all, all for one," corrected John.

It wasn't far-fetched, they mirrored like an echo the famous novel, The Three Musketeers. Ben, the disillusioned Athos; Wellington, the elegant Aramis; and Nabokov, the resourceful Porthos.

"A man without a sword," said John.

"But we have one," said Wellington.

"I've decided to pay up," said Ben.

"Ok but with a condition," said Wellington.

"And what's that?

"That they leave Chen and Jasmine and all her family, if not, we will pursue them until we will hunt them down, one by one."

"Would that really function?"

"Usually, it does."

"It might, intervened John, "a few years ago I met a Spanish businessman, who claimed he had contacted the Mafia in Marseilles. In the case his family would be hurt, they would hunt any potential assassin from ETA," said John, "it seemed to function."

Wellington looked with curiosity and appreciation at John. and said, "I've heard about it."

"That's a hard road to take," said Ben.

"I believe this thing about Jasmine's grandmother was a trick, they spread a smokescreen. The Triad knew about the refugees and her grandmother thinking they could scare the shit out of her, black mailing with the knowledge that Chen is working close to the Dunbar, who would through up the money" sentenced- like Wellington.

"This thing about threating the guy like you just said, is this within the legality of the MI6?" asked Ben.

"These guys have been troubling us and the negotiation with China and Hong Kong too long too often." Which wasn't an answer but they preferred to leave such a sensible matter and solve what was at hand. "One of them is called 14K and based in Hong Kong with around 20,000 members. They are involved in illegal gambling, money laundering, arms trafficking, prostitution, human trafficking etc."

If someone knew about these things it was Wellington was obvious. He continued; "since the 1990s, alliances have grown between triads and the Chinese government, which enhances government's control over the city."

Nabokov interrupted him to add.

"There are interactions between the government and Triad societies infiltrating the police force and bribing police officers."

"It's called "Mainlandization", Triad societies co-opt and neutralize potential opposition before and after the handover. In return, the Chinese government offers protection and business opportunities."

"Do we have the right to do what we now consider?" asked John, surprised by his audacity to speak as if he knew what the limits are in these cases.

"We can interfere and put leverage on the authorities. There are quite a few very important projects going on between China and the UK, which they don't want to be messed up with and this little thing is not worth it for them."

"Okay, how do we proceed then, looking at Wellington Ben asked."

"I suggest in the terms what we've just said, we are going to pay and agree with the meeting place. Nabokov and I with a few friends will be in place and watch over the proceedings in case there are any wrong doings."

"Why does he come with a helicopter," wondered John?

"It's easier to escape and difficult to follow them."

"Are there many helicopter-lines doing this here?"

"Mostly it's the company doing Hong Kong and Macao."

"Might be a coincidence but I happen to know a Swedish pilot who flew Copenhagen and Helsingborg a few years back and now flies Hong Kong Macao, maybe he is the pilot and could give an indication if Chen really is in that helicopter, speaking Swedish, no one would understand."

"John, you do surprise me, that's would be a big coincidence," said Wellington." If it comes to that we can check which line it is, not a bad idea. Finally, you are beginning to be useful," he said smiling and continued, "we have an Ops Center, which our analysts can immediately provide vital information about where the flying birds are located at any moment."

"I could have use of it you when doing business," said Ben smiling.

"My suggestion is, you accept to pay the ransom with the condition I just mentioned and see how they answer."

They agreed and crafted the message, cooperative and resolute at the same time telling the kidnapper that Ben's conditions must be met. A risky game.

They sat in silence a while, waiting for an answer.

"Beers for everyone?" asked Ben.

A waitress came with much desired beers, the tense situation had got them thirsty. After about five minutes an answer appeared on the screen of his mobile.

"You are not in position to negotiate anything."

Wellington told John to answer, *"Actually I am."*

"Give me proof. Don't believe you."

"Give me proof you have Chen."

A photo appeared on John's screen of Chen, looking miserable, sitting in a local which could be a barbershop or a shop of some kind. The kidnappers didn't seem to have objections of the conditions, perhaps they didn't believe the threat was real.

"Okay, agreed then?"

"Agreed, how and where are you going to deliver Chen?"

A few moments of waiting.

Tomorrow, alone, at 19 hours at the rooftop of the Peninsula with the money," was the answer on John's mobile.

Strangely they felt elated.

"When we have information about their whereabouts, we contact both of you". Wellington and Nabokov stood up.

"Do you think they have Stewart also?" asked Ben.

"No," said Wellington, "it seems the stripper-guy is a competitor to this little shit" in an unusual lapse of sincerity of his lack of affection towards the kidnapper.

"My son always had a thing for putting himself in danger," said Ben grudgingly now standing ready to leave.

"Call me when you know something" said Ben and left. Before leaving Wellington, took John aside.

"There is another thing we have to solve, I talked to Eric, we think you ought to go to Tallinn."

Quite an understatement thought John.

"I've told Erik, I'm ready to go."

"Good, it's becoming urgent."

"We'll see," said John with a shrug.

"Don't worry, we'll cover you. You won't be alone out there."

"How comforting."

Wellington checked his watch, "right, have to go now good luck and all that." He gave a quick nod and walked away.

Alone John called Jasmine.

"How is it going?"

"Better than I thought. My grandmother told me everything."

"Can I see you now?"

"I come to your apartment in an hour or so."

John was relieved but at the same time heartbroken, he was leaving Jasmine.

CHAPTER 42

He sat trying to concentrate his thoughts, when he got a message from Wellington; *"We know where they are and will go in and take them, think you should come.*

"When? responded John.

"In an hour at 18.45 hours.

"I'll come, where do I go?

"It's in Kowloon, close to the Shangri-la hotel, go to a bar called Happy Joe.

John rushed out on the street and grabbed a taxi, a sent short message to Jasmine he'll be late.

Sitting in the cab a message came through with details of a flight, first to Helsinki, then Tallinn and Stockholm. That was fast, John thought, must have been Eric, together with Wellington.

It took him half an hour to get to Happy Joe. When he arrived, Wellington and Nabokov were there with eight guys, who didn't look the typical Chinese-clients. More like a gathering of English football-fans but not the ones with a beer in their hands. These were ripped muscular guys with short haircuts, no bulgy stomachs, could only be Special Forces dressed as civilians.

No social small talk, just a focused silence. Nabokov and Wellington both wore safety-vests. This meant there wouldn't be any paying of the ransom. Wellington now in command, displayed a reassuring authority, a man meant to lead, who you follow. In a wink they were all in combat gear and weaponry to their teeth. Eight hardened special forces operators, prepared for a surprise assault. John understood that each man was a veteran, trained for missions just like this—fast, precise, and lethal. Superficially the atmosphere was like as if they were going for a walk in the park, although he noticed a cocksure focus in the eyes of the men.

"Is Ben aware of this?" asked john.

"Yes. "The idea is that one of our guys goes knocking on the door asking for a haircut, we go in from the backdoor, the moment he rings the door," he said pointing to a guy looking capable of violence of any sort, "we go in from their backdoor and a side-door, we got it covered," added Wellington,

The mission briefing was clear: get in, neutralize the kidnappers, and extract the hostage unharmed, banking on the element of surprise. The kidnappers thought they were safe, hidden away in the low-profile establishment, but what they didn't know was that the clock was ticking. It was almost seven in the evening, the sun setting, casting long shadows on the quiet street where the barbershop was situated, an unremarkable building on the outside. The kidnappers were unaware of the impending strike, maybe they had become complacent thought and no idea their fate was about to be sealed. A tense standoff was underway. Wellington handed John a helmet and safety-vest saying, "Put these on, you might need them," then with a nod, added, "come along and see how we get things done." The effect on John was almost visible, he began to sweat nervously. Nabokov gave a sign and there was movement. Stealthily this bunch of fighting men rustled and got going with Nabokov in the lead. The team moved into position with calculated precision, clad in dark gear that made them blend seamlessly into the afternoon shadows. They had done their reconnaissance, mapped out the layout, and identified weak points in the building's security.

At precisely 1900 hours, the signal came. John followed from behind closely observing as the attack began and unfolded before his eyes. The man posturing as a man in need of a haircut walked the thirty or so meters to the front-door of the barbershop, at the same time, silently placed a small breaching charge on the side entrance, while two snipers took position on a nearby rooftop, ready to provide overwatch. The man who wanted to cut his hair had to call sharply several times until someone showed up. A conversation was taking place, which seemed to be about whether the shop was open or closed, when a sudden burst was heard, followed by several explosions and what seemed like a volley of shots. The breaching charge exploded with a controlled bang; the door blown off its hinges as the first wave of operators rushed in. Flashbang grenades followed, flooding the room with blinding light and deafening sound. Chaos erupted. The kidnappers, caught off guard, scrambled for their weapons, but it was too late. The special forces moved with deadly efficiency, clearing the room in a matter of seconds. One operator, a hulking figure, grabbed a disoriented kidnapper and slammed him into the ground before he could even draw his gun. Another team member, moving with surgical precision, put down two more kidnappers with suppressed shots to their legs, incapacitating them without killing. They wanted them alive for interrogation. As the operators advanced deeper into the shop, two kidnappers made a last- ditch effort to barricade themselves in the backroom with the hostage. But the special forces team was relentless. A swift strike breached the room with a battering ram, and in an instant, they flooded the room, bursting in to find the last two criminals standing, their weapons trained on Chen, sitting tied up on a chair. One of the operators, a skilled marksman, took the lead. With one precise shot on the man's leg, he neutralized the kidnapper who held a gun to Chen's head. The second kidnapper, panicked, fired wildly, but the team was already on him. He was tackled to the ground, disarmed, and cuffed before he could do any more harm. It was the same man who had held John in prison in Shendi. Chen was dressed in a trainer's suit looking older than his seventy-five years.

"Hi," said John to Chen who didn't show any emotion only looking tired.

Wellington appeared with the ward from Shendi hand-cuffed.

"Here is our friend," said Wellington.

"We meet again," said John satisfied.

The Chinese said something which wasn't a buenos días.

"We got them, and no ransom-money paid" said Wellington happily.

"How many were they?"

"Five."

John was going to ask in what condition but halted himself when he heard Police sirens sounding and getting closer and closer, they would be there in a minute.

"We'll take care of this when the police arrive, you can go now".

A hasty goodbye, it wasn't the moment to talk about the weather or ask if the other two were injured or dead.

"See you," said John.

"Bring your racket when you come to London,." said Wellington

"Ok, and you tell me about your famous ancestor."

"Deal."

As they were saying their goodbyes, a sudden urge compelled John to speak. "I fly to Tallinn in a few hours."

"I know, talked to Eric about it. Might see you there," said Wellington.

"You are coming too?" said John surprised.

"It's possible."

"It's that serious then?"

"Yes, it is."

Onlookers were now arriving due to the explosions, thus John distanced himself and searched for a cab. Texted Jasmine and told her in subdued version what had happened with Chen, they agreed they would meet at the apartment.

CHAPTER 43

In the quiet intimacy in the apartment and by the weight of recent events both needed to share their respective stories. Eventually, when things got cleared and out of the way, they decided to go to the beach, the same place they had been two months ago. Watching the sunset, this time it was different, aware that this might be it. They sat in silence looking for answers or a miracle, which would make it possible for them. Close by two birds flew in formation in a disciplined and synchronized manner, like war planes in complete harmony as if joined together, like us, but we have to spread John thought.

"It couldn't be," she said looking straight at the water. "Will we get over it?"

"You will."

"And you?"

"I'll stay a while then I might go to America."

John didn't know what to say or comment anymore.

They sat in silence until she said.

"Let's go."

"Hungry?"

"No, not really."

They began to walk without knowing where the next steps would take them, both physically and spiritually.

"Let's go to the apartment and spend the night together."

He had never seen her like this before. Spend the night together knowing that it would be the last one maybe wasn't the best of ideas and he had a flight the day after.

"I'll come with you," she said without enthusiasm.

Both sensed a feeling of suspense once they arrived at the apartment but as lovers always have done and always will do, unconsciously by the force of their love, seized the moment and did what they had done many times with intense passion. Strangely they felt closer than they ever had been.

"I'll never love again like this," she said.

"Me neither."

Strong affirmations but that was both felt at this very moment. John had a strange sensation that all had been mapped long ago.

It wasn't a quest anymore, it was decided, they would give up their love, it couldn't be. The question wasn't to be or not to be, it was Hemingwayesque; to have or not have. John wasn't Bogart in Casablanca where he let go his love, this was John who was going to leave and his love stayed.

"How many renounce their love," said John looking to the ceiling. She didn't answer.

Exhausted because of too much thinking they slept. When they woke up both were conscious that in a few moments it was the end, making it impossible to say something. Just a powerful quietness. Console with words would be superfluous. There are different forms of silences, this one told so much exasperating of their most feelings. She dressed, searched for her bag, and went to the door. He stood still then went forward to her. There were tears in her eyes.

"Don't say anything Johnny," and she gave him a last look and fumbled with the door and began to walk a few steps, stopped and turned and gave him a kiss and said; "I'll never love like this again." John didn't find words to express his thoughts, instead he tried to reach out at her and gently touch her when she turned away. He just stood there, in a silent goodbye, his eyes traumatized filled with a mixture of pain and love. She pushed the button for the elevator, and she was gone. It was over.

John returned inside and saw his mobile vibrating. It was Jessica.

"Wake up dad, it's your daughter. I'm coming in two days," she said happily.

"Wonderful," answered John with a bland voice.

"Are you okay?"

"Yes, of course."

"You sound strange."

"No no, I fly in a few hours to Stockholm." We'll see what happens in Tallinn first he thought nervously.

"I'll be there in two days."

"I'll be at the airport to pick you up."

"Good flight Dad."

The word Dad made him gradually return to his usual self.

"Will be wonderful to see you again," sounded hollow even to his own ears.

Inside, a storm of conflicting emotions raged. Regret gnawed at him. The thought of Jasmine, of the connection they could have shared. He berated himself, a harsh internal monologue echoing with accusations of cowardice and self-sabotage. The weight of not being man enough pressed down on him, a crushing sense of failure. He knew this regret would linger, a persistent shadow haunting his memories. He wished he could turn back time, to rewrite the past, to be the man he knew he could be, the man who had the courage to seize the moment and embrace the love that had been. Mechanically he began to do his luggage, with a mix of emptiness and joy of seeing his daughter again.

Must say good-bye to Ben and sent a message. They agreed to meet at the Mandarin. When he was finished, he had a last look of this place where so much happiness of supreme love had flourished. He walked with his Samsonite to the hotel at a slow pace. When he arrived to the hotel Jasmine wasn't to be seen in the lobby. The Italian came forward when John entered the hotel, he had a something in his hands. "This is for you."

It was a letter not to be opened until you are in the air it said.

John didn't care, opened the envelope with force and began to read eagerly. *From the first moment I saw you something happened, and it has continued every time I see you. It was wonderful. Our story doesn't have a Hollywood happy ending, it's like the book by Han Suyin. I will always love you, don't call me, it'll make it worse.*

Jasmine.

He didn't have time to reflect on this when Ben appeared.

"What the hell happened back there?" Ben was referred to the stealth attack to liberate Chen.

"I still don't understand how they pulled it off. It all happened so fast."

"Those fighters… they must be good those men."

"Good? They were incredible, precise too. Every move was coordinated like clockwork."

"You are leaving?

"Yes, have a flight in three hours.

"Let us sit down a while. is that a letter there? Is it from the one I think it is?

"Yes, a kind of goodbye," said John sulking.

"Kind of?"

"Too many obstacles."

"The age difference or the geographics?"

"The easy answer would be geographic, at least to begin with. Age? With time I suppose the age difference will take its toll and count."

"Choose wisely is difficult when strong emotions are involved," said Ben as if he had understood John's mental battle.

"Suppose it was dead before it even started.,"

"Don't say that John, leaving someone you love is never easy, but sometimes it's necessary."

"It just feels…wrong. Like I'm betraying what we started. I still love her, but I know staying isn't the right for neither of us. My mind is pulling me in different directions."

"It's natural to feel torn. But love alone doesn't always mean the relationship is sustainable. You must ask yourself: what is the long-term impact of staying?"

But John was still stubbornly resisting the idea he must surrender his love towards Jasmine.

"I just keep thinking, what if I walk away and regret it forever?"

"That's a fear we all face when making big decisions. But think about this: sometimes the hardest decisions are the right ones. Staying just because you're afraid of regret isn't a strong foundation for a relationship. Focus on what brings you inner peace."

"But still, letting go… it feels like I'm giving up on something I promised."

"Letting go isn't giving up, John. Perhaps the relationship is not the right one for either of you."

"But how do I stop feeling like I'm failing her? Or failing myself?"

"You're not failing her or yourself. It's brave to acknowledge when staying might do more harm than good."

"I just want to be sure I'm doing the right thing."

"You won't always feel certain right away, but trust that your instincts led you to this decision for a reason. Over time, clarity comes, healing comes."

"I'm not so sure, this has been the perfect match."

There was a moment of silence.

"Anyways, it's your decision, not circumstance, that determine your destiny," said Ben," our life is the sum result of all the choices we make."

"Well put but it doesn't make me feel better."

"Think about your daughter," said Ben to animate John.

"Yeah, he said blandly, "must do that, talked to Chen yet?

"I'll go and see him now."

"Where is he?

"Wellington took him to a private clinic I know" said Ben, "What shall you do now, over there?

"Try to figure out my life, find a job", there was no reason for John to hide that there was no concrete assignment to go back to. "I have an offer from a think-tank or write a book."

"After all this you have stuff to write about." said Ben laughing.

You don't know how much John thought, thinking of the Tallinn-thing.

"Dangerous waters could be a title."

"Anyways, when things will be cleared with Chen and our project I'll contact you. What I mentioned the other day working for me is still intact, if you are interested of course."

They exchanged possible venues for a while and agreed to be in contact. Ben gave John a big hug.

"Good flight," said Ben looking straight into John's eyes, "we'll miss you here."

"Thanks, me too," trying to maintain himself straight. Both men gave the impression with a wish to continue their talk, there was much more to say that and unpronounced, instead they shook hands and said their goodbyes. John went towards the exit, feeling lonely and wretched as his life was like he was surfing on a wave in the sea, with its highs and lows, not knowing how to tackle it with rhythm, not understanding the why's. The Italian came forward.

"The hotel has a limousine for you."

"It's been a pleasure," said John.

"As they say here, I hope you find happiness and a long life."

"I wish you the same. "She gave this to you?" showing him the envelope.

"Yes," he answered looking guilty as if he having done something wrong.

"Was she okay?"

"Not her usual self no."

"Okay, thank you," and went outside to the waiting limousine.

CHAPTER 44

Sitting in this giant car he began to absorb these lasts events. An incoherent inner dialogue began, jumbled in disarray, convinced himself she is from a too far away place, in addition, too different culture and too young for you. A man should follow his instincts he had pledged many times but now John was loose and drifting, a rolling stone, he felt miserable. The car glided smoothly through the city's nights, neon lights flickering across the window as John occasionally gazed out in fleeting moments. Then his phone buzzed, a message from Erik snapping him back. It was clear and methodical, detailing exactly where to go, each instruction carefully crafted to guide him safely, once he landed, to keep him safe and keep the plan on track. During the flight, first to Helsinki and then to Tallinn, John dealt with life's obstacles as best as he could, contemplating the emotions and passions that whirled in his inner self and despite the disordered state he had been in before takeoff, he tried to see things in a positive light and with a certain fortitude. Years ago, he had read that reason is the highest and the most powerful human capacity. That reason rules over the other passions and directs the individual to a virtuous life. But to John, a belief that reason should be the supreme guide of human behavior was dubious and thought there is a fickleness in such an unabashed suggestion, even if it came from such a giant like Plato.

With Jasmine, reason had been elsewhere. Was he a rolling stone who gathers no moss, a man who never stays in one place, always moving with no roots while avoiding responsibilities? Looking out he and felt exactly as the Gobi-desert, isolated, dry and ugly. What could have a beginning was really an end, he felt more alone than ever in his life. He was running out of mental fuel in this mishmash of thoughts.

He slept turmoiled a while and woke up thinking of his daughter, he would be a good father, let her feel it. He had many things to take care of, there was the matter of Dennis, and the bank account he was the beneficiary of. There was the issue of his unemployment and the looming challenge with the press. He tried to read a book he couldn't remember how it had come into his hands and decided it was pure trash about killers and people in dire straits and began to consider writing a book intertwine his tangled love life into the fabric of history, blurring the lines between fact and fiction. For sure he didn't need to find a purpose that felt too grand but a path, yes, that was what he sought. In truth, he knew exactly what he wanted; the simplest pleasures were sometimes the most extraordinary, a good shot on the golf-course, dinner with friends filled with raucous laughter echoing through the night, skiing the slopes like the wind, rhythmically in tune with the elements. At the same time, not just fleeting pleasures. It was something deeper, something simple yet profound. He wanted to love and be loved, to share his soul with another, and in that exchange, find meaning in the quiet, unwritten spaces of life. The rest—everything else—could follow. He realized that life stretched before him like a blank page—that everything is to be done, like developing a film-roll you dip into water, and you get a negative, untouched, waiting to be written. Destiny is not deterministic although Sartre said we could decide our own destiny, well that depends my-dear-know-it-all, who must have missed that the environment has a lot to say, as the genes not to forget if you are born a shit or a king for instance. Now, Stockholm waited with the uncertainty of a life that had unraveled—no career, one lover lost to time, and another who may have already slipped back into the arms of her husband. But foremost, there was a bank account to fix, before anything else.

John's plane descended toward Tallinn, the city's skyline and coastline sprawling out beneath him. As they approached the airport, he was relieved to see the clean, modern design of the terminals—nothing like the gray, Soviet architecture he'd half-expected. After a short ride through the airport, he disembarked and moved quickly through customs, keeping his eyes peeled for anything out of the ordinary. He couldn't shake the feeling that someone might be watching. Outside, he hailed a taxi to the hotel Erik had booked. The driver didn't ask questions, which John appreciated. He stared out the window, scanning the streets for any signs of a tail. The city seemed quiet, but his nerves kept him on edge. Every shadow, every unfamiliar face, made his pulse race.

When the taxi arrived, the hotel was unremarkable. Not bad, but not impressive either—just a place to sleep. After checking in, he headed out for a quick bite, sticking to something simple before calling it a night. Tomorrow was the day. The bank. The account. He just hoped Erik's people had him covered because he knew the Russians might be waiting for him too. The plan was simple, there would be no direct contact with Erik to avoid tipping off any prying eyes. Whoever was watching, wasn't a fool, and Erik's face was likely known to them. Instead, a woman with a labrador would shadow John as he neared the bank, a quite sentinel prepared to intervene if anything went amiss. Erik would be close by but unseen while John walked into the bank. John woke up after a nervous night, got a simple breakfast and prepared himself for the bank.

CHAPTER 45

He took a deep breath as he approached the bank, its imposing facade doing little to calm his nerves. In the recent attack of the Triad-boys he had been a spectator, now the plan rested on his shoulders. This was a different ball-game. What if all went wrong? Then what?

The five-minute walk had been enough to clear his head, but now that he was here, the weight of what lay ahead settled on him.

The bank's revolving doors seemed to mock him, spinning him closer to a truth that might shatter everything he thought he knew. He felt the weight of his father's name, the weight of the unknown, pressing down on him, stealing his breath.

Erik's warning echoed in his mind: Russian thugs or British spooks, might be watching. They want those documents.

The bank loomed ahead, a stark, imposing structure against the pale Tallinn sky. It looked ordinary enough, yet every window seemed to glare at him, every passerby a potential threat. He imagined eyes watching him from across the street, from the shadows of doorways, calculating, assessing.

He scanned the square in front of the bank. A group of men huddled near a parked van, their faces obscured by shadows and the brims of their hats. Were they just waiting for the bank to open, or something more sinister? His gut clenched. The air crackled with unspoken tension. He could almost taste the danger, a metallic tang on his tongue. He felt exposed, vulnerable, like a lone chess piece on a board where the game was already rigged. He took a deep breath, trying to steady his racing heart. This was it. He was walking into the lion's den. He just hoped he wouldn't become the lion's lunch.

The thought of Jasmine, her laughter, her vibrant energy, felt strangely out of place now, like a frivolous melody played during a funeral march. Could he afford such distractions when his father's legacy, hung in the balance?

The urgency to reach the bank eclipsed everything, even the memory of Jasmine's touch. He felt a sudden, sharp clarity. This was his path, his alone. No one else could walk it for him.

He entered, presented his passport to the receptionist, and was led into a secluded room without much fanfare. A few administrative hiccups delayed the process, but eventually, a bank clerk arrived with a key. John was shown to a secure vault where a small, unassuming box waited.

Left alone, John fumbled with the lock, his hands unsteady. When the box clicked open, he was greeted by the sight of an old envelope on top of a stack of cash. The exact amount was hard to estimate, but it was a substantial sum. Ignoring the money for now, he gingerly opened the envelope. Inside were documents. As he scanned them, English and Russian names jumped out at him. His breath caught when he saw his father's name. Further down, he froze again—an old, prominent foreign minister's name was listed. The implications were staggering.

John gathered everything, his mind racing, and called for an employee. When a bag was brought, he swiftly emptied the box, closed it, and left the bank with his heart pounding in his chest. The moment he stepped outside, he sensed he wasn't alone. A glance over his shoulder confirmed it—two bulky men were trailing him.

Panic surged. He quickened his pace, but they followed. Then, a shot rang out. John felt a sharp pain in his leg and looked down to see blood staining his trousers. He staggered, trying to keep moving, but his body was betraying him. As he sought cover behind a car, Wellington appeared out of nowhere. More shots were fired, and John could barely comprehend what was happening. Another man crouched next to him, whispering urgently, "I'm on your team."

The gunfire stopped as abruptly as it had begun. Wellington approached, smiling, with a triumphant glint in his eye. "I told you I'll watch you," he said. "Did you get what we wanted?"

John, wincing from the pain in his leg, nodded. "Yeah, I got it. But we need to get to a hospital."

Wellington paused only for a moment before agreeing. Together, they hurried to a car, the weight of the documents in John's bag suddenly feeling heavier than before.

At the hospital, they acted quickly, and John's injury turned out to be less severe than feared. He was told he could be discharged within a few hours. Wellington had been waiting for him and, after a brief conversation, revealed he had managed to read parts of the documents. To John's relief, the truth was finally out: his father was innocent. It had all been an ugly cover-up orchestrated by the Foreign Office to hide their mishandling of the Philby case.

"And Erik?"

"Erik will meet you at the airport."

"So, he was there?"

"Yeah, and a team of his. He had to talk to the local police about the incident."

John went silent, lost in thought, wondering about the strange world of spying.

"Well, it's goodbye for now. We'll be in touch," said Wellington giving his now customary smile.

"But what about the documents… and the cash?"

"We'll take care of that."

"And how do I know they're in good hands?"

Wellington smirked, "I photocopied them while they operated on you. Here it is."

"Thanks." He took the papers, a fast look to see if they were the correct ones giving a faint smile. "And what happens after this? I mean they guys that shot at us?"

"We'll deal with them. They won't be a problem for long. See you on the tennis court next time."

"We'll see," said John looking at his leg.

"John, about that position we discussed…"

Wellington began, his voice trailing off slightly.

"There might be a role for someone with your talents."

Wellington fixed his gaze on a point somewhere over John's shoulder, with a flicker of something mischievous in his eyes. John raised an eyebrow, with skepticism.

"What?"

"There are, we have…other avenues. Other opportunities. Things that require a certain…discretion. And a certain…adaptability." Wellington leaned forward, his voice dropping to a conspiratorial whisper.

"Let's just say, the world isn't always what it seems, John. There are shadows, and within those shadows, there's work to be done."

"Shadows?" John repeated, his brow furrowed. "What kind of work?"

Wellington smiled, a thin, almost enigmatic expression. "The kind that requires a keen mind, a steady hand, and a… willingness to embrace the unexpected. Let's just say, we deal with matters that don't always make the front page. Matters of national security, shall we say?"

"National security?" John's eyes widened slightly. "You mean...MI6?"

Wellington chuckled softly. "Let's not be too specific, John. But yes, something along those lines. You might find a path, a meaningful work which gives you satisfaction and adventures. Think of it as...a different kind of service. One that might suit your talents rather well."

John hesitated, a whirlwind of thoughts swirling in his mind. He had always been drawn to the idea of adventure, of making a difference. But this...this was something else entirely. "Adventures?" he echoed, a hint of disbelief in his voice.

"Indeed," Wellington said, his eyes gleaming. "Adventures, John. And a chance to contribute in ways you never imagined. Think about it. The world needs people like you. People who aren't afraid to step into the shadows. People who can make a real difference, even when no one is watching. It's not just about the task itself, but the sense of purpose, the feeling of contributing to something larger than yourself." He paused, letting the words sink in. "And, of course, there's always the excitement."

John said, glancing at his watch, a nervous habit he'd picked up recently.

"Look, this...this is a lot to take in. I appreciate the offer, I really do. But I'm...I'm not sure. MI6?

That's...intense."

Wellington's smile widened, a knowing glint in his eyes. "Think about it, might just change your perspective on things."

John managed a weak smile.

"Right. I'll...I'll think about it. Really. But I need to catch this flight."

He extended his hand. "Thanks, for everything."

Wellington shook his hand firmly, his smile unwavering. "Safe travels, John." And don't be a stranger. The shadows are always waiting." He gave a small, almost imperceptible nod. "And do consider the adventure."

John nodded back, a mix of apprehension and intrigue swirling within him. He turned and walked towards the door, a lingering sense of unease and excitement following him. Wellington was conspicuously amused, smiled left him standing there.

Touching the photocopied version of the documents, it felt good, an insurance for him and his father. He decided to not overthink, it wouldn't lead anywhere, be instead like Anna Karenina's brother, who put on a smile and adapt to whatever there was to adapt to. Settle in Stockholm, rely on your buddies and battle the net storm head-on. The true picture will only emerge when all is said and done.

CHAPTER 46

John left the hospital with the help of two crutches, without them he wouldn't be able to walk after the gunshot and surgery. Found a cab and went to the airport, Erik was waiting, smiling.

"We fly together."

"I heard you were there the whole time."

"I told you we'd cover you."

John grimaced, "a bit late though."

"Yeah, sorry for that," he nodded towards the boarding gate. "You'll be flying first class to Stockholm".

"Well that's uplifting."

After a somewhat arduous ascent up the airplane stairs, they finally settled into their first-class seats. During the flight, Erik surveyed the documents, his expression growing more serious as he read. Finally, he said a bit grim.

"For us, this is just the beginning. We still need to find the people behind all this."

John, exhausted and wanting to put everything behind him, shook his head. "I think I need some time to digest all this."

After a moment of silence Erik sighed,

"Such a shame this flight is so short." John chuckled, "No time for a proper drink."

Erik raised an eyebrow, "What are you up to these days, anyway? I heard the job you were supposed to start fell through."

"Seems that way," John replied, sounding a bit uncertain. "Wellington mentioned the Hong Kong incident, didn't he?" John asked.

"Yes," he said "you behaved brilliantly,"

There was a moment of silence. John admitted; "Not sure what I'll do now."

"You could always join our team," Erik suggested. "No big bucks, but it's incredibly exciting, almost aphrodisiac."

John grinned, "Money's not really my primary concern."

John had a roughly clear vision for life; set goals that could be achieved, towards confined horizons, a stable, comfortable existence without the constant hassles of financial worries. He wasn't obsessed with wealth but appreciated the freedom that financial stability offered. His goal was simple, rebuild his life with fresh ambitions.

A self-made man, John was driven by guts and a love for learning like a sophomore. His positivity was infectious, yet his mind often raced with restless thoughts. Not switches of bipolar extract or out of control like a sprinkler-garden machine gone mad, it just happened swinging between philosophical insights and trivial reflections. His mental elasticity was both a strength and a flaw, allowing him to adapt but sometimes leaving him scattered. Life was full of chain-reactions, small changes could ripple into unstoppable outcomes. He decided he mustn't sink into a mental quick-sand and lose the path.

John drifted off to for a bit until the pilot informed the passengers, they would land in about ten minutes, on the forefront of his mental screen; that is Marianne, with the same speed as the plane's velocity. When they arrived at Arlanda, Erik helped John towards the exit. As they reached the outswing doors, Erik turned to him.

"Thanks for your help, I'll leave you here."

And with that, Erik was gone, leaving John to contemplate his next steps. Wellington's offer would have to wait.

CHAPTER 47

Each dragging step out of the airport was a conscious act of postponement. A way to hold back the uncertain moment of seeing Marianne or not, was she even waiting? Be composed like Djokovic and above all, don't think of Jasmine. Install her to a place where everything is good but hasn't anything to do with you anymore. The understanding of the impossible relationship with Jasmine was a cold hard fact, as hard as the floor he walked. Yet, amidst the melancholy, a flicker of understanding began to emerge and a resolve took hold, in spite of the pain in his leg after the shooting in Tallinn, a sense of liberation and surge of elation washed over him, as the documents clutched in his hand would clear his father's name.

Then from a distance he saw Marianne, wearing a light blue skirt just above her knees, a marine-blue blouse which suited perfectly combined with light blue high heels. Objectively she looked perfectly fine so don't compare now, this isn't about superficialities, this is life, it's not about looking good it's much more he thought.

John approached with a tired smile "I wasn't sure you'd come."

When Marianne saw John approaching on crutches she gaped in shock.

"What happened?"

John grinned slightly, "I'll tell you on the way."

Still surprised, Mariannes expression softened int a warm smile and said, "I said I would wait for you."

"You did."

"I wasn't sure you'd ask me to."

She reached for his hand. John paused, searching her eyes while squeezing her hand gently "I didn't expect this."

"But something about this feels like... a new beginning."

With warmth in her eyes "Maybe it is. You don't need all the answers right now. Just one step at a time."

John nodding, letting out a breath, nodding at the crutches, "Yeah... one step at a time."

As they walked together, John felt elated as the weight of his past began to lift, realizing that maybe, just maybe, he's exactly where he's meant to be.

"Have you solved what you needed to solve?"

"Yes, at least parts of it," and strangely he felt elated.

He looked at her and sensed a deeply set affection.

"Me too," she said.

"You know where I'd like to go?"

She raised an eyebrow, "with crutches?"

"Grand Hotel?"

"Not tired after the trip?

"I'm fine."

It dawned on him the quest of love was over, not entirely but enough for the moment. What happened in Hong Kong stays in Hong Kong. He understood, it's more important the resolution than the content in a decision as the essence of life can never be fully understood anyhow, the best would be to let life intervene. He realized there had been a butterfly effect in everything that had happened to him, and he had emerged not only physically intact in spite of the shooting in Tallinn but hopefully stronger mentally.

www.ingramcontent.com/pod-product-compliance
Lightning Source LLC
Chambersburg PA
CBHW020053310726

48970CB00002B/296